Dear Readers,

This spring, we're willing to bet a *woman's* fancy will turn to love—with four brand-new Bouquet romances full of passion and laughter.

Award-winning author Vivian Leiber begins a three-book series titled "The Men of Sugar Mountain" with **One Touch,** as high school sweethearts confront the past—and dream of a shared future. Beloved Silhouette and Zebra author Suzanne McMinn offers **It Only Takes a Moment,** a charming present-day fairy tale in which a feisty woman proves that even a prince must remember he's a man.

Nothing stays the same forever. In **Charmed and Dangerous,** Silhouette author Lynda Simmons presents a woman who never thought her childhood buddy would ever offer anything more than a shoulder to lean on—until she discovers he's willing to give so much more. Last is Anna DeForest's **The Cowboy and the Heiress,** the passionate tale of a woman searching for independence and finding that true love is the greatest freedom of all.

With spring flowers ready to bloom, what could be more fitting than a Bouquet of four fabulous romances from us to you?

Kate Duffy
Editorial Director

"IT'S TIME TO TRY A LITTLE DANCING CHEEK TO CHEEK."

Lang stepped close and pulled Beth into his arms. She went, a little stiffly at first, for all sorts of warning bells were going off in the back of her mind. Jitterbugging with Lang Nelson was one thing. Dancing so close their bodies were going to touch was something else entirely. Lang, damn his laughing eyes, knew exactly what she was thinking.

"Relax," he told her quietly. "We can't get into too much trouble during just one slow dance."

Of course they couldn't, the rational side of her mind told her. As she relaxed and let him pull her closer, though, she knew in her heart that touching Lang in any sort of intimate way wasn't a wise idea. Her nerves hummed every place their bodies brushed together.

Despite her nervous system's peculiar reaction to Lang, she liked being held by him. Because he was so big, she expected to feel engulfed and intimdated in his embrace. Instead, she felt safe and protected within the circle of his arms. Her mind began to drift, and she almost forgot she was dancing in the kitchen while two fourteen-year-old girls watched her. How wonderful it would be someday to have a man she loved, trusted, and liked as her lifetime dance partner. For the moment, it would surely do no harm to pretend Lang was that man.

THE COWBOY AND THE HEIRESS

ANNA DeFOREST

Zebra Books
Kensington Publishing Corp.
http://www.zebrabooks.com

ZEBRA BOOKS are published by

Kensington Publishing Corp.
850 Third Avenue
New York, NY 10022

Copyright © 2000 by Polly Holyoke

All rights reserved. No part of this book may be reproduced in any form or by any means without the prior written consent of the Publisher, excepting brief quotes used in reviews.

If you purchased this book without a cover you should be aware that this book is stolen property. It was reported as "unsold and destroyed" to the Publisher and neither the Author nor the Publisher has received any payment for this "stripped book."

Zebra and the Z logo Reg. U.S. Pat. & TM Off.

First Printing: April, 2000
10 9 8 7 6 5 4 3 2 1

Printed in the United States of America

For my sister Julie.
Thank you for caring about my writing since the beginning.

ACKNOWLEDGMENTS

I'm grateful to Denny and Jill, two good friends who survived alcoholism in their families to become remarkable, loving women; to Jeanne Maas, for coming through on music titles in record time; to Mr. Joe Vilane, for graciously sharing his shag and jitterbug expertise; to Kristin and Mark, for their enthusiastic birding suggestions; and to Carol, who has lived the ranching life and made certain I kept the details accurate. Many thanks as well to Dawn, Joyce, Theresa, and Nana Jane for their terrific proofreading.

ONE

Lang Nelson liked his coffee cowboy strong—hot, black, and thick enough to float a horse's shoe. Having lived in Perrytown, Colorado, all his thirty-six years, he knew exactly where to go this time of morning to find a cup brewed just the way he liked it. Lang smiled to himself in anticipation as he pulled up beside the eighteen-wheeler in the parking lot of Danny Parson's diner.

Moments later, the passenger door of the big rig banged open and a small black suitcase came flying out. Lang swore aloud when the case almost hit his truck. Not that his old Chevy didn't already have its fair share of dents. It was the principle that irked him. No one ought to start launching suitcases without looking first to see where they were going to land.

Lang glanced up and forgot all about his anger and that cup of coffee he'd been thinking about for the past hour while he shuttled dudes to the airport. Above him sat the most beautiful woman he had ever seen. After a long stunned moment, he decided she was a dead ringer for Grace Kelly back in her movie star days. With a shove, she sent a second black suitcase tumbling out to land beside the first. She followed her suitcases down out of that cab as if someone had set her tail afire.

Lang wasn't one to go poking his nose into someone else's business, but he was hardly going to close his eyes or roll up the window of his pickup. So he settled back in his ringside seat to enjoy the show.

"Just where the hell do you think you're going?" Lang caught a glimpse of the red-faced trucker who had bawled this question from behind the wheel.

"Look, Mr. Broden, I already thanked you for the ride. You know I didn't offer you anything else when you picked me up. This is as far as I'm going to travel with you." With that, she picked up her suitcases and strode toward the door of the diner. Lang grinned as he admired her graceful, long-legged stride. Score one for the lady. He liked the cool way she had just told the trucker off.

"You come back here, you little tease, or you'll be damn sorry."

The blonde never faltered. If anything, she walked faster toward the door of the restaurant. *Smart girl,* Lang thought. He sighed when he realized the trucker was climbing down out of the cab. *Lang Nelson, you've never been one to interfere in other people's affairs, but you can't let this jerk hurt a woman.*

By the time the man came around the hood of his truck, Lang stood blocking his path to the diner. "You might want to think twice about following her in there," he told the trucker mildly.

The man paused and eyed him belligerently. His blue eyes were bloodshot, his greasy blond hair thinning, and a fold of his belly bulged over his leather belt. He was a big man, easily as tall as Lang, with some muscle in his beefy arms, but he also looked out of shape. Lang figured he could take him if he had to.

"This ain't none of your business, cowboy," the trucker growled.

THE COWBOY AND THE HEIRESS

"I reckon I'm making it my business. Folks in these parts don't take kindly to men who treat ladies rough."

"She ain't no lady, and she owes me."

"Seems pretty clear the lady in question feels differently."

"Just who's planning to stop me from going in there?" The trucker planted his feet and curled his hands into fists.

"Well, there's me, for one. If you manage to take me down, there're likely ten or twelve more cowboys sitting in that diner right now who'll keep you from getting anywhere near her. Of that you can be damn sure."

That news gave the trucker pause, just as Lang had hoped it would. He never liked to dodge a good fight, but he did have a mountain of work ahead of him this summer on the Rafter N. The last thing he needed to do was get laid up for a few weeks.

"Aw, hell, she ain't worth it," the trucker swore after a long moment. He spun about and stalked back toward the driver's side of his cab.

"Wise choice, amigo," Lang murmured under his breath, sorry he wasn't going to have a chance to bury his fist in that bulging gut, after all. He waited until the trucker drove off before he went inside the diner.

He spotted her at once. She was sitting at the counter, her suitcases right beside her feet. She glanced toward him when he opened the door, her expression anxious. Her cheeks colored faintly when she recognized him, and she ducked her head.

Because she was sitting with her back to the window, she probably hadn't even seen his little talk with the trucker. *So much for hoping the lady would be grateful.* Lang smiled ruefully at himself and went to take a seat in a booth that gave him a good view of her profile. *After playing white knight, you at least deserve the pleasure of looking at her when you drink your coffee.*

She was the kind of woman who would draw notice wherever she went. With her creamy skin and fine elegant features, she looked like a model or a movie star straight from the pages of one of those fancy fashion magazines. She wore her golden hair tied back in an intricate braid. Her jeans set off her long graceful legs to perfection.

Although she was dressed simply, the black suitcases she carried and the black leather boots she wore cried money. People didn't often see a woman like her in northwestern Colorado. This was ranching country, and the closest city where a woman like that belonged was hundreds of miles away.

What on earth is she doing here? Something damn peculiar is going on. He knew from his own bitter experience that women who looked like her didn't ride with truckers. Usually they had chauffeurs or hot little Porsches or Mercedes of their own.

Unless they were on the run.

As the thought occurred to him, Lang studied her more carefully. There were telltale circles under her eyes and lines of strain about that perfect mouth. If she was impatient or nervous, though, she gave no sign. Instead, she waited quietly for someone to wait on her. At last, Sally Kurtz, one of Danny's two middle-aged waitresses, stopped hustling from table to table and asked for her order.

"Actually, ma'am, I'm not here to eat. I was hoping I might speak to the owner of the restaurant." Her voice was cool and cultured, but the respectful way she addressed Sally surprised him.

"Danny's back in the kitchen. Are you a friend of

THE COWBOY AND THE HEIRESS 11

his?" Having married and divorced three husbands, Sally was never one to pull her punches, and everyone liked Danny.

"No, I'm afraid I'm not. I was wondering if he needed a cook."

"Danny does most of the cooking around here." Something in the blonde's expression must have made Sally relent. "I'll go fetch him for you, hon, and you can talk to him yourself. The coffee's on the house. You look all in." With that, Sally poured her a cup of coffee and hurried off to the kitchen.

Danny Hernandez Parson emerged from his kitchen just a few minutes later. An ex-college linebacker, ex-marine, ex-mercenary, Danny was a formidable sight. He weighed in at two hundred pounds plus, and he wore his long black hair tied back in a ponytail. To give the blonde credit, she didn't even blink. She slipped from her stool, extended her hand over the counter, and said, "Hello, Mr. Parson. My name is Beth Richards and I'm looking for work as a cook."

"Just call me Danny," Parson rumbled as he shook her hand. "I'm afraid I don't need a hand in the kitchen right now. Don't really need a waitress right now, either. You might give the classifieds in the *Perrytown Register* a look. Sometimes one of the bigger ranches around here needs a cook. In fact, Lang Nelson from the Rafter N was in here just the other day asking if I knew of anyone who could sling hash."

Lang cursed inwardly and slumped down in his booth. The last thing he needed out at the Rafter N right now was a gorgeous blonde who didn't know a potato from an onion.

Sally, who had been listening in on the conversation, brightened. "Why, hon, you're in luck. That's Lang Nelson sitting right over there in that booth."

The blonde looked over her shoulder. Lang sat up again, just as their gazes met. Her irises were a lovely gray blue, the color of an alpine lake beneath a clear Colorado sky. Her eyes should have been cold and haughty. Instead, they were amazingly expressive, tinged with a desperation that pulled at him. *Why was she desperate, and who was she running from?*

He wrenched his gaze away and stared at the white Formica tabletop before him, annoyed by the wave of heat rising in his cheeks. What the hell was the matter with him? Instead of wondering about her past, he should be figuring a way out of this fix.

"Say, Lang, are you still looking for a cook out at your place?" Sally called to him.

He was tempted to lie through his teeth and tell them all the job was filled, but lying just wasn't his style. Too many people had lied to him in his time. "Yes, Sally, I am," he got out through gritted teeth.

Sally was already shepherding the blonde in his direction. Danny Parson, doggone his miserable hide, sent him a wink and smiled hugely. Lang rose to his feet as she approached his table. The manners his mother had drilled into him were second nature, even though he was feeling as flustered as a thirteen-year-old boy on his first date.

"Hello, Mr. Nelson. My name is Beth Richards."

"Call me Lang," he replied automatically as he reached out to take her proffered hand. The skin of her palm was soft and smooth. She might be looking for work as a cook now, but the softness of her hand told him that wasn't how she'd made her living recently.

"I'll call you Lang only if you will call me Beth,"

THE COWBOY AND THE HEIRESS 13

she replied with a tentative smile that made his blood pound faster in his ears.

"Have you had breakfast?" he asked her abruptly. Close up, she was even more lovely. He scanned her features, searching for some imperfection. If she was wearing makeup, he could see no sign of it. Her lashes were long and golden brown, the same color as her fine arching brows. Her cheekbones were high and slanted, her nose regally straight. The fullness of her lips made a man think of sinful things done in dark rooms on big soft beds. Her chin some might consider a flaw. It was a trifle on the square side, hinting at a strength at odds with her dreamy eyes. All in all, she was far too alluring for his peace of mind.

"No, I haven't."

"Sally, could you fetch us a couple of menus?" he asked the waitress hovering nearby.

"I don't need to look at a menu," Beth countered. "I'd like a sweet roll and more coffee please."

Although he'd eaten a quick breakfast at the ranch, Lang decided he could find room for some of Danny's fried eggs and hash browns. After he placed his order, Sally beamed at them. "All right. I'll get Danny to hurry that right up so that you two can eat a nice cozy breakfast together. I'll tell you this, hon: You'd be real lucky to hire on at the Rafter N. Lang Nelson is as fine a man as you'll find in these parts."

Lang glowered after Sally. *Why do half the folk in Perry County feel like they have to matchmake for me? Just because I'm thirty-six and still single doesn't mean I'm doomed to be a bachelor forever. Marrying is serious business. I'm just taking my time finding the right lady.*

He glanced back at Beth Richards. She was eyeing him quizzically, a smile playing on her lips. Was Beth Richards really her name? She looked more like an

Elizabeth or a Katherine to him. Oh well, it wasn't really his business what her name was. It was time he started discouraging her from the crazy notion of cooking for his outfit.

"Have you ever worked as a cook before?"

Her amusement over Sally's obvious matchmaking quickly faded. "No," she admitted slowly. "I have attended several excellent cooking schools, though."

"My ranch hands don't want to eat canapés and quiche lorraine."

"I didn't think they would," she replied with a quiet dignity that made him regret his sarcasm. "I can cook anything from haute cuisine to biscuits and stew. Cooking is the one thing I'm good at."

He wondered at the bitterness in her tone. Surely a woman of her background was good at lots of things, from playing tennis to having her nails and hair done each week. *Sonya had certainly been good at those things.* As soon as the memory came to him, he tried to banish it from his mind. Sonya was past history—old history, at that. It wouldn't be fair to tar the woman across the table with same brush. It wouldn't be fair at all.

He was grateful when Sally arrived just then with their food. The way Beth Richards dug into her sweet roll made him think it had been a long time since she had last eaten. Always one to appreciate good food, Lang did likewise, and they were both quiet for a time.

While they ate, he thought to look for a wedding ring. She could easily be a runaway wife. He soon discovered she wore no rings. Her hands were lightly tanned, with no telltale whiteness on her ring finger. So there was no Mr. Richards. Lang was dismayed by how much pleasure that notion gave him.

THE COWBOY AND THE HEIRESS   15

Looking at her hands was a mistake. They were long and slim and elegant. It was all too easy to wonder what her touch would feel like. Disgusted with the track his wayward thoughts were taking, Lang made himself concentrate on Danny's crispy hash browns.

"Could you tell me a little more about the job?" she asked at last.

He looked up from his plate to find her watching him with an earnest expression at odds with her cool, sophisticated facade. He was beginning to think the lady truly did need a job for some mysterious reason of her own. "The Rafter N has always been a cattle ranch, but this summer we just started taking guests. I need a cook who can feed my hired hands and the guests."

"Do you expect your cook to prepare two separate sets of meals?"

"No, the guests who come to our place expect simple hearty food, and the Rafter N has always fed its hands well. The same menu will be fine for all of us, including me and my family. In fact, we all eat in the same room together."

"How many people would I be cooking for?"

"We never have more than twelve guests at a time, and I have two hands. That would be about twenty all told, counting yourself. My housekeeper, Elsie, will help you with the washing up, but she's so busy keeping the guest quarters and the ranch house clean that she won't be able to help much with food preparation."

"I think I can handle that. I've cooked dinners for a hundred."

"Cooking three meals a day, six days a week, for twenty people is damned hard work."

"I still believe I can perform this job to your satisfaction. Would Mrs. Nelson like to plan the menus or would you want me to?"

To his chagrin, he felt his face heat again. "There is no Mrs. Nelson."

"But you mentioned a family." When she was puzzled, her fine arching brows drew together, making a delightful little pucker over her nose.

"My two nieces live with me, along with my uncle."

"Your Rafter N sounds like a busy place," she said with a small smile. "Would I need to find an apartment in town or do you have lodging available at the ranch?"

Lang found the formal, precise way she spoke deeply arousing. He wondered what it would take to shake that poise of hers.

"The Rafter N is a good thirty miles from town, and my hands need to be fed right at six o'clock in the morning. That's why my cooks usually live on the ranch. Would that be a problem for you?"

"On the contrary, it sounds like a most satisfactory arrangement."

"The cook's cabin isn't much," he warned her. He was going to have to find a way to scare her off and find it fast.

"I'd have a log cabin all to myself?" For the first time, he saw a spark of eagerness in her lovely eyes. Suddenly, she looked much younger and less world-weary.

"It's just a single room with a small bath added to it. That cabin will get mighty cold come wintertime. The only heat you'll have is from a woodstove."

"Will I have to split my own wood?" she asked with misleading sweetness. "I've always wanted to learn how to handle an ax." Then he realized that

THE COWBOY AND THE HEIRESS 17

she knew he didn't want her to take the job, and that fact amused her.

"I expect we can provide you with wood," he replied gruffly.

"How much are the wages?"

As they discussed what he was willing to pay, Lang wondered if he needed to have his head examined. He was actually considering hiring her. He had to find a good cook—and soon. The future of the Rafter N now depended on the success of the venture he had begun this summer, and his guests wouldn't be returning if they weren't fed well.

Two weeks ago, when his last cook had quit and run off with a handsome bull rider she met at the Perrytown rodeo, Lang had placed ads in every paper within two hundred miles. Summer was a busy time in ranch country, though, and he hadn't received a single reply.

Beth Richards will quit in a week when she realizes what grueling work it is cooking for so many. Then you'll be stuck looking for a cook all over again.

Even if Beth did only stay for a week, Elsie and he would get a break from kitchen duty, and perhaps someone else would answer one of his ads in the meantime. Hopefully Beth Richards wouldn't give anyone food poisoning in the brief time she stayed at the Rafter N.

Lang leaned back and looked Beth over again. Even the meager wages he paid didn't put her off. Every instinct he possessed told him this woman meant trouble. Life was crazy enough at the Rafter N these days without taking more home with him.

She must have sensed his reluctance, for she leaned forward and clasped her hands together. "I know I don't have references or experience of the sort you want, but I promise I am a good cook. I may make mistakes, but I'll learn from them, and I am a hard worker." She hesitated for a moment. "Please, I need this job. Just try me for a week. If you don't like my cooking, I'll move on."

Lang blinked. *It had cost her to ask outright for the job that way.* He could see the pride in her. It showed in the way she held herself and the way she spoke. He doubted she often had to ask anyone for anything. The telltale huskiness in her voice and the shadow in her eyes finally convinced him. If she needed a place to hide, the Rafter N could take her in for a time. Hell, it had been a safe haven and hideout for various sorts since his great-granddaddy had stopped robbing banks and gone straight over a hundred years ago.

He'd just make damn certain the trouble dogging her heels wouldn't hurt him or any of his own.

"All right, Beth Richards," he found himself saying. "You've got a job. When do you want to start?"

She sent him an odd smile he couldn't quite interpret. "I'm between engagements presently. I can start today, if you wish."

Lang thought of the mountain of dishes he had left in the kitchen sink and smiled for the first time. "Lady, I most definitely wish. Let's get you out to the Rafter N before you change your mind." He reached down for his wallet. When he glanced up again, she was staring at the bill lying on the table between them, and she was blushing.

"I'm sorry. I can't pay for my share," she said haltingly. "Could you take it out of my wages?"

"This one's on the house," he replied shortly and threw the money on the table for Sally. Picking up his white straw cowboy hat, he wondered how Beth Richards had landed in Perrytown without enough money to pay for breakfast. No wonder she was desperate for work. Whatever situation she was running from, she must have left it in a hurry.

She started to reach for her suitcases, but he picked them up and waited for her to precede him. Although he nodded to several folks he knew, he didn't stop to chat with anyone. They all watched him with great interest. The news that Lang Nelson had hired a beautiful stranger to be his cook would be all over Perrytown before the day was over.

When they passed by the cash register, Danny stuck his head out the door of his kitchen. Beth paused and smiled at him with such warmth and sweetness that Lang swore under his breath. She hadn't smiled at him that way, and he had just given her a job.

"Danny, that was one of the best sweet rolls I ever tasted. Would you consider trading the recipe? My grandmother used to make a pecan pie that would make your mouth water."

"You've got yourself a deal." Danny grinned at her. "Bring that recipe by anytime you want. Good luck out at the Rafter N."

"Thank you. And thank you, Sally," she called out to the waitress. Sally smiled and waved. Afraid his cook might spend the rest of the day at the diner chatting with her new friends, Lang impatiently opened the door for her. After they stepped out into the cool, sunny Colorado morning, he led the way to his old Chevy pickup.

He grimaced when he looked down at her elegant leather suitcases and then at the dusty bed of his truck. "I'll put your suitcase up with us. The cab is cleaner."

He took the suitcases around to the driver's side and hefted them onto the bench seat. Beth had already climbed up on the passenger side. She sat quietly, looking straight ahead, her beautiful features composed and controlled.

While he settled the suitcases between them, he noticed the engraved initials beside the handles. KEH, they read. He pondered those letters as he started up the truck and headed out of the parking lot.

E could stand for Elizabeth. He had probably been right to think she looked more like an Elizabeth than a Beth. He also had been right to think she was running from something or someone. Either she had stolen the suitcase or she was lying about her last name.

Neither possibility made him feel particularly confident about the mysterious young woman he had just hired to be his cook. More worrisome was the way he reacted every time he looked at her. Just sitting this close to her in the cab made his blood pound in his veins and his body tighten uncomfortably. Wondering if he had just made a major mistake, Lang turned the truck onto the road leading toward home.

TWO

Beth watched the emerald green hay meadows and rolling gray hills dotted with sagebrush flash past the windows of the truck. In the distance the rocky pinnacles of the Zirkel mountain range rose wild and beckoning. *It's all just as vivid as you remember.* She was finally here, on the western slope of Colorado, about to start a new life. Her dream had come true at last, but she was almost too tired to enjoy it.

A large handsome cowboy with sandy blond hair and compelling brown eyes had never been a part of that dream. Beth bit her lip and risked a quick glance at her new employer. Lang Nelson was watching the road, his big competent hands relaxed on the wheel, his mind obviously on other matters. *He's probably thinking about the ranch he spoke of with such pride in his voice.*

She shifted slightly so that she could study him without being obvious. He was the kind of man most women dreamed about, but she wasn't like other women. Too many handsome men had courted her for the wrong reasons over the years, and sheer looks could no longer turn her head. He was tall and lean, his face weathered to an appealing shade of teak by years of work out-of-doors. His worn denim jacket framed his broad shoulders perfectly. The plaid shirt, cowboy hat, and boots he wore all looked natural and right on him.

His hair was a wonderful blond-brown color. Thick and shaggy, it had a tendency to fall across his forehead. Rimmed round by long dark lashes, his eyes were the color of coffee with amber glints in them. His eyebrows were thick and straight. His jaw was strong, his chin had just a hint of a cleft in it, and his lips were beautifully shaped. When she found her gaze lingering on his mouth, she forced herself to look out the window once again.

All in all, Lang Nelson was a dangerously attractive man. Many of the women in the world she had just left would do anything to entice him to their beds. She guessed the women guests at his ranch probably vied to attract his attention.

But she wasn't interested in a man right now, particularly the sort who liked to organize and control others' lives. She didn't know a great deal about her employer yet, but she did know he was the kind to make decisions quickly and act on them. He could hardly run a ranch successfully and not be a controller. *If you try to control one moment of my life outside of work, Lang Nelson, I'll leave the Rafter N so fast your head will spin.*

She had never realized what a cage her life had been, but now that she had broken out she was never going to let anyone cage her in again.

She hoped and prayed she had covered her tracks well. She had cut up all her credit cards, for she knew they could be used to trace her movements. Instead, she had withdrawn all the cash from her checking account, money she had earned on her own over the years, and used it to leapfrog her way across the country, buying tickets on small commuter planes and buses and staying in cheap hotels. She had doubled back several times since she left New York, hoping to leave false trails and obscure her final destination.

There was no doubt in her mind that such measures were absolutely necessary. Her father and her ex-fiancé were going to try to find her, and the resources available to them were formidable. A little shiver ran down the back of her neck. She didn't want to imagine her father's anger when he found her gone. But she didn't mean to be found, and she didn't mean to go back.

Lang slowed the truck and turned off the main road. They drove under a large wooden Rafter N sign with the ranch brand burned into the planking on either side of it. She smiled when she realized the Zirkels were a great deal closer now. The ranch spread across the meadows beneath the first ridges of the wilderness. She promised herself she would go on a long hike up in those mountains on her first day off.

"What a beautiful place," she breathed. "How long have you owned it?"

"My great-grandfather started the ranch back in the eighteen seventies. He bought the land here from the Utes for a hundred horses. An enterprising fellow, he decided to give up robbing banks to sell beef to the miners. Fortunately for his descendants, his sense of timing was good. If he'd kept on robbing banks, he probably would have gotten his neck stretched. Instead, he jumped into the cattle business just when the mining towns were booming and people were willing to pay a lot of money for beef."

Beth smiled at the dry humor in his tone. Lang sounded quite fond of his colorful ancestor.

"My family has run horses and cattle here since

that time," he continued. "It's been a profitable operation until relatively recently. Unfortunately, too many folks from out-of-state have discovered how beautiful it is here on the western slope. Some come in for the skiing and stay and buy vacation homes. Property taxes in our county have been rising steadily, while cattle prices have fallen. Labor costs have gone up, too, as most of our young folk find jobs in cities or resort towns."

He hesitated for a moment, and then he added, "The bottom line is, if I can't make the guest business work I'm going to have to sell out."

Beth stared at him in dismay. His face was grim, his brown eyes dark as their gazes met. "That's why I had to find a good cook, and find one fast. Guest ranches are a dime a dozen these days. I'm not the only rancher who's trying to save his place by catering to dudes. I studied the industry for a long time before I decided to try it. Folks remember the food and service. That's what sets the successful guest ranches apart from the rest and keeps people coming back.

"What I'm trying to say is, if you can't handle the work after a few days, I'd appreciate your letting me know."

"You mean, you'd rather I quit than give your guests heartburn five meals in a row."

He cleared his throat. "Something like that."

"Your confidence in my abilities is heartwarming." Beth didn't try to keep the bitterness from her tone. *Didn't anyone believe she could be good at something?*

"I'll be the first one to sing hallelujah if you're as good a cook as you claim to be. It's clear you've got your own reasons for needing this job." He glanced meaningfully at the suitcase sitting between them. Beth felt her cheeks begin to burn.

THE COWBOY AND THE HEIRESS 25

"I'm just letting you know I have my own reasons for wanting you to do your job well," he finished quietly after a long moment.

Beth took in a deep breath to steady herself. She could see the man's point. He had a lot riding on this guest venture of his, and he had no way of knowing whether or not he had just hired a decent cook. He had only her word, which he obviously didn't trust. She sighed inwardly. She would have to let her cooking speak for itself.

"All right. I understand what's at stake. I'll tell you right away if I'm in over my head."

"Thank you," he said simply. He smiled at her, the first real smile he had given her with no restraint or reserve in it, and her heart began to race. *Lang Nelson, you are even more lethal than I realized.* Suddenly the cab of the truck seemed far too small and intimate. She was casting about desperately for some neutral topic they could talk about when she realized they were approaching the ranch buildings.

Taking in the main ranch house in a single glance, she smiled in delight. Lang Nelson's home looked just like a Colorado ranch house ought to look. A two-story dwelling built from logs and granite, it had a long porch that wrapped all around the base of the first floor. Large windows on both floors would have spectacular views of the hay meadows in the foreground and the mountains in the distance.

Suddenly, the big front door opened, and several people spilled out to greet Lang. In the forefront were two pretty teenage girls dressed in jeans and plaid western shirts. They ran up to the driver's side door and began speaking the second he opened it.

"Uncle Lang, did you get it? Did you get it?" they sang out in chorus. Beth realized she was looking at identical twins. Both girls had fine even features, wayward brown curls, and lively blue eyes.

He grinned at them and reached for a parcel behind the seat. "It was there at the post office. But before you two go rushing off to listen to your music, I want you to remember your manners and say hello to Beth Richards, our new cook."

"Hi," they said obediently.

"This is Stacy, and this is Tony." Lang gestured to each twin. Even as she smiled and nodded, Beth looked at them despairingly and wondered how she was ever going to tell them apart.

"We've been waiting all month for this CD to come." Stacy flashed her a smile which suddenly made the resemblance to her uncle obvious.

"We'll come down to the kitchen and catch you later," Tony added. The two of them disappeared back into the ranch house, Stacy clutching the parcel Lang had handed her.

Lang smiled at Beth a little sheepishly. "They're so crazy about music that I let them subscribe to a teen music club. Soon it will be boys, and then I'm going to miss this music phase."

Beth looked at her employer with new respect. If he was raising those two girls on his own, he had his hands full. When Lang got out of the truck, Beth followed his example. An older man stepped forward. His face was wrinkled, his hair sparse and grizzled, but his light blue eyes were shrewd and clear. He addressed Beth directly before Lang could begin the introductions.

"Beth Richards, you're the purtiest cook we've ever had on the Rafter N. If you can cook half as good as you look, my belly is going to be mighty happy this summer. My name is Harry Tuckett, but most folks just call me Tucker. This young whippersnapper here is my nephew." The old man gestured to Lang with a grin.

Beth held her hand out and quickly discovered surprising strength in Tucker's grasp.

Tucker turned to face Lang then, his expression all business. "That bull you bought last winter in Denver is sick. We may have to call Doc Burton. Before you go haring off to look at that bull, though, you best spend a half hour or so with the Petersons. They want you to show them a good fishing hole. I told 'em I knew every good fishing spot on the ranch, but Mrs. Peterson wants you to take them."

Lang's face tightened at this news. Beth smiled to herself. She had been right to think the women guests were going to be all over this rugged rancher.

A trim, gray-haired woman with lovely cornflower-blue eyes and rosy cheeks spoke up last. "Lang, why don't you let me take Beth to the cook's cabin? I'll help her get settled, and you can get right to work."

"Thank you, Elsie. I'd appreciate that. Beth, I'll probably see you at lunch. If you have any questions, Elsie here probably knows more about this ranch than anyone."

Feeling sorry for her harassed-looking employer, Beth picked up her suitcases and followed Elsie toward the outbuildings. She was going to make sure the food at the Rafter N was one area of ranch operations that Lang no longer had to worry about.

On the way to her new cabin, Beth learned that Elsie was Lang's housekeeper, and she had worked on the Rafter N for over twenty years. After giving her a quick tour of her new cabin, Elsie said, "Take your time getting settled. Come down to the main house when you're done. I'd love to stay and chat, but we have four guest cabins changing over today, and I have my hands full."

With that the friendly woman slipped away and left Beth to her explore her new lodgings. Smiling happily to herself, Beth prowled about the cabin. It was perfect—small enough to feel snug, but not cramped.

Enjoying the fresh scent of pines, she quickly unpacked her suitcase and took a shower. She glanced at herself in the mirror and frowned at the circles under her eyes. She had been traveling for three weeks straight, and last night she had talked with the trucker who had given her a lift from St. Louis about his marital problems for hours—to avoid his groping hands.

Although she was bone-weary, she was too excited about her new job to linger. As soon as she had changed into clean jeans and a simple work shirt, she hurried down to the main ranch house.

When she opened the large front doors and stepped inside, she discovered Lang Nelson's home was rustically but comfortably furnished. The house seemed light, spacious, and welcoming. Strains of music with a deep base beat echoed from upstairs someplace. Beth grinned at the notion of the twins enjoying their new CD. What fun it must be to have a sister to share crazes like music. Her own childhood had been a lonely one.

She found her way to the kitchen easily enough. It was a large open room with two big picture windows looking out at the mountains in the distance. A small breakfast table sat before one of the windows. Beth smiled when she saw the fireplace set along the interior wall, and she smiled again when she discovered a new, industrial-grade stove and dual ovens.

Going through a set of swinging doors, she found a large dining room. She sighed when she returned to the kitchen and spotted the stack of pots and pans in the sink. *No wonder Lang Nelson is so eager for you to start today.*

Shaking her head, she rolled up her sleeves and set to work. An hour later, she had finished tidying the kitchen and was taking inventory of the supplies in the pantry when Elsie hurried into the kitchen bearing a large armful of linens.

After a quick glance around, she smiled approvingly. "I see you've been busy. You won't usually have to do so much washing up—it just gets a little hectic around here on changeover days. The twins will set the tables, serve the food, clear, and put the dishes in the dishwasher. You and I will do the rest of the cleanup."

"What's for lunch, and when should I serve it?"

"Sandwiches are fine. You should be feeding twelve today, since eight of our guests went home this morning, and Lang won't be picking up the next set until late this afternoon. We usually serve lunch right at noon and dinner at seven. We're glad to have you aboard. You're like the cavalry coming over the hill in one of those old westerns." With that declaration, Elsie bustled out of the room.

Beth was happy to have the kitchen to herself again. She hummed under her breath as she whipped up some brownies and made sandwiches. The twins arrived fifteen minutes before lunchtime and set the tables for her. As the girls worked, they still managed to pepper her with questions about herself. She told them the truth when she could. They were fascinated to discover she was from the East Coast. They seemed to think anyplace was more exciting than Perrytown.

At first, Beth wasn't certain if she was supposed to eat in the dining room, but the twins made it very clear in their friendly exuberant way that they wanted her to sit with them. She was still standing awkwardly behind her chair, wondering if it was truly appropriate for the cook to eat at the family's table, when Lang arrived with Tucker and the two ranch hands. Hank and Jim, young cowboys in their twenties, greeted her diffidently before they sat down at a different table with Tucker.

Lang came in and sat down next to Stacy. When Elsie arrived and took the chair beside him, Beth at last slipped into her own chair. The Rafter N was obviously a very casual place. Although she had often made friends with her family's staff, she couldn't imagine her father sitting down to a meal with his chef or housekeeper.

After starting in on their food, the twins continued questioning her where they had left off. "Why did you come to Perrytown?" Stacy asked with the directness of a teenager.

Although Lang was making quick work of his sandwich, Beth noticed that he paused between bites to hear her reply.

She chose her words carefully. "When I was just about your age, my family went to a dude ranch here in Colorado. I fell in love with this country, and I always promised myself I would come back here someday to live."

She was relieved when the twins accepted her simple explanation. She was aware that Lang was watching her curiously, but she didn't offer any further information. He looked as if he was about to ask her a question when the Petersons arrived and took the last places at the table. Elaine Peterson promptly proceeded to monopolize the conversation. An attractive woman in her forties, she obviously spent a great deal of time trying to keep her age at bay. Beth had known too many women like her in her old life, women who devoted hours every day to their appearance.

At first Beth was grateful to Elaine Peterson, for she wanted someone else to be the focus of the conversation. Unfortunately, listening to the others talk gave her too much time to look at Lang, who sat directly across the table from her. There was no doubt that he was an impressive specimen of western manhood. *Advertising executives in New York would flip over him,* she thought. *He would make a perfect cowboy model for anything from Levi's to men's cologne.*

This afternoon he wore his sleeves rolled up, and she could see the dusting of dark hair on his tan, muscular forearms. His hands were big and capable. *They would be gentle handling horses, or when he touched a woman he loved.* When she realized she was staring at his hands her cheeks warmed, and she forced herself to look away.

He was much more genial and talkative with the rest than he had been with her this morning. She was charmed by the way he teased the twins. He treated Elsie like a good friend, and he handled Elaine Peterson's efforts to attract his attention with considerable aplomb. He spent much of the meal talking with Henry Peterson about his morning of fly fishing.

She felt Lang's gaze on her several times during the meal. Only at the end, however, did he speak to her directly.

"These are mighty fine brownies you made, Beth," he complimented her as he reached for a second one.

"A cook can't go too far wrong with brownies," she replied tartly, still miffed that he had doubted her cooking abilities.

"I suppose not," he admitted, "although Stacy

here made a batch so bitter not even our pig would eat them."

"That's not fair," Stacy replied indignantly. "How was I supposed to know that I had to use sweetened chocolate?"

"Reading the recipe might have helped," he countered with a grin.

Tony flew to the defense of her twin. "What about that cake you made for our birthday last year?"

"So I left out a little baking powder. You two had a fine time using my cake as a Frisbee, as I remember."

Beth smiled to herself as they all rose and the twins began clearing the tables. It was hard to imagine Lang baking a cake for his nieces, but she was touched that he had made the effort. She wondered what had happened to the girls' parents. She was surprised when Lang stayed after lunch and helped her wash up. She was even more surprised when he brought up the topic of the twins when everyone else had left.

"You're probably wondering why the twins are living here," he said as he handed her the brownie pan to dry.

"As a matter of fact, I was," Beth replied, trying not to smile at the incongruous sight of one of the most macho men she had ever seen up to his elbows in soapsuds. "Are the girls just staying for the summer?"

"No, their parents died in a car crash two years ago. I'm their legal guardian."

"Those poor girls," Beth said softly after a long moment. "What a terrible shame." She had lost her own mother when she was fourteen, and she still missed her to this day.

"I'm trying to do my best by them. They miss their parents, but they adore Elsie."

"From what I saw today, Stacy and Tony are crazy about you. They're lucky you wanted to take them in."

"I'd hardly let anyone else raise my own kin," he said so abruptly that Beth swallowed hard and turned her attention once again to the last pan that needed drying.

While the awkward silence stretched between them, Lang quickly finished up at the sink. He turned away and took a clipboard down from the wall.

"Here's the menu for this week," he said in a brisk impersonal tone. "Feel free to make some changes if you want. It's your kitchen now. We put simple appetizers out for the guests at six o'clock, and serve dinner promptly at seven." With that he handed her the clipboard and strode from the kitchen.

Beth took the clipboard over to the table and sat down. She tried to concentrate on the menu, but it was no use. Instead, she found her mind drifting to her new employer and the tragic information he had just shared with her. She thought she had heard anger in his voice when he spoke of the accident which had claimed his brother and sister-in-law's lives. That anger made her wonder how the accident had happened.

The man certainly had plenty of responsibilities and challenges. Keeping the ranch he loved and raising teenage nieces on his own was a full plate. She wondered why he had never married. Had he been too busy working on the Rafter N? Were the women in these parts blind?

Beth sternly turned her thoughts away from Lang Nelson. A handsome rancher and his family's tragedies were none of her business. She had come to the West to find out who Beth Richards was, and to reclaim her independence. Only time would tell if the Rafter N was the haven she had been searching for.

THREE

Her body ached with fatigue by the time Beth sat down to dinner that night. She ate at a table with Tucker and the Petersons and two new couples Lang had picked up at the airport that afternoon. Tucker kept everyone entertained with his colorful yarns about life on the Rafter N.

After the meal, Beth received several compliments on the simple pot roast, mashed potatoes, vegetables, and carrot cake she had prepared, but she was too worn out to truly appreciate the praise. When she went into the kitchen to help with the washing up, Elsie took one look at her and said sharply, "You should go back to your cabin right now and go to bed. Lang, look at her. The poor girl is exhausted."

Through a weary haze, she saw Lang peering down at her. Moments later he took her by the elbow and ushered her from the kitchen. She did her best to answer the chorus of cheerful goodnights from Tucker, Elsie, and the twins.

"I can find my own way back to my cabin," she said with a flash of spirit when they reached the front door.

"I'm sure you can, but I'm so happy to have a cook who can make a carrot cake like that, I'm not going to take any chance of your getting lost." He

THE COWBOY AND THE HEIRESS   35

kept his hand under her elbow as he guided her down the front steps of the ranch house. Despite the claim she had made, Beth wasn't entirely sure she could have found her cabin. She was glad to have a guide now, for everything looked so different in the dark.

"You honestly liked my cake?"

"I'll probably dream about it tonight," he replied lightly. Actually, he was far more apt to dream about her, but Lang wasn't about to admit that fact aloud, not for a million dollars. The last thing he wanted to do was let a woman like her know he was attracted to her. They said nothing more until they reached her cabin. He opened the door for her and switched on the overhead light.

Lang glanced down at her and cursed mentally. Elsie was right. Beth was so tired she was almost asleep on her feet. She clearly had been exhausted that morning when she came into the diner. He was sorry she'd had to do so much on her first day. Then again, he reminded himself grimly, they all were pushing themselves hard these days on the Rafter N.

Beth stumbled forward and sank down on her bed. Lang watched in some amusement as she yawned, closed her eyes, and toppled back on the pillows.

"Oh, no, you don't. You'll sleep much better if you change into your nightclothes first." He reached forward and shook her foot.

"I don't want to change." She curled up on her side and grumbled into her pillow, "I want to go to sleep right now."

How did she manage to sound regal, sleepy, and childlike all at once? "I'll make you a deal. You hustle yourself into your bathroom and change, and I'll pull the covers down for you. You can be sound asleep in two minutes."

She lifted a bleary face from the pillows and shot him a disdainful look. "I knew you were the managing type. I knew it from the first moment I laid eyes on you."

Why did she seem to think being a managing person was such a terrible thing? "So everyone tells me. Right now, I'm trying to manage my tired cook into a good night's sleep so that I can get three more delectable meals out of her tomorrow."

She sat up on the bed again, looking partially mollified. "I'm not sure I'd go so far as to say dinner was delectable. I thought it was tolerable, all things considered."

"Taking into account the amount of time you had to prepare it, and what you had to work with, you mean," he suggested ironically.

"Exactly," she said with another yawn. "I'll do better tomorrow."

Before she collapsed back onto the bed, he went over to the small chest of drawers and rummaged through it until he found a surprisingly plain and serviceable blue flannel nightgown. He did his best to ignore the piles of white lacy lingerie laying beside it. He caught up the nightgown and tossed it to her.

She caught it reflexively. "Why, thank you, Lang."

It was the first time he had ever heard her say his first name. Once again, he found her low, slightly husky voice and her cultured accent tremendously arousing. His body tightened reflexively. He was shocked by how much he longed to tumble her back on that bed and cover that gorgeous body of hers with his own.

"Get in the bathroom and get that nightgown

on," he said through clenched teeth. He was relieved when she finally rose to her feet and did as he asked.

While she was in the bathroom, he tried not to imagine her wearing some of those lacy bits of underthings he had just seen in her drawer, but it was no use. He was acutely aware of the fact that she was taking her clothes off that very moment behind the bathroom door. He leaned over and flipped back her bedspread and blanket, just as he had promised he would. Touching the sheets that would cover her this night didn't help matters any. He was hard with need by the time she emerged again.

That girlish blue nightgown she was wearing should have helped to cool his ardor. With its high neck and long sleeves, there was absolutely nothing revealing about it. Wearing her long blond hair down around her shoulders, though, she looked like a dangerously seductive angel, and his blood boiled hotter.

"I don't think you should consider a career in service," she announced and sat down on the edge of the bed. "Humble doesn't seem to be in your repertoire."

"Since I wasn't considering being a butler, I think I'll live," he gritted out. He saw a flash of a slim shapely calf as she lifted her legs and slipped them under the covers.

"You did say you wanted breakfast served at six o'clock, didn't you?"

"That's when my hands and I will want it. The guests usually eat at eight." He was surprised to see she was awake enough to reach over and set a small traveling alarm clock beside her bed.

"Very well. I'll have your breakfast ready by six.

Good night, Lang, and thank you for showing me back to my cabin."

He had to smile at being dismissed so properly by his own cook. As long as he was playing the role of lady's maid, he decided he damn well ought to tuck her in while he was at it. Besides, he wanted to see if he could disturb her as much as she disturbed him.

He sauntered forward and stood beside her bed. Her eyes widened, and she shrank back against the pillows. He leaned across her and pulled her covers up higher. His hand brushed a lock of her silken hair in the process, and it seemed to burn against his hand.

He quickly realized the game he was playing was going to rebound on him. She smelled like wild roses in the spring. He forced himself to continue with the charade and tucked the sheet and blanket in on his side under the mattress. It took every ounce of willpower he possessed not to touch her.

"Do you usually tuck in all your cooks?" she asked him warily.

"Only on their first night, and only when they look as tired as you do." He wrenched his gaze away from her lovely lips. As much as he was tempted to kiss her, he needed a good cook even more. He had a feeling that if he gave her any indication of how much he wanted her, she would load up her suitcases and leave the Rafter N before Elsie's rooster started to crow in the morning.

He felt a pang when he stepped back and saw her lying in the bed, looking frail and defenseless, the blue shadows under her eyes more obvious than ever. What was so awful in her past that had made her push herself to the edge of exhaustion to escape it? The urge to protect defenseless folk had always been strong in him. *Beth Richards is hardly defenseless,* he told himself sternly. *She's too poised, too sophisticated, and too elegant to need any help from a hick cowboy like you.*

"Thank you for hiring me, Lang Nelson. I like your family, and I like your Rafter N." Her eyes were already shut, her precise diction slurred by sleepiness.

Damnation. He would not, could not, let her get past his guard, but the woman was making a dangerously good effort. He wondered if the sweet spontaneous side of her was all an act.

"Good night, Beth Richards," he replied. *Or whoever you are,* he added silently. He turned around, shut off her light, and closed the door behind him.

When Beth woke the next morning, it took her several moments to realize where she was. The air chilling her nose and cheeks was too cold for her to be in her beautifully furnished, perfectly heated bedroom at home. After she opened her eyes and saw log walls all around her, she realized she wasn't waking up in another seedy hotel room, either.

Ah, now she remembered. She was at the Rafter N, just the sort of place where she had dreamed of finding work. Unfortunately this ranch came with a handsome but domineering rancher, just the sort of man she had hoped to avoid.

She blushed when she remembered him tucking her in last night. She had been so exhausted that she wasn't really sure what she had said to him. When he leaned over her to tuck in her covers, the temptation to reach up and touch his sandy blond hair and kiss his beautiful mouth had been perilously strong. Thank heaven she had managed to control herself. Much of the time, her new employer looked at her as if he considered her the lowest form of life. Somehow he must know or guess her rich indulged background. *Considering how susceptible you seem to be to him, you would be wise to spend as little time as possible with Lang Nelson.*

Suddenly, she realized that the sunlight pouring through her curtains was far too bright. It couldn't possibly be five o'clock in the morning. Frantically, she reached for the alarm beside her bed. The damning numbers 9:00 flashed at her. She groaned and covered her face with her hands. She must have slept right through the alarm. Swearing under her breath, she hustled out of bed and hurried into her bathroom.

When she entered the ranch house fifteen minutes later, she found Elsie tidying up the living room. Beth felt her cheeks starting to warm as she approached Lang's housekeeper.

"Good morning," Elsie said with her easy smile.

"I'm so sorry I slept in. I swear I'll never do it again. Someone should have come and woken me."

The older woman just waved off her apology. "We all knew you needed the rest. The twins wanted to get you up just so they could talk to you, but Lang wouldn't hear of letting the girls bother you. He made breakfast for the hands and guests himself."

Beth was torn between dismay and surprise. The surprise won. "Lang Nelson can cook?"

"He's a better cook than I am," the older woman said with a chuckle. "You can sample his buttermilk pancakes. There's a plate of them warming for you in the oven."

"I can't believe I slept in my first full day on the job." Beth shook her head with chagrin. "I wonder if I'll still have a job by dinnertime tonight."

THE COWBOY AND THE HEIRESS   41

"Something tells me Lang wouldn't let you go now for a million dollars. He happens to be very partial to carrot cake. He also needs a good cook desperately."

"So he said. Well, I'd better get to work, especially since I've gotten such a late start."

"There's plenty of time between now and lunch. Make sure that you eat your breakfast first," the housekeeper called after her.

Beth did exactly that. She turned on the radio to a wonderful, honky-tonk western radio station while she devoured Lang's delectable pancakes. After mixing some cookie dough to chill, she took time to pour through a cookbook of frontier recipes.

As the morning progressed, she decided she was in heaven. She had her own kitchen. She had wonderful ingredients to work with, like fresh eggs, fresh milk, and beef. She was earning her own way at last, with no safety ropes or nets to catch her—and the glittering world where she had never been happy was thousands of miles away at last.

When Lang came in early to check on his guests, the smell of baking drew him to the kitchen like a magnet. He paused in the doorway to watch his new cook expertly flipping a batch of cookies off a cookie sheet. She was singing—slightly off-key but with real enthusiasm—along with an old Hank Williams song on the radio. Her cheeks were slightly flushed, a few tendrils of golden hair escaping from the simple braid she wore down her back.

Beth Richards continued to surprise him at every turn. He had never met an easterner who truly liked western music. More startling was how at home she looked in his kitchen. She ought to be lounging on a yacht or having her body wrapped and pampered in a spa. Yet here she was, clad in Levi's, sneakers, and a flannel shirt, putting together lunch for his guests and ranch hands as if it were the sort of job she did every day.

He thought he might find her out of sorts because of the pile of pots and pans he and Elsie had once again been forced to leave her. Yet, if Beth's singing was anything to judge by, she was quite content this morning. As he moved closer, intent on stealing a cookie, he was pleased to see she looked much better rested.

He reached around her to snatch a cookie from the counter. She dropped her spatula and spun about to face him, her body crouched in a fighting stance, her arms raised as if to ward off a blow. The fierce strained expression on her face shocked him.

Slowly she lowered her arms. After a long moment, she turned away and picked up her spatula again. As she started flipping cookies once more, she said in a cross tone, "Do you usually sneak up on people like that?"

"I wasn't sneaking. You were just singing too loudly to hear me. Do you usually react that way when you're startled?"

She was quiet for so long that he didn't think she was going to answer his question. "I took a self-defense class last year. The instructor trained us to react that way when we sensed someone stealing up behind us."

He reached out and placed his hand on her shoulder. Gently, he turned her to face him. He studied her face carefully. She was still pale, and she was trembling.

Her irritation was all an act. He had really scared her. He longed to ask her why she had decided to

THE COWBOY AND THE HEIRESS 43

take that self-defense class. He wanted to ask why she had been so frightened when he surprised her from behind. It made him furious to think she might have been attacked. Was that part of the reason why she had run away from her old life?

Now's not the time to ask the lady these questions. She didn't trust him yet. He made himself a promise then and there. One day soon he would find out all the secrets Beth Richards was hiding, and he would protect her from her dragons, if he could.

"I'm sorry that I startled you." He raised his hand and cupped her cheek.

She gazed up at him, her silver-blue eyes wide and wary, but she didn't move away from his touch.

Her skin was intoxicatingly soft against his palm. Telling himself he wished only to offer comfort, he traced the line of her cheek with his fingertips. The rose scent she wore mingled with the sugar and cinnamon of the cookies she had baked. All of a sudden, his mouth watered. He wanted to taste her, he needed to taste those lips which had tempted him from the moment he'd first seen her.

His hands tightened on her shoulders. Her eyes warmed and darkened with a longing which matched his own. The sun-drenched kitchen was quiet except for the sound of a plaintive love ballad playing quietly on the radio.

He lowered his head. She closed her eyes and swayed closer.

And Tucker called out from the dining room, "I smell fresh baked cookies. Beth Richards, I swear it was our lucky day when Lang found you at Danny's place."

Beth's eyes flew open. Lang swore under his breath as she pulled away from him. When Tucker walked into the kitchen, Beth was busily removing the last of the cookies from the baking sheet, and Lang was leaning against the counter munching on one.

"I should have known you'd beat me to it." Tucker snorted with disgust. "I hope you left a few for the rest of us."

"It was a sacrifice, but I left you one or two," Lang replied while he studied Beth out of the corner of his eye. Her cheeks were tinged with color, her expression set. When she glanced at him, her gaze was distant and cool once more.

As he strode off to find his guests, Lang wondered if he had imagined the longing in her eyes a moment ago. One thing was for damn sure. It was going to be twice as hard to stay away from her if the attraction was mutual.

FOUR

Beth gave the little bay mare she rode a nudge with her heels, for they were starting to lag behind the horse and rider ahead of them. She was very aware that Lang rode right behind her on the narrow trail. He was bringing up the end of the long column of dudes—"guests," as Lang preferred his employees call them. They were on their way to a cookout at Beaver Lake, a lovely glacial cirque in the mountains above the ranch, and she didn't want her new boss to think she couldn't keep up with the rest. When the little mare obligingly shifted into a jog, Beth kept her seat easily.

She had liked the riding lessons that were part of her weekly regime growing up, unlike the classes in dancing and deportment, which she had loathed. She felt so comfortable on a horse's back, in fact, that she could look about and enjoy the spectacular view over the valley floor below and the way the late afternoon sun bathed the pines and aspens beside the trail with golden light.

It had been nearly a week since she had arrived at the Rafter N. She had seen relatively little of Lang over the last few days, which was just as well for her peace of mind. Her cheeks warmed every time she thought about that moment in the kitchen when she had come far too close to kissing him. *Just because you like the packaging,* she told herself tartly, *doesn't mean you have to go sampling the contents.*

What puzzled her most about that incident was the light she thought she had seen in Lang's eyes when he bent his head toward hers. She could have sworn he was on the brink of kissing her. It was the first, and only, hint he had let slip in her presence that he might be attracted to her. If anything, she had received the distinct impression that her new boss disapproved of her. When she saw Lang at meals, he was polite toward her and very distant. His guests, his family, and his cowhands received more warmth from him than she did.

It surprised her, therefore, that he had suggested that she ride with him at the back of the column this afternoon. Then she had noticed that particular order placed her between Lang and Elaine Peterson. At mealtimes, she had seen the way the woman had been pursuing Lang relentlessly. Beth's lips twitched. If her riding at the back of the line bought Lang a few moments of peace, she was happy to oblige him.

In the short time she had been at the Rafter N, one thing was already apparent to her: Lang Nelson worked harder than anyone else on his ranch. She wasn't entirely sure she liked her employer and his forceful managing ways, but she couldn't help admiring how determined he was to keep the Rafter N afloat.

"Are you settling in all right?" His deep voice suddenly interrupted her musings.

Beth glanced back over her shoulder at him while she considered the question. "Yes," she replied simply. "I love your ranch."

"My guests love your cooking, so I guess we're

THE COWBOY AND THE HEIRESS 47

even," he said with a humorous twist to his mouth which surprised her.

That smile made her bold. "I saw you take three helpings of my chicken pot pie last night."

"Fishing for compliments?" he said with a raised eyebrow. "All right, I'm mighty partial to your cooking, too. I'm damn glad I stopped by Danny Parson's place that morning, and I thank my lucky stars that your truck driver friend decided to pull off the road in Perrytown."

"Why, thanks, boss." Beth turned back to watch the trail in front of her, warmed through and through by his words. She had received more flowery compliments on her cooking, but somehow his meant a great deal more.

"You look comfortable in that saddle," he commented a few minutes later.

"I've always liked riding," she replied carefully.

He was quiet for several moments, but when she didn't add anything more he spoke again. "Beth Richards, you're the first woman I've ever met that didn't prattle on about herself when given half the chance. I just gave you a fine opportunity to tell me how and when you started riding, and you didn't take it."

"Is that a compliment?" She glanced over her shoulder again. He looked amused, puzzled, and aggrieved all at once.

"It's a statement of fact," he replied shortly, and he didn't speak to her again for the rest of the ride.

Wondering if Lang was irritated at himself for being curious about her, Beth did her best to ignore his brooding presence behind her and to enjoy the scenery instead. This wasn't the first time she had stonewalled his questions about her background.

Her past was her business, and the less he knew about her the better.

When they reached the lake, Tucker, who had been riding at the front of the column, came back to help Beth unload the dinner fixings from the packhorse. She was pleased to discover that there were four sturdy picnic tables on which she could prepare and serve dinner, and an old oil barrel near them which had been converted into a barbecue grill. Beth couldn't help but look around her from time to time as she worked. Beaver Lake was the perfect setting for a cookout. Storm Peak rose steeply above its clear waters. The mountain's sheer ridges and cliffs made Beth wish she'd thought to bring her camera.

While Tucker helped her get the coals started, Lang and Hank looked after the guests. Within minutes, Beth saw with some amusement that Elaine Peterson had attached herself to Lang's side while he helped the rest find good fishing spots around the shore of the lake.

Beth was hip deep in the dinner preparations when Lang suddenly appeared by her table.

"Please, tell me you need some help here."

Beth glanced up to see the look of a hunted animal in his pecan-colored eyes. It was so out of character that she had to laugh.

"You wouldn't by any chance be trying to avoid Mrs. Peterson, would you?"

"You're damn straight I am," he returned with a rueful grin. "That woman will not take 'no' for an answer. I'm beginning to feel like a trophy buck with one hell of a determined hunter on my trail."

Lang Nelson, that smile of yours is way too lethal. No wonder Elaine Peterson is hot on your trail. Beth shook her head and slapped another burger on the grill.

THE COWBOY AND THE HEIRESS 49

"Well, if you plan to hang around in my kitchen, boss, I'll definitely put you to work."

"That's fine by me," he said. "I'm a pretty fair hand at barbecuing."

"Somehow that doesn't surprise me. What is it about men and searing meat?"

"It's a ritual that goes back to our caveman days," he said with great seriousness. "The men used to go out hunting large dangerous game. When they succeeded in killing a mammoth, they brought it home and had a big party while they cooked the meat over an open fire outside the cave. They probably lied about their feats of skill during the hunt, and danced, caroused and celebrated, while the women had to stay inside their dark stuffy caves tending babies."

"Hmm, it sounds as if I would have enjoyed being a caveman more than being a cave-woman. Where did you learn this fascinating theory?"

"I minored in anthropology at the University of Colorado," he replied promptly.

She blinked. So much for assuming her rough tough cowboy boss had never been to college.

"All right," she said swiftly to cover her surprise, "here are your mammoth burgers, and here's the chicken. The chicken's already partially cooked, so don't dry it out."

"Yes, ma'am," he said with surprising meekness as he deftly laid the rest of the burgers and chicken out on the grill. In the meantime, Beth finished placing the garnish for the burgers out on platters.

Beth couldn't resist teasing him a little as she worked. "Mrs. Peterson is a very attractive woman."

"She's married," Lang said shortly.

"I don't think Mr. Peterson would notice if you did take her up on those invitations she's been offering you. He's too obsessed with catching the trophy trout of his dreams."

"A barracuda would be more my type than Elaine Peterson is, and men in these parts prefer to do the hunting," he said with such disdain Beth had to grin, but she decided to let the issue drop.

During the next hour, Beth discovered they worked well together. Between flipping burgers, Lang helped her spread out red-checkered tablecloths on the other tables and set them with silverware and wineglasses.

After they finished, he stepped back and surveyed the three neatly set tables. "So much for roughing it in the Rockies," he commented dryly.

"Well, your guests are about to sit on real pine benches," Beth pointed out. "They are running a real western risk of getting slivers in their soft, rich, eastern posteriors."

Lang let out a short deep laugh. Beth found she liked the sound immensely. She also liked the way the skin about his eyes crinkled when he smiled.

"I sure hope not. I'd probably get sued if that happened."

"I bet Mrs. Peterson wouldn't sue you," Tucker commented slyly as he strolled up. "She'd be more than happy to let you pull a sliver from her posterior, and a mighty shapely posterior that is."

Lang snorted in disgust. "Why don't you go do something useful, like rounding up some of our guests for dinner?"

"Anyone ever tell you that you're getting downright touchy in your old age?" Tucker smirked at his nephew, showing no inclination whatsoever to call the guests.

"The only person anywhere near old at this lake right now is you," Lang countered.

Tucker looked at Beth with a sorrowful expression. "It's a crying shame. My own sister's son, and this is the way he treats me. An old gent like me gets no respect anymore."

"An old gent like you is going to find himself walking back to the ranch if you don't round up our guests before their supper gets cold," Lang growled.

"All right, I'm a-going, I'm a-going." Tucker made a great show of stomping away. Beth looked after him, amused by his bowlegged gait.

"He's the real thing, isn't he?" she commented softly. "He's a cowboy through and through, western humor and all."

"There aren't many of his kind left," Lang said with a shake of his head, "which on some days I tend to think is a good thing."

It didn't take Tucker long to round up the hungry dudes. Soon they had made real inroads on the heaping platters of barbecued chicken, burgers, potato salad, and biscuits Beth had put out for them. Beth cleaned her own plate quickly. The ride and the fresh mountain air had made her hungry, too.

After dinner, the guests sat around the fire where Lang and Beth served them fresh blueberry pie and coffee. As the sun sank toward the mountains in the west, Beth started to clean up. She was surprised when Lang insisted on helping her. Then she assumed he was still trying to avoid Elaine Peterson. With Lang's help the work went quickly, and soon she had everything packed up again.

"Tucker will keep them happy for the next hour or so with his yarns," Lang said when they had finished. "Do you want to take a walk along the lake? It will be real pretty at sunset."

"I'd love to," she was surprised to hear herself say.

She rose to her feet and fell into step beside him as they walked toward the lake shore. It was chilly away from the fire now that the sun was setting. She had forgotten how cold even summer nights could be in the mountains, but the cold made her feel alive. The way the mirror-still water reflected the brilliant orange and red clouds overhead was lovely. Only the occasional slap of a trout leaping from the lake to catch its supper broke the stillness.

All the while, she was keenly aware of the tall man walking beside her. He didn't make any effort to strike up a conversation, but the silence between them was comfortable.

"I think your guests are having a wonderful time," she offered after a time.

"They sure can't complain about the food. I didn't think anyone could make a potato salad to match my mother's." He set her a sideways look. "But tonight you proved me wrong. Of course, if she heard me say that, she's probably rolling over in her grave right now. That woman took some pride in her potato salad." He had deepened his Western drawl, which should have sounded corny, but coming from him sounded exactly right. "You are one hell of a fine cook, Beth Richards."

There it was again, the unaccountable warmth a compliment from him gave her. "The food is only one part of your guests' experience. You and Tucker make sure they enjoy themselves, and Elsie has a special way of making people feel welcome and pampered. Your guest ranch is going to be a rousing success."

"As much as I like your prediction, I have to point out that the Rafter N has only been a guest ranch for three weeks now. We have a whole summer ahead of us, not to mention the hunters we have to

THE COWBOY AND THE HEIRESS 53

keep happy come fall. There's still a lot that could go wrong between now and then."

"That's an awfully pessimistic outlook on things."

"I don't know that it's so much being pessimistic as it is being realistic," Lang said as he rubbed a hand along his jaw. "One thing being a rancher teaches you is to never take things for granted. Take haying season, for example. That's a real busy time of year for us, and an important one. If we can get our hayfields mowed and the grass dried at just the right time, our hay will be much better feed for our cows through the winter.

"It's a complicated process, though, with a lot of different factors involved. One moment you can feel like you've got it all under control, and the next moment your hay baler breaks, your crew comes down with stomach flu, and Mother Nature cuts loose and rains for weeks until the hay you just mowed rots on the ground. That's why I have to take life one day at a time."

Beth studied him, wondering if he wasn't talking about more than just hay season and the ranching business. She wondered about the accident which had taken the life of his brother and his wife, the accident he and the twins never seemed to mention.

Because she wanted to keep Lang talking, she thought of another question to ask him. "If your guest venture is a success, what next?"

"I'll pay off the loans my father took out years ago and stop worrying that the bank is going to end up owning my ranch instead of me," he replied promptly.

"Besides that." Beth waved off his answer and planted her hands on her hips. "If you had enough money to do anything with the Rafter N you wanted, how would you spend it?"

"Paying off the bank would be about the best thing I could imagine," he pointed out with a whimsical smile. "But after that, if we were running solidly in the black, I'd buy five good Brangus bulls and a hundred Brangus cows."

"There, I knew you had to have a dream of your own." She felt triumphant, having finally pried it out of him.

"I have plenty of dreams, all right," he said. "I come from a family that is big on dreams."

Beth was puzzled by the bitterness in his voice. Why did he seem to think possessing dreams was such a bad thing? "What on earth are Brangus?" she asked.

"Some of the wildest, most ornery cows on the face of this earth, but they're hardy and they carry plenty of beef. They're a cross between Angus and Brahmin cattle," Lang said, obviously warming to his topic. "I have a friend up in Wyoming who's doing well with them."

As she gazed up into his serious eyes and the planes of his strong face, she knew right then and there that he'd do it. He was the sort of man who could accomplish whatever he set his mind to.

"I'm going to make another prediction," she said slowly. "Ten years from now the Rafter N will be running as many Brangus as its range can hold."

"Time will tell, I suppose." He was staring down at her now, and she received the strong impression that his mind wasn't on his words. She felt her cheeks start to warm under his steady perusal. "Did anyone ever tell you how sweet you are, Beth Richards?"

He reached out a hand. She thought he was going to touch her cheek. He obviously thought better of it, for he pulled his hand back and shoved it into the pocket of his jeans.

"So," he said gruffly, "turnabout is fair play. What would you do if you had all the money in the world?"

Beth let her breath go in a trembling sigh. *I had more than my fair share of all the money in the world, and it never made my dreams come true.*

"Exactly what I'm doing now."

That reply earned her a skeptical look. "You've always dreamed of working long hours for little pay cooking for other people?"

"I wanted to do some sort of work which mattered, at least a little. I don't need to change the world, but I do need to make a contribution of some sort." She knew her words probably didn't make any sense to him. He lived in a world where everyone worked, a world where everyone's contributions were vital.

"And most of all," she added hurriedly, "I wanted to find that work here, in the West, in these mountains. I've loved Colorado ever since we came here when I was young."

"So you said before. Tell me more about that summer you spent at a dude ranch."

She considered his question and decided that answering it seemed safe enough.

"It was the most magical summer of my childhood." She turned away from him to look out over the still waters of the lake. "We were supposed to come for a week, and we ended up staying for a month. My father has always been a workaholic, and that dude ranch was one place I saw him relax and forget about his work. We hiked and rode horseback, and went fishing and river rafting." *It was the last time my parents were truly happy. It was the last time I was truly happy.*

"My mother died the next spring." All the millions her father threw at his wife's cancer treatment couldn't stop the spread of that cruel relentless disease. It was one of the few times in his life Peter Harrison had ever been thwarted. Beth didn't think he had ever really recovered from the shock, or his sorrow at losing a wife he had loved—as much as he could love anyone.

"We had meant to come back the next summer, but neither Dad nor I had the heart for it."

"I'm sorry that you had to lose your mother so young."

"It was hard. It's still hard. That's why I feel so for Stacy and Tony. I miss my mother every day. I never realized until she was gone how much she had given me, how much joy she gave us all, and how much she had tempered the more driven side of my father."

"Is he a part of the reason why you landed in Perrytown with hardly a cent to your name?"

The question, even though it was uttered in such a quiet sympathetic voice, brought her up short. "My reasons for ending up in Perrytown are my own business."

He looked up at the high pinnacles and towers of Storm Peak. "I figured you probably felt that way. I just wanted to say this. It's pretty obvious that you were on the run when you came here. I might be willing to help you face down whatever trouble you've got in your past, but you'll have to trust me enough to tell me about it first. And I know full well it takes time for that kind of trust to grow between people. I'll listen anytime you're of a mind to tell me why you were running. Most problems don't solve themselves. You have to stand and face them."

He'd started to reach her, there at the beginning of his little speech, but by the end she was ready to shove him into the lake. Lang Nelson knew absolutely nothing about her or the glittering stifling world she'd escaped. She was hardly a coward to have run. Walking out on her old life to face a world she'd never once been alone in was the most courageous thing she'd ever done.

She wanted to tell him he was a sanctimonious busybody, but then she looked up into his sober, sherry-brown eyes, she didn't have the heart to say the words. Lang Nelson honestly cared. He cared about his nieces, his uncle, his ranch, and—for some odd amazing reason—he even seemed to have space in his large heart to care about her. *He probably wants to keep his cook happy, and he doesn't want to go through the trouble of hiring himself another one if you decide to leave.*

"I'll keep that in mind," she said tightly. She stood up and started back toward the campfire. Somehow she sensed the moment he turned to follow her. Wondering why she had to be constantly aware of this particular man in such a particularly sensual way, Beth refused to look over her shoulder and kept right on going.

FIVE

The next morning Beth vigorously whipped a bowl of egg whites into a froth. What had gotten into her last night? If she had stayed talking with Lang by that lake any longer, she probably would have given him her whole life story. He had stood there looking at her, his face earnest, his beautiful eyes so serious and concerned, and for one brief moment she had actually considered telling him everything. Lang Nelson was a good listener, a dangerously good listener, and she would do well to remember that in the future.

She had already mentally reviewed everything she had told him. She knew she hadn't given much away about herself last night, but she might have, and the less he knew about her the better. That pull of attraction she felt whenever she was around him was just plain dangerous. For one treacherous moment she had hoped he would reach out and touch her. For some crazy reason she had wanted to feel his hand against her cheek and his lips pressed against her own.

Crazy, indeed. She didn't want anything to do with a man who ran his ranch like an army outfit. She was going to make darn sure she didn't go on any more walks with a cowboy with thick, sandy blonde

THE COWBOY AND THE HEIRESS 59

hair and a voice as smooth and rich as the finest malt whisky.

She was so busy giving herself a good talking-to that she jumped when the subject of her lecturing suddenly materialized in the doorway to her kitchen. Today he was wearing a blue denim shirt beneath his jean jacket, and he held a pair of leather work gloves in one hand. Big, vital, and undeniably masculine, he somehow suddenly made her large kitchen feel a great deal smaller. The closed expression on his handsome face made her wonder if he, too, was regretting having such a personal talk with his help last night.

"I'm heading into town after lunch," he declared coolly. "I thought it would be a good time for you to stock up the pantry."

Beth felt her stomach lurch. The last thing she wanted to do was go into town. Too many people would see her. "When I signed on as a cook for your ranch, you didn't mention anything about having to do the grocery shopping."

"I'm sorry I left it out of your job description," he said with a trace of impatience in his tone, "but cooks usually do the shopping for their ranches. You're the one planning the menus, and you're the only one now who knows what we need."

"Well, this cook isn't going into town. I'll write you up a list."

"And I'll spend two hours in the store trying to fill your order, two hours I don't have right now to do my cook's work for her."

The anger kindling in his eyes was unmistakable now, but Beth refused to back down. In the past she had rarely stood up to angry men, and she was determined now to hold her ground.

"I still have dinner to cook tonight," she protested.

"Tell Elsie what you want her to do. She can get dinner started. I'll have you back by four, and you can handle the rest."

She was still trying to form an argument which would persuade Lang to let her off the hook when he turned on his heel and walked out of the kitchen. No one had ever simply walked away from her. She stared at the whisk in her hand, aghast to realize how much she longed to throw it after him.

After a long moment, she went back to whipping her egg whites even more vigorously than before. She had a feeling her boss wasn't going to budge on this one. The fair, objective side of her mind had to admit that it made a world of sense for a ranch cook to do his or her own shopping. She'd just make sure she did it as quickly and as efficiently as possible, and then she was going to sit in Lang Nelson's truck until he was ready to come back to the Rafter N.

It would be best if as few people as possible saw her when she was in town. She tried to ignore her cold, creeping fear that her father's detectives had already traced her to northwestern Colorado. She had covered her tracks well. They wouldn't find her. They couldn't find her.

Even though Lang Nelson was a domineering bully, she'd do her job for him, and do it well. In the meantime, she could only hope that fulfilling all her responsibilities as a cook for the Rafter N wasn't about to endanger her hard-won freedom.

Lang glanced from the road ahead of his truck to sneak a sideways look at his passenger. Beth Richards sure was pretty, even when she was pouting. As she stared straight ahead at the road, she gave him a fine view of her profile. Her creamy, even skin fascinated him no end. It was all too easy to imagine what that skin would feel and taste like beneath his lips. He longed to reach over and tug off the tie at the end of her long braid.

He had only seen her hair loose once, when she was getting ready for bed that first night in her cabin. In his own bed this past week, waiting impatiently for sleep to come, he'd found himself remembering how innocent and searingly tempting she'd looked in her plain blue nightgown, her hair cascading over her shoulders in a rich fall of gold.

Feeling a familiar stirring in his groin, he shifted his weight and decided it was time to think about something else, like how angry she had made him this morning.

It was the damnedest thing—a ranch cook thinking her boss had nothing better to do than go shopping for broccoli and potatoes. He had a half-dozen important errands to do in town this afternoon, and he was going to be lucky if he got them all done. Yet she was acting as if she was the injured party because he'd put his foot down and insisted that she do her job.

Yes, sir, Beth Richards had her ice princess routine down to a fine art. A man would be a fool to cater to it, and Lang was no fool. Still, Perrytown was a good forty-mile drive from the ranch, and after a time the strained silence in the cab began to wear on him.

"You got something against towns in general, or this town in particular?" he asked her at last.

"I don't know what you mean," she replied with frosty politeness.

"You know exactly what I mean," he fired back, and then he cursed himself. Starting a fight with her wasn't going to help matters any.

"If it makes you feel any better," he decided to try again, "folks in Perrytown mind their own business. I expect you're thinking everyone's going to be watching you, but people in these parts mostly care about their own affairs. No one's going to ask you anything about where you're from, unless you want to tell them."

That was only partly true, but he figured his saying it might make her feel a little better. A new woman in town, and a beautiful one at that, was going to cause a stir. Elsie and Danny had already told him folks had been talking and wondering about his cook, and he'd asked them both to tell everyone to give her some space. The way news traveled in Perrytown, word should have gotten around by now that Beth wanted to be left alone. Or so he hoped.

She didn't say anything in response to his comment, but he thought he saw her relax, just a little.

"I liked Perrytown, what I saw of it," she offered suddenly.

"It's a nice place, even if it's on the small side. We still have a parade on the Fourth of July. Almost every child in town is in it—either riding on horseback or on bicycles."

"Do children actually decorate their bikes?"

He wondered at the wistful note in her voice. He was willing to bet that Beth Richards had never seen a Fourth of July parade, much less been in one. A pang went through him at the thought. He had no business feeling sorry for Beth, but every child ought to ride a bike in a parade at least once in his or her life.

"The kids riding bikes cover them with red, white,

and blue ribbons, and the horses in the parade get red, white, and blue streamers braided into their manes and tails. The firefighters polish up every piece of equipment the fire department owns to drive them in the parade. After the Elks put on a big barbecue in the park, the Kiwanis members put on a heck of a fireworks display. Then there's usually a big dance over at the VFW hall. All in all, Perrytown usually does a pretty good job of celebrating the Fourth."

"It sounds wonderful."

"Well, you're going to have a chance to see it all firsthand. The Fourth is just ten days away, now."

"So it is," she said quietly.

From her guarded reaction, he guessed she had no intention of returning to town to watch the festivities. Right then Lang promised himself that Beth Richards was going to celebrate a proper western Fourth of July with the rest of Perrytown, even if he had to hog-tie and haul her into town himself.

They talked more easily then, discussing the guests and happenings at the ranch. More than once Beth made him laugh with her dry comments about the guests. Although she spent relatively little time with them, Lang was surprised by how well she seemed to understand them all.

"You should have been a psychologist. You've got a good handle on what makes people tick," he commented.

"I am good at watching people," she said with a shrug, "another one of my few sterling accomplishments."

Lang frowned. "That's the second time I've heard you belittle yourself. Why do you do it?"

She looked startled by his comment. "Perhaps," she said slowly, "because all my life I've been told how little I know how to do—and that what I can do is worthless."

He was surprised by the sudden anger he felt on her behalf. He'd like to give a piece of his mind to whoever had helped Beth to form such a poor opinion of herself. "Anyone who can keep twenty people blissfully well fed for a week is hardly worthless."

"I know deep down inside that you're right, but most of the people I used to know would have disagreed with you. I suppose a lot of them lead worthless lives in their own right, so I probably shouldn't mind what they think of me."

She crossed her arms and looked out the window. From her closed expression, he guessed she wouldn't let him charm anything more about her past out of her today. He sat back and chewed on what she had told him. Clearly, Beth hadn't been happy in the world she had fled from, but was being unhappy the only reason she had left? He still couldn't forget the strained look in her eyes that morning he'd first seen her at Danny Parson's diner. He also couldn't forget the way she had turned on him on the kitchen when he had startled her.

More than simple unhappiness had made her run away, but he still wasn't any closer to figuring out who or what she was running from. *Lang Nelson, that's her business, and you'd do well to leave well enough alone.* The hell of it was, he was starting to care about Beth, and he wasn't sure he could hold to that resolution. He wasn't sure at all.

As she pushed the shopping cart down the aisles at the grocery store and began selecting her purchases, Beth considered the conversation she had just had with Lang driving into town. After a lifetime of watching other people live while she existed in a protected unreal bubble, she had become adept at reading others. Or perhaps she had inherited the gift of empathy from her mother, a woman who had been a people person through and through.

Beth made a face at a can of tomato paste and tossed it into her cart. She understood people well, all right, except for the two men who were closest to her, the men she was supposed to be able to trust. *I'll never understand how my father and my fiancé could place so much value on money and power, and so little on me.*

With a sigh, Beth promised herself not to think about her father, her ex-fiancé, or her infuriating employer for at least five minutes and went back to shopping.

An hour later, she was just about to roll her first cart of groceries out through the open glass doors of the grocery store when she spotted two state troopers parked three spaces away from Lang's truck. Blood rushing in her ears, she stopped dead in her tracks. The last thing she could afford to do right now was to let two lawmen get a good look at her face. She had been right to think it was a bad idea for her to come to town. Now her first trip into Perrytown could turn into a complete disaster.

SIX

Lang whistled as he strolled to his truck. He had gotten his errands done in record time. He was actually looking forward to the ride back to the ranch. Even though he knew his cook was completely off limits, he could enjoy looking at Beth on the way home.

He glanced toward the store just in time to see Beth stop suddenly in the doorway. For a long moment, she stared at the parking lot. Even from this distance, he could see her face pale. Abruptly, she darted back inside, pulling her shopping cart with her.

Lang glanced around him, puzzled. For the life of him he couldn't understand what had scared her so. The lot of the grocery store looked much the way it always did at this time of day. It was full of cowboys' battered pickups, minivans which belonged to mothers who lived in town, and a few tourist rental cars. In the middle of the lot, State Patrolman Charlie Walsh talked with his fellow officer Earl Broward.

Lang swore under his breath when he realized Charlie and Earl must be the ones who had spooked her. There were plenty of reasons why a person might not want to be noticed by cops—and most of those reasons were bad news. The most obvious one of all seemed ridiculous. Although he didn't know her well, Beth Richards didn't seem like a criminal. However, it was possible she had gotten herself tied up in some sort of trouble, bad trouble which could threaten his family, and that was a possibility he couldn't tolerate.

Still debating with himself, Lang went to lean against the wall of the grocery. He'd wait and see if the state patrolmen were truly the reason why Beth had ducked back inside the store. After fifteen minutes or so, Charlie and Earl drove off. Sure enough, a minute later, Beth emerged from the store and pushed her shopping cart straight to the truck.

Lang straightened up and came away from the wall. He ignored Beth's start of surprise when he came up behind her and began lifting the bags into the bed of the truck. She went back to the store and brought out a second cart of food while he continued to unload the first.

"Did you get all your errands done?" she asked when they had finished.

"In record time," he replied absently, wondering if he should confront her now or wait until after they returned to the ranch. He was surprised and worried by how much he wanted to wait. *Lang Nelson, if she tells you she's wanted by the law, you're going to have to let her go.* He didn't want to let her go. He wanted to keep her safe. He wanted to help her sort out whatever trouble she had gotten herself into.

After they climbed up into the cab he started to turn the key in the ignition, but then his common sense stopped him. It was better to get this over with right now.

He cleared his throat and stared at his cracked dashboard. "I saw what happened just now. I saw you take one look at those two cops and bolt like a scared jackrabbit for cover."

He forced himself to look at her. She was watching him, her gray-blue eyes wide and wary. She looked so lonely, proud, and frightened that his heart twisted for her.

"Look, I know you're on the run," he continued, hating himself for the ultimatum he was about to give her. "I know you don't want to tell me who you're running from, or why. After what I just saw, though, I have to ask you this. Have you broken the law, or gotten yourself into the kind of trouble which could get anyone hurt out at the Rafter N? Stacy and Tony mean the world to me, and I can't let you stay on with us if there's a chance you'd put anyone I care about in danger."

She drew in a deep breath and stared at her hands.

"Those are fair questions," she said after a long moment. "I know how much the girls mean to you, and I could never live with myself if something happened to them because of me."

She lifted her chin and stared him straight in the eye. "I swear to you, I haven't broken the law. I'm not involved in the kind of trouble you mean."

"I'd feel a hell of a lot better if I did know what you were running from."

"If you have to know that, I'll go find myself another job." The way her jaw was set, he knew she meant what she said.

Lang cursed under his breath. He'd been right that first day to think she'd have a stubborn side. Calling himself ten thousand times a fool, he turned the key and slammed the truck into first gear.

"You're going to let me stay on," she said wonderingly as they drove out of the lot and started back toward the ranch.

"You gave me your word," he said gruffly. "That's

THE COWBOY AND THE HEIRESS 69

good enough for me." *And I'm probably an idiot for believing you, but somehow I don't think you're a liar, Beth Richards. There's something in your past that scares you, but I don't think you can look me in the eye like that and tell me an out-and-out whopper.*

Ten miles down the road she said in a low voice, "Lang Nelson, there are times you make me so angry I want to break a rolling pin over your head, but I am coming to think that you are one of the most remarkable men I have ever met."

Lang brooded about that comment, and the woman who had made it, most of the way home. One thing was for sure, he decided with an inward smile. He was going to be careful from now on not to rile Beth when she had a rolling pin within reach. He hoped the fact she thought he was "remarkable" was a good sign. Maybe he was one step closer to getting her to trust him. But should he be trusting *her*? He so desperately wanted to. There was a sweetness and a caring in her that he found tremendously appealing. Only time would tell if he'd just been played for a sucker.

"Hey, Beth, am I making these right?" Stacy called from where she stood at the kitchen counter, decorating a cake she had baked and frosted. "They look more like white blobs than flowers to me." She stared doubtfully at the globs of white icing she had just squeezed onto her cake.

"That's because they are blobs," Tony informed her twin with little sympathy. She went back to work on the cupcakes she was icing.

Beth looked up from Tucker's birthday cake. As soon as they heard she was going to make a fancy cake for their great-uncle, the twins had asked her for a cake decorating lesson. They often wandered into her kitchen and helped her while she cooked, especially before dinner. She encouraged their visits, for she enjoyed the girls' company no end. She liked listening to the way they constantly teased and argued cheerfully with each other. During her lonely childhood, she had often imagined she had a twin sister to play with.

"They probably would look more like flowers if you squeezed the bag a little less hard each time," Beth pointed out as diplomatically as she could. During the ten days she had spent at the ranch she had come to realize that Tony and Stacy, for all they looked so much alike, had very different personalities. Tony was more serious, careful, and thorough. Stacy laughed easily, took more risks, and tended to be careless at times. Both had always been polite and friendly to her. Lang, and their parents before him, had done a fine job of raising the girls.

"At least I have most of my cake decorated," Stacy tossed at Tony. "At the rate that you're going, your first cupcake won't be done by dinner." Beth had to bite her lip to keep from laughing. Stacy had a point. Tony was so meticulous about her decorating that it was going take her all night to get her cupcakes finished.

Beth decided it was time to provide a diversion. "So, do you girls have dates all lined up for the Fourth of July dance yet?"

"Uncle Lang won't let us go on dates," Stacey said with a pout. "He says we're better off at our age doing things with groups of friends."

Oops, I forgot that they're only fourteen. They seem so mature. "Well, your uncle probably has a good point," Beth loyally backed Lang. "You've got a lot of years ahead of you yet to go on dates."

THE COWBOY AND THE HEIRESS 71

"Stacy's hoping that Billy Ferguson is going to ask her to dance. She has a serious crush on him," Tony offered with a sly look at her twin.

"Is Billy cute?" Beth asked Stacy, already guessing what her answer would be.

"He's only the most gorgeous guy in the whole tenth grade." Stacy hugged her bag of icing dreamily and leaned against the kitchen counter.

So Billy was a grade ahead of Stacy. Lang wasn't going to like that. Beth tried to keep her expression noncommittal. "More importantly, is he nice?" Beth looked to Tony for a more objective opinion.

Tony shrugged. "He's okay, I guess. The guys he hangs out with can be a little wild."

"Hmm. Define a little wild for me."

"Well, you know, they like to smoke cigarettes and drink beer whenever they can talk older kids into buying for them."

Stacy flew to her beloved's defense. "Billy told me he hardly ever smokes anymore. And all of the sophomores drink beer."

"I hope they don't drink and then get behind the wheel of a car," Beth said firmly.

There was a long silence. Tony and Stacy exchanged odd looks which Beth couldn't quite interpret. "They don't. Or most are smart enough not to," Tony said at last in a subdued voice.

Puzzled by the sudden tension in the twins, Beth decided to change the topic. "Do you girls know how to jitterbug?"

"We know how to do cowboy dancing, but I don't think they're really the same thing," Stacy admitted.

"I don't know how cowboys dance, but I took plenty of dancing classes growing up, and jitterbugging is one thing that I do know how to do." Along with the fox-trot and the cha-cha, and any number of dances she didn't particularly enjoy. Jitterbugging had been different. She had loved the beat of the music and the more athletic moves that she and the rest of her classmates had persuaded their instructor to teach them.

Beth went to the radio and found an oldies station which played mostly hits from the fifties. As luck would have it, they were playing "In the Mood."

"What do you say to taking a break from cake decorating for one very quick dance lesson?" she asked the girls with a grin.

"Way cool." Stacy put down her bag of icing and bounced over to stand beside Beth.

"I think I'll just watch," Tony said, but she looked intrigued.

"Most of the basic moves start from the two dancers having their hands joined like this." Beth demonstrated. They successfully navigated the first few simple maneuvers, but as soon as Beth tried to get Stacy to do a pretzel slide, they became hopelessly tangled.

"If this is supposed to be a jitterbug lesson, it looks to me like you two ladies could use a hand here," Lang drawled from the doorway. "Mind if I cut in?"

Giggling, Stacy quickly retreated to the kitchen counter, leaving Beth standing alone in the midst of the kitchen with her employer. Before she could voice an objection, he grabbed her hands and began whirling her about in time to the music. Within moments, she was too out of breath to protest, and she was having too good a time to ask him to stop.

Despite his size, Lang Nelson was a marvelous dancer. He was light on his feet, the cues he gave her were clear and precise, and a giddy girlish side of her couldn't help responding to the cocky appreciative grin he gave her each time they successfully

THE COWBOY AND THE HEIRESS 73

completed another move. They even managed a passable hip toss, which made the twins whoop with delight, and when the song came to its finale they ended by locking their elbows and Beth rolled over Lang's back with a big fan kick.

When Beth stood upright once again, she was panting and laughing all at once. She had a feeling her arms and shoulders might be a little sore tomorrow from the unaccustomed exercise, but the excited looks on the twins' faces made the effort she and Lang had just made all worthwhile. The girls deserved more happy silly times in their lives.

"Beth Richards, you are a woman of surprising talents," Lang said with a smile which made him look ten years younger. "You are one heck of a dancer."

"Why, thank you, sir. And so are you." With a small pang, Beth realized she rarely had a chance to see Lang smile in such a carefree fashion.

"Have you ever done any cowboy dancin'?"

"No," Beth admitted. "But the girls tell me it's quite an experience."

"After this little session, I predict you'll set the dance floors in Perrytown on fire. If you can jitterbug like that, you can cowboy dance just fine."

Although she didn't plan to risk setting foot on a single dance floor in Perrytown, she did appreciate the compliment.

"A lot of those jitterbugging moves are like cowboy dancing," Stacy admitted, "but what do we do at the sock hop when they play a slow song like this one?"

With a small start, Beth realized the radio was now playing "Come Softly to Me" by the Fleetwoods.

"Ah, then it's time to try a little dancin' cheek to cheek," Lang said. His eyes never leaving hers, Lang stepped close and pulled Beth into his arms. She went, a little stiffly at first, for all sorts of warning bells were going off in the back of her mind. Jitterbugging with Lang Nelson was one thing. Dancing so close their bodies were going to touch was something else entirely. Yet she couldn't see any way to back out without causing an embarrassing scene in front of the twins. Lang, damn his laughing eyes, knew exactly what she was thinking.

Within moments that strange electric awareness she always felt when he stood close to her returned. She could feel the calluses on his large hand as he held hers. His shoulder was hard and muscular under her fingers. He must have been fixing one of the tractors, for he smelled faintly of diesel oil and hay.

As he stared down at her, the laughing light in his brown eyes vanished.

"Relax," he told her quietly. "We can't get into too much trouble during just one slow dance."

Of course they couldn't, the rational side of her mind told her. As she relaxed and let him pull her closer, though, she knew in her heart that touching Lang in any sort of intimate way wasn't a wise idea. Her nerves hummed every place their bodies brushed together. His plaid shirt was soft against her cheek, the chest beneath it hardened from years of hard physical work in the out-of-doors. They moved well together, as if they had been slow dancing together for years.

Despite her nervous system's peculiar reaction to Lang, she liked being held by him. Because he was so big, she'd expected to feel engulfed and intimidated in his embrace. Instead, she felt safe and protected within the circle of his arms. Her mind began to drift, and she almost forgot she was dancing in a

THE COWBOY AND THE HEIRESS 75

kitchen while two fourteen-year-old girls watched her. How wonderful it would be someday to have a man she loved, trusted, and liked as her lifetime dance partner. For the moment, it would surely do no harm to pretend Lang was that man.

Then, as he swayed even closer, she suddenly realized he was fully aroused. Her eyes flew open and she found he was studying her, a kind of pained alarm in his own glance. Lang Nelson wanted her? Her cheeks began to burn, and she tripped over his foot. When she pushed against his arms, he cleared his throat and let her go.

"I think that gives you girls the general idea," Lang told his nieces, who were eyeing them both with considerable interest.

"Can I let Billy Ferguson hold me like that?" Stacy asked with a too innocent expression on her face.

Lang's brows drew together, and he sent Stacy a thunderous look. "If you let any boy hold you like that, you won't be doing any slow dancing at all." With that Lang stalked from the kitchen and left them to their cake decorating.

SEVEN

Beth studied the seam she had just sewed with Elsie's sewing machine. The twins had talked her into helping them make matching poodle skirts for the sock hop. Elsie had warned her that Stacy and Tony often tackled ambitious sewing and craft projects beyond their skills and their patience.

Beth glanced wryly at Stacy, who had completely abandoned the piece she was supposed to be cutting out. Instead, she stood staring longingly out the window, toward the horse barn. Tony was still plugging away, pinning a piece, but she had begun to glance at the door more and more frequently during the past half-hour.

Beth decided to take pity on both girls. "I think you've done enough for today," she informed them briskly. "I'm going to be plenty busy for the rest of the morning sewing the pieces you've already cut and pinned."

Stacy reached the door in three seconds. "C'mon," she said impatiently to her twin, "if we hurry, you might still catch Tad down at the barn." Tad was one of the guests, a handsome seventeen-year-old from Ohio on whom Tony had developed a hopeless crush.

Tony glanced at Beth, her gaze doubtful. "Are you sure you don't mind us leaving?"

THE COWBOY AND THE HEIRESS 77

"I'm positive." Beth grinned at them both. "I think you've got great taste. Tad is gorgeous. If he were seven years older, I'd make a play for him myself."

Tony smiled at her in that serious way she had. "Then I wouldn't have a chance. He'd never look at me with you around."

"Sweetie, I don't believe that for a moment. I bet you and Stacy are two of the prettiest girls in Perrytown. When you get a little older, it's the boys around here who won't stand a chance. Now, get out of here before you miss Tad."

The twins needed no more urging. Moments later, Beth found herself alone in a room strewn with partially pinned pattern pieces and yards of pink felt. She smiled and lined up the next seam. She didn't mind being abandoned by the girls, for she loved to sew. During the past few years, she'd rarely had a chance to do it. At least the twins were appreciative of the fact that she was helping them, and they were very excited about the skirts.

She envied their enthusiasm. She couldn't remember ever being so happy or exuberant when she was fourteen. "Young ladies don't run. They walk sedately. Young ladies don't shout. They speak quietly at all times." Beth winced at the memory of the admonishments she used to receive from Miss Bertram, the Englishwoman her father had hired to look after her when her mother died. For four long, agonizing years Beth had endured Miss Bertram and her unbending notions about proper behavior. At last Beth had been able to escape—to the elite private women's college her father had chosen for her.

Teenagers should be allowed to run and shout. If she ever had children of her own, which she very much wanted to someday, she meant for them to enjoy a great deal more freedom than she ever had. Last night the twins' high spirits had added greatly to the simple party they had thrown in honor of Tucker's sixty-second birthday.

She would have enjoyed the evening more, however, if she hadn't been so aware of Lang watching her broodingly throughout the night. Just thinking about their slow dance in the kitchen made delicious shivers trace down her back. Just remembering the moment she discovered how much he wanted her made her body tingle.

Bryce Townsend, her ex-fiancé, had claimed she was frigid. The handful of times when they had made love she hadn't been able to climax, and he clearly thought that failure was entirely her fault. He had even suggested diplomatically, to her extreme chagrin and embarrassment, that she see a sex therapist. Although she had never gone, she had been inclined to think Bryce was right in his claims. Whatever it took to be strongly attracted to a man, she simply didn't have it. Whenever Bryce took her in his arms, she had liked it. She relished the sensation of being close to someone, for there had been few hugs in her life after her mother died. When Bryce kissed her and touched her more intimately, though, she had felt self-conscious and uncomfortable.

Lang Nelson made her realize that she'd been wrong about herself all these years. She could feel desire, a desire so intense that it made her body burn. Unfortunately, he was the wrong man, at the exact wrong time in her life. Why did a handsome cowboy with an overdeveloped sense of responsibility have to be the first man to arouse these sorts of feelings in her?

"So this is how you spend the first day off I've given you."

Beth started in surprise. She looked up to find Lang filling the doorway, his arms crossed against his chest. He must have just come in from working outside, for he still wore his denim jacket. Some of his sandy hair had fallen across his forehead, the gold in it forming a vivid contrast to his weathered skin. The first two buttons on his plaid western shirt had come undone, and she could see a dusting of dark chest hair. Once again she was overwhelmed by the sheer male presence of him, and she could feel her treacherous pulse start to race.

It's just not fair. Why does he have to be the first man to make your heart beat faster?

His expression was quizzical as he studied her. "I thought you'd sleep in, or go for a ride. And here I find you sewing poodle skirts for my nieces."

He shook his head sadly. "You, Beth Richards, are a complete fraud."

"I beg your pardon," she said, falling back on haughtiness to hide the fact that she was feeling cornered and confused.

"Lord, woman, I love it when you talk that way," he said with a devastating smile, his own Western drawl more evident than usual. "I love it when you use that lady-of-the-manor tone which puts me firmly in my place."

"I'm glad you like my accent. I find yours very quaint, as well."

Lang gave an appreciative chuckle at her quick rejoinder and sauntered several steps into the room. He stood, hip shot, one thumb hooked through his belt, looking so cowboy-handsome that it was hard for her to concentrate on his words.

"I'll tell you why I think you're a fraud. You look as if you ought to be on the cover of *Town and Country* magazine. You speak as if you were educated at one of the finest colleges in this country, and I'm willing to bet good money that you actually were. You walk like royalty. Yet the times I've seen you look happiest, you've been elbow deep in vegetables you're slicing up for stew, or surrounded by sewing patterns and yards of pink fluffy fabric."

"That makes me a fraud?'

"Someone who looks like you, talks like you, and walks like you shouldn't be so domestic. You should be happiest getting that gorgeous body of yours wrapped and manicured at expensive clubs and spas. You should spend your days pampering yourself and buying designer dresses to wear to society functions where you would outshine some of the most beautiful women in the world."

She stared back at him, wondering how he had known or guessed so accurately how she used to spend her days. Hearing her old life described in his words made it sound so completely worthless and hedonistic. Something puzzled her, though. Where was the anger she sensed in his tone coming from? Surely it wasn't all directed at her.

"I'm sorry if I don't fit your image of me," Beth said stiffly. That had been a major problem all of her life. She never had fit the life or body she had been born to. She had never fit in anywhere. "But I won't apologize for my domestic skills." She stared down at her clasped hands, appalled to realize that tears were beginning to well in her eyes. "You may not value them, but I've come to realize that sewing and cooking are among the things I do well, and I'm proud of them." There at the end, she couldn't quite hide the quiver in her voice, despite her best efforts.

He crossed the remaining distance between them

THE COWBOY AND THE HEIRESS 81

in two quick strides. He knelt before her and took her hands gently in his.

"Beth, honey, please don't cry," he said, his tone of voice completely different now. "I'm so sorry. I don't know what got into me. You should be damn proud of what you can do. I'm damn proud of what you can do."

He tipped her face up so that she had to look at him, his hand gentle beneath her chin. When she forced herself to look into his eyes, she was surprised to discover he appeared stricken. Had he really just called her honey? She was close enough to see the most lovely hints of gold within his velvety brown irises. There should be a law against a man having eyes that beautiful.

"It's just that you look as if you ought to be one sort of a person, but you keep acting like someone else," he confessed. "You've got me all tied up in knots trying to sort you out."

She blinked at the blunt honesty of that admission. "I guess that makes us even. I can't sort you out, either."

She didn't know him well yet—on the surface, Lang Nelson appeared to be the last male on earth she'd be attracted to—but she knew that she wanted him, and the whole idea of desiring a man, this man, with such intensity was disturbing. It was a strange heady feeling to have large capable Lang Nelson kneeling at her feet. Involuntarily, her gaze went to his mouth. She was so tempted to lean forward and kiss him. She longed to feel his lips against hers, with a deep visceral kind of wanting that was almost painful.

Perhaps he read her mind, for his hands went up and cupped her head. Gently he urged her toward him, but she needed no urging. It was a tentative kiss at first, questioning and curious. His mouth nibbled at hers, seductively gentle, sinfully skilled. She already knew he was a thorough careful man, and he kissed with a kind of single-minded intensity which made her head swim.

Uncertain what to do with her hands, at last she placed them on top of his broad shoulders. They were rock-hard beneath her touch. She tightened her grip as he deepened the kiss. Caution and gentleness suddenly vanished, replaced with something much more dark and urgent. She forgot the quiet, sun-filled sewing room. She forgot the pink felt scattered all over the floor. She forgot everything but Lang. Her awareness narrowed to this man, and to this moment.

Her head fell back against his shoulder, and she let him taste and plunder the insides of her mouth. She had been kissed before, but it had never felt like this. She had never felt completely consumed. And Lang wouldn't be satisfied with mere compliancy. He coaxed and compelled until she kissed him back the same way and became lost in the taste of him.

With an impatient sound, he broke away from her lips. His mouth roved across her face, kissing her eyes, her cheeks, the line of her jaw. With a shock, Beth realized she was panting, and his breath was coming in ragged gasps. *Had this blazing need been banked under the surface all this time?* she wondered dazedly. She promised herself that she would never take Lang's bluff good-natured cowboy act for granted again.

He shifted his weight, and let go a sudden startled curse. He jumped to his feet, a piece of pinned fabric dangling from his knee. "Hell, I just got a pin stuck halfway inside my kneecap." Gingerly, he plucked the pin and the fabric away from his leg.

He looked so offended that she had to stifle the urge to laugh.

"Here. You should keep better track of your pins," he said, thrusting the fabric at her. "This whole room is probably a damn minefield."

Cautiously she took the piece of fabric, pins and all, from him. "I'm sorry, but I do need to point out that they aren't exactly my pins," she declared, not knowing whether to laugh or cry at the sudden shift in the mood between them. "I've tried to make the twins be more careful, but you know how the girls are."

He sighed and ran a hand through his hair. "Yeah, I do know. I suppose they ran off and left you with this mess."

Beth made a noncommittal sound. She didn't want Lang chasing off after the twins and getting angry at them on her behalf. She was also appalled at the way her whole body was tingling after sharing just one kiss with him.

"I won't go chew them out, if that's what you're worrying about," he reassured her. "I just want them to realize that it's not fair to ask for your help on a project like this, and then leave you to clean it all up." He swung about and headed for the door.

He hesitated in the doorway, and his gaze met hers a final time. "I suppose it's just as well that pin stuck me when it did," he said.

"I suppose so," Beth agreed. Lang Nelson was trouble. Her body's strong response to him was proof of that. Of course it was a good thing their kiss had gone no further.

After a long awkward moment, he left.

Beth went back to her sewing, wondering if it was regret or relief she'd just glimpsed in his eyes.

"I need to speak with you for a few minutes after lunch," Lang informed Beth the next day as she fixed a plate for herself at the lunch buffet she had set up in the dining room. Before she could ask him what they needed to talk about, he had already walked past her and taken the last place at one of the tables.

While she smiled absently at a guest, Beth fought her irritation and anxiety. It was so like Lang not to ask if after lunch was a convenient time for her. *He is your employer,* an aggravatingly fair voice in the back of her mind pointed out. *He's one busy man, and he's got a right to assume that you'll be available when he needs to talk to you.*

Beth toyed with the sandwich she'd been looking forward to eating just moments ago. Beneath her irritation at Lang's high-handed ways lurked a nagging fear. After what had happened between them in the sewing room, she was afraid that he was going to ask her to leave. She knew he had his hands full this summer. A torrid affair with his cook would only complicate Lang Nelson's already immeasurably busy and complicated life.

Not that she was willing to have a torrid affair with him, of course. She ruthlessly repressed the pulse of pleasure radiating through her at the very idea. Yet, she might have given him that impression from the enthusiastic way she had responded to his kiss.

Well, if she had to move on, she would. The past few weeks had given her confidence. She now knew that she could do the job of ranch cook, and do it well. Surely she could find work at some other ranch

THE COWBOY AND THE HEIRESS 85

on the western slope. It was hard to imagine she would find a ranch as beautiful as the Rafter N, though, or a place where she felt so at home.

After lunch the twins appeared in the kitchen and were more diligent than usual about helping her clean up. Beth was willing to bet her first paycheck that sometime during the last twenty-four hours Lang had talked with them about responsibility and doing their chores well. The girls had just left, and Beth was peeling potatoes for dinner when Lang came into the kitchen and leaned against the counter.

"Are you planning to come into town with us on the Fourth of July?" he asked with no preamble. "The twins are counting on it, you know."

"Actually, I was planning to stay here," Beth replied, keeping her tone light.

"If you come watch the parade with us and eat at the town barbecue with my family, the folk of Perrytown will know you're a part of the Rafter N. You'll belong to the whole community, then, and the people of Perrytown protect their own. If any strangers come asking about you, I guarantee they'll be met with blank stares."

She looked up from her potatoes, wondering why her going seemed to matter to him so much. Celebrating the Fourth of July the real, old-fashioned way did sound wonderful. She'd been thinking about the town's festivities ever since Lang had described them to her in his truck on the way to town the other day. However, when she thought of what she risked, her resolve hardened. She would be far wiser to stay close to the Rafter N.

"I still would prefer to remain here that night," she said, and hated herself for sounding so priggish. Whenever she felt uncomfortable, which around

Lang appeared to be most of the time, she found herself talking like an uptight snob.

"Stacy and Tony are going to be mighty disappointed to hear that. After all the work you've all put into their poodle skirts, the girls are just assuming you'll be there to watch them dance up a storm."

Despite herself, Beth felt her resolve weakening. "I don't want to disappoint Stacy or Tony."

"Then don't," he said briskly. "Come into town with us. You'll have fun, and they'll have a terrific time. Your coming to the Rafter N has been good for the girls. I haven't seen them laugh so much in a long time." With that, he caught up an apple from the fruit bowl on the counter and strode from the room.

Beth stared after him, wondering if anyone ever got the last word with Lang Nelson.

EIGHT

Beth stepped out of the door of her cabin and paused to admire the sunrise. What a wonderful way to begin the Fourth of July. The clouds along the horizon burned brighter scarlet than any fireworks she had ever seen.

She buried her cold hands in the pockets of her down vest and hurried down to the ranch house. Although she always rose before 6:00 A.M. to make breakfast for the rest, this morning she was up extra early to put the finishing touches on a large sheet cake she was taking to the barbecue.

After giving the matter a great deal of thought, she had decided she would go into town with everyone. She had been tempted not to go, just to show Lang that she wasn't going to give in to him. Every time she thought about the way he had tried to use the twins to change her mind, she wanted to do something particularly violent and vengeful to her handsome employer.

Her father had used her emotions to manipulate her all of her life.

"Now, Beth, sweetheart, you know you care too much about Agatha Harrington not to come to the symphony with us. Now, Beth, you know if you take a job in California you're going to make your lonely old man even more lonely."

And she had always given up her own plans, to do what he wanted.

Sometime last night she had come to realize she mustn't let her strained relationship with her father affect the decisions she made in her new life. She wanted to go see the Fourth of July in Perrytown, regardless of Lang Nelson, his nieces, or anyone else. She was taking a risk, but she would face the consequences of being found if and when that moment came. Her new life certainly wasn't going to amount to much if she hid like a scared rabbit all the time.

She had just reached the porch of the ranch house when she heard the sound of galloping horses. Tucker, Hank, and Jim came racing past and then circled the guest cabins, firing pistols into the air and letting go a chorus of wild cowboy yells. Beth grinned as she watched the sleepy startled guests appear at their doors. Thanks to Tucker's Fourth of July salute, everyone on the Rafter N was going to be awake early.

By eleven o'clock Lang had loaded up his guests, family, and hired hands and started for town. The twins had insisted that Beth ride in Lang's pickup with them, and somehow she ended up squeezed in next to Lang. Every time he had to shift, his hand grazed her left knee, sending frissons of excitement through her. The twins were in such tearing spirits, they talked constantly on the way into town.

Beth tried to concentrate on their chatter rather than the fact that her shoulder rested against Lang's, and she could feel the heat from his leg where it brushed against her own. It was unsettling to realize that just sitting next to her boss in a dusty pickup could send her senses into overdrive. The more she tried not to think about him and the places their bodies touched, the more keenly aware she became. The one time she risked glancing directly at him, she was so close she could see those amber highlights in his eyes again. She could also see the knowing amused expression in his gaze, as if he guessed just how uncomfortable she felt sitting so close to him. Beth was relieved when they reached town and they could finally pile out of the truck.

She had a wonderful time at the parade, just as Lang had promised. She laughed and waved at the beaming youngsters riding bicycles and horses festooned with red, white and blue ribbons. The twins were in the parade, too, marching with the Perrytown Panthers, in the high school band. Lang whistled and clapped louder than anyone in the crowd when the girls came past the place where the Rafter N group stood.

Beth found herself grinning as she watched Lang. He looked so proud of his girls. Lang must have felt her gaze on him, for after the band had gone by he glanced at her and said a little sheepishly, "Well, I have to make noise for two parents, you know."

"I do know," she said quietly, and she wondered if the twins would ever realize how lucky they were to have a man like Lang raising them. With a twist of her heart, she realized she had never managed to make her father look that proud.

"I'm glad now that Tony hung in there with those clarinet lessons," Lang declared in a lighter tone, "but when she started up with that thing, you never heard such terrible caterwauling in all your life. Stacy sounded pretty good on her flute early on, but that clarinet could have put a pack of yipping coyotes to shame."

After the parade ended, the Rafter N contingent headed to the stockyards behind the old railroad station to watch the rodeo. The twins wanted Beth to sit with them in the stands, and Elsie joined them. Lang slipped away after he got everyone, including his guests, settled. Beth was surprised to learn from Stacy that Lang was going to compete in several of the events. After the rodeo started, the twins gave her an entertaining running commentary on the events and the people riding in them. Of course, after a half-hour, the twins spotted friends they wanted to talk with and they bounced away, leaving Beth and Elsie sitting together.

Beth drew in a deep breath when the announcer declared the bareback riding event was next. This was Lang's first event. She could see him easily, for their seats were located just above the stock area. He was standing spraddled over a chute where a wild-looking horse shifted about restlessly. Lang's face appeared cool and calm as he concentrated on the horse under him. Her stomach lurched when the bronc Lang had drawn began to lunge and kick.

Moments later, after the horse had settled briefly, Lang gave a nod to the rodeo crew. The chute gate swung open, and the bronc exploded into the arena. Beth held her breath as the horse dove, kicked, and twisted, madly trying to rid himself of his rider, who refused to be thrown. An eon later, it seemed to her, a loud buzzer went off, and Lang slipped from the horse's back. A loud cheer went up from the crowd, for Lang had stayed on for a full ten seconds. Shortly, the judges gave him a high score for the style of his ride, as well.

After his score was announced, Lang grinned and waved to the crowd. She saw him glance around and then focus on her area of the stands. Her heart did a flip-flop when their eyes met, and he sent her a cocky, very male, and very self-satisfied smile. Then he strode from the arena.

Beth let go her pent-up breath.

"How can you stand to watch him?" she turned to ask Elsie. She knew the older woman loved Lang like a son. Elsie had never said it in so many words, but Beth had received the strong impression that Elsie had been in love with Langdon Sr. She stayed on at the Rafter N because Lang, Stacy, and Tony were like her own flesh and blood.

"It's not easy. It's never been easy," she admitted with a shake of her head. "It was worse when he was only sixteen and he rode in the bucking events. I draw some comfort from the fact that Lang has a great deal of common sense now. I know he'll do his best to bail out before he comes to any serious hurt. He knows he can't afford to get laid up right now. In fact, I'm surprised to see he entered the bucking events today. During the past few years, he's usually just entered team and calf roping. I'm guessing there might be someone here today he wants to impress."

Beth glanced at Elsie sharply, but the older woman had turned away to watch the stock chutes. Elsie honestly thought Lang possessed a great deal of common sense? Since that notion seemed to give Elsie some comfort, Beth decided not to point out that anyone who voluntarily tried to ride a bucking bronco had to be a little crazy.

"In his twenties, Lang used to compete in rodeos all over Wyoming and Colorado," Elsie added after a few moments. "People always told him he had the talent to do well on the pro circuit, but he never wanted to be too long away from the ranch."

"Why would he want to be anywhere else? His heart was always at the Rafter N," Beth said softly.

Elsie gave her a long, steady look. "If you've already figured that out about Lang, you're well on your way to understanding him. There's something else, though, that you need to know about Lang to understand why he became the man he is today. His father, Langdon Sr., was an alcoholic. He was one of the most wonderful and charming men I ever knew, and he was one of the weakest. I don't know how much you know about alcoholism, but it changes everyone in a family. It changed Lang, in ways I'm just beginning to understand myself."

Elsie sighed and looked away at the arena, where young women were racing horses around barrels now. "Langdon was always full of great plans and schemes for the Rafter N, but somehow nothing ever became of them. Some of those schemes were expensive, and Langdon borrowed against the ranch, loans which Lang is still fighting to pay off today. After his father died Lang gave up a promising career on the rodeo circuit to stay close to his mother and the Rafter N. He had to drop out of college after his junior year because his mother developed breast cancer. We lost Elaine two years later. Lang has essentially been the foreman of the Rafter N since he was twenty.

"The rest Lang needs to tell you, in his own time and in his own way. I just wanted you to understand there's a good reason why Lang tries to take charge and look after everyone around him. He's been doing it ever since he realized his father was incapable of doing it for his family."

Beth found herself completely at a loss for words. Why had Elsie chosen to tell her such difficult and personal things about Lang and his father? There was only one reason she could think of, and it made her cheeks warm.

"I think you may have gotten the wrong impression about Lang and me." Beth said at last, choosing her words carefully. "I respect Lang a great deal. I'm even starting to like him." *Even though he makes me crazy half of the time.* "But I don't believe the opposite is true at all. I mean, if you're worried that there's something going on between us, you don't need to. Lang doesn't even like me."

Elsie met her gaze steadily, a quizzical look lighting her intelligent blue eyes. "I think you honestly mean that, dear. Lang probably thinks the same thing, too. All I know is that he looks at you the way I've only seen him look at one other woman, and she broke his heart. Because I love him so much, I'm asking you to be careful. I think you are a very kind person. You would never mean to hurt Lang. But he has a generous heart, and I don't want to see it broken again."

After making that remarkable statement, Elsie changed the subject and began to talk about the rodeo and Perrytown happenings. Beth followed her lead with relief. As they watched the rest of the rodeo together, Beth found herself considering what Elsie had said. Surely she was wrong about Lang's feelings. Despite the kiss they had shared in the sewing room, Lang usually looked at her with more dislike and distrust in his eyes than affection. She couldn't deny the strong attraction they seemed to feel for each other, but being in lust was a far cry from being in love, or having any sort of lasting relationship.

Resolutely, she pushed her worries about Lang to the back of her mind and concentrated on the rodeo. She cheered with the rest when Lang received his first place prize for the bareback riding and took second place in the calf roping. She was also heartily relieved when he managed to survive the saddle bronc contest and won that event, as well.

Elsie's words were still very much on Beth's mind when the rodeo ended. She followed the older woman down to the open area behind the stock chutes. Lang came striding up to them, his brown eyes still dancing with excitement. In that moment, she could easily picture the mischievous boy he must have been.

"Three prizes in three events. Not bad for an old rancher, eh?" And with that, he pulled Beth into his arms and gave her a long, exuberant kiss.

NINE

Lang felt Beth's surprise. For one long, heady moment she let him taste her, and then she stiffened in his arms. He knew he had no business kissing her in front of Elsie, his nieces, and the rest of Perrytown. She had looked so pretty, though, and he was so fired up from riding those two broncs well that he just couldn't resist. When she started to push against his arms, he let her go. To cover his tracks, he went over and gave Elsie a big buss on the cheek, as well.

"You don't fool me for a moment, you rascal," she told him with a chuckle, "but I appreciate the kiss just the same."

Then Tony and Stacy pounced on him, demanding to see his prizes and making a big fuss. The guests came forward to congratulate him, too, excited to be part of such a thoroughly western event. Beth hung back on the edges of the crowd of well-wishers around him, looking heartbreakingly beautiful, and very cool and aloof. She wasn't comfortable right now, he realized with a flash of insight. She used that haughty look to disguise the times she felt most ill-at-ease. He understood that about her now. He was just about to seek her out and drag her to the barbecue with him when Danny Hernandez Parson appeared at her side.

The smile she gave him was dazzling. Lang gritted his teeth and turned away before he marched over and rearranged Danny's face for him. Pure male jealousy burned in Lang's veins. The fact that he felt any jealousy at all when Beth smiled at another man shocked him. He had no claim on Beth Richards. He had absolutely no right to resent her smiling at Danny—or at anyone else, for that matter.

That still didn't keep him from wanting to plant a fist in Danny's face, especially when Beth walked away with him, clearly headed toward the barbecue. *Lang Nelson, you need to have your head examined. Wanting to start a fight with Danny is just plain loco. He's one of your best friends and with all that Special Ops training he's had, he could probably tear you apart with one hand if he wanted to.*

During the next few hours, while Beth sat next to Danny at the barbecue, Lang had to remind himself of those facts many times. Trying to concentrate on making conversation with his guests, he was keenly aware of Beth at the next table over, laughing and talking with Danny, his waitress Sally, and several of their friends. He was also aware of the admiring glances Beth was drawing from every single man present, and plenty who were married, too.

Why on earth had he been so keen on bringing her into town today? Now that the local fellows had seen she wasn't too standoffish to talk with Danny, she was going to be besieged with partners at the dance. Lang stared glumly at his half-eaten portion of barbecued ribs. He knew exactly why he had wanted so much for her to come today. He had wanted Beth to enjoy a real Perrytown Fourth of July celebration. Even more than that, he had wanted to dance another slow dance with her. He wanted a socially acceptable reason to hold her in his arms again.

Beth's clear musical laugh rang out, and Lang stabbed at a chunk of potato salad with his fork. Even if he had to wait in line, he was damn well going to have that dance with her.

Beth collapsed into a chair beside Elsie, panting and laughing at the same time.

"I've never danced so hard in all my life," she gasped to the older woman. "If these cowboys don't leave me alone, I may end up at the Perrytown health clinic with cardiac arrest."

"You could say 'no' to them," Elsie suggested with a smile.

Beth glanced about the crowded, well-lit hall. During the past three hours she had danced with cowboys of all ages, from Elsie's twelve-year-old nephew Hal, to Tucker, who was sixty-two. Most, though, were in their twenties and thirties, and the admiration she had seen in their eyes had done her morale a world of good.

"But they're always so polite, and they look so hopeful when they ask me. I can't bear to hurt their feelings," Beth admitted.

"Then I expect you're going to dance tonight until your feet are sore. Better take a couple sips of water, dear. Here comes another one," Elsie warned her with a grin. "On second thought, here come two. This should get interesting."

Beth glanced up and saw one of Danny's friends— Glen, she thought his name was—coming toward her with a shy expectant look in his eyes. Just when Glen reached her chair, Lang appeared beside her, his face set in harsh lines. The band began playing the opening notes of "Love Me Tender."

"The lady promised this dance to me," Lang told Glen shortly, his brown eyes hard and cold.

Beth felt a surge of irritation when the younger cowboy stopped dead in his tracks. "Why sure, Lang. Now that I think about it, I'm feeling mighty thirsty. I'll just go fetch myself a beer." Glen turned away and beat a hasty retreat for the table where volunteers were selling beer.

"I don't remember promising you any dances," Beth told Lang coolly to hide the fact that, beyond her irritation, she was glad he had asked her to dance. She'd been wondering for the past hour if he would ever get around to it.

"Didn't anyone ever tell you that it's a good idea to dance with your boss when he asks you?"

"Have you ever heard of sexual harassment in the workplace?" She smiled back at him sweetly.

"Sweetheart, this isn't your workplace, and I'm way too busy to have time to harass my female employees—all two of you. Besides, I'm too smart an hombre to even think about it. Elsie would probably plug me with that old twelve bore she keeps in her cabin, and you already told me that you're handy with a rolling pin."

Lang held out a hand to her, and smiled that devastating smile of his, and the whole hall full of people seemed to vanish. All she could see was Lang and his coffee-brown eyes with a look in them which made her knees melt.

Beth took Lang's hand. After he led her to the dance floor, she slipped into his arms as if she was meant to be there. Dreamily, she allowed him to pull her close against him, until her cheek rested against his chest. They moved together in time to the music,

THE COWBOY AND THE HEIRESS 99

their bodies brushing and touching tantalizingly until that familiar ache began to pulse deep inside her. Beyond the pull of desire, though, was the simple pleasure and contentment of being held by him.

As much fun as she'd had this evening, she realized this was the moment she had been waiting for all night, and for most of the day, as well. That realization was a sobering one. Lang Nelson was coming to mean too much to her. Feeling a strong physical attraction to a man was one thing. Growing emotionally involved with him was something else entirely. She had to figure out if she could live life on her own.

Because today had been such a magical day, she decided to put her worries about her independence aside for the moment and let tonight be magical. She closed her eyes and let the music take her. How could it be that she had never enjoyed dancing with anyone as much as she did with Lang? Being with him took her someplace dark and romantic, miles and worlds away from the brightly lit VFW hall in Perrytown, Colorado.

She felt a little disoriented when the music ended and Lang eased away from her. When she opened her eyes again, he still held both of her hands and made no move to leave the dance floor. Beth sighed inwardly when she saw Danny approaching, clearly intending to cut in. She liked Danny very much, but she had hoped to steal just one more dance with Lang.

"Go away, Danny," Lang growled, never loosening his hold on her. "And you can tell the rest of the boys the lady's dancing with me until this shindig is over."

"So that's the way the wind's blowing," Danny said with a grin. He raised his beer bottle in salute to

Lang. "I admire your taste, Nelson, but you just dashed the hopes of twenty young cowboys here."

"They'll live," Lang said unsympathetically, his gaze never leaving Beth's face. There was something so intense and searching in his gaze that she felt relieved when the music started up again, a fast song this time.

They danced together for several more songs, jitterbugging hard and fast, slow dancing in an exquisite sensual haze together. She was aware of laughing and talking when the twins came to dance beside them, but most of all she was aware of Lang, broad-shouldered, dynamic, and quietly imposing. The way he looked at her made her feel like the most cherished woman in the room.

When the band paused to take a break, Lang steered her over to the bar and bought them beers. He kept a possessive arm about her waist the entire time. They were leaning back against the wall of the hall, drinking their beers and simply enjoying each other's company, when Lang suddenly straightened up and frowned. "Hell, I haven't seen Stacy in the hall for a good half-hour."

"Is that bad news?"

"With Stacy, you never know," he replied in a clipped tone. "You stay here. I'll be back in a bit."

He strode to the door of the hall. She tried not to mind his abandoning her so abruptly. The safety and well-being of his nieces certainly had to be his first priority. She saw several young cowboys looking her way wistfully, but now that Lang had staked his claim on her they obviously were reluctant to approach her. She left the wall and went to sit with Elsie and several of her friends, who were all happily exchanging Perrytown gossip. Elsie promptly intro-

THE COWBOY AND THE HEIRESS 101

duced her to the group, who soon included her in their conversation.

"Uh-oh," Elsie commented, looking over toward the door several minutes later. "Stacy must have gotten herself into another scrape. I wonder what she's been up to this time."

Beth twisted around in her chair, just in time to see Lang coming toward them, his eyebrows drawn together in a furious frown. Stacy waited by the door, looking both scared and defiant while poor Tony hovered beside her.

"I'm leaving now with the twins," Lang informed them all. "Elsie, can Beth catch a ride with you if she wants to stay here for a while longer?"

"Sure thing," Elsie replied.

Although she didn't want to get involved in a family argument, Beth knew that she didn't want to stay at the dance. Of course, her wanting to leave had nothing to do with the fact that Lang was going now. She was worn out from the long exciting day, and she wanted nothing more than to tumble into her soft bed in her cozy cabin.

"I'd like to go back now—if that's all right with you," she added hastily.

"That's fine," Lang said shortly. "I've already said everything I needed to for the moment to Stacy." He turned on his heel and stalked from the hall. Beth rose to her feet and followed more slowly behind him.

The trip back to the ranch was strained and quiet. This time Beth made certain she climbed up into the cab last so that she didn't have to sit next to Lang. Stacy was clearly pouting, and Tony looked miserable because of all the tension.

Beth tried to ignore them and relive her wonderful day. She had loved the parade, and the fireworks the Kiwanis members had set off after the barbecue. Despite her best efforts to keep her mind busy with her memories, it was still a relief when they finally pulled up before the ranch house.

As Lang helped Beth climb out of the pickup, he asked quietly, "Would you come in and make some coffee while I get the twins settled?"

She knew it wouldn't be wise to spend any more time with him, but she was reluctant to let the night end just yet.

"All right," she agreed, and went to the kitchen. After she finished making coffee, she built a fire in the fireplace, just to keep her hands busy.

He came to the kitchen a half-hour later. Wordlessly, she handed him a mug of coffee, black and strong just the way he liked it.

"I expect you're wondering what happened back there," he said after he took a long swallow from the mug.

"I expect I am, but I'm not sure it's any of my business."

"Such a diplomatic reply. You should have gone into the foreign service," he said with a glimmer of his usual dry humor. Then he sighed and stared down into his mug.

"You see so much of the twins these days, I suppose it probably is your business." When he met her gaze once more, his eyes were dark and troubled. "I found Stacy drinking a beer with Billy Ferguson behind the hall. It's the first time I've ever caught her doing that. Kids do start drinking young in these small, western towns, but I thought Stacy and Tony knew better."

"Teenagers are going to experiment with alcohol sooner or later."

"Fourteen is sooner than I want, and I'm damn

THE COWBOY AND THE HEIRESS 103

sure that boy is a good part of the reason why Stacy decided to try beer now. He's one of the wildest kids at the high school. That tenth grader is just about the last boy in Perrytown I want Stacy to spend time with."

Beth decided this probably wasn't the time to point out it was a tricky business telling teenagers what friends they could and couldn't see. Lang didn't look like he was in the mood to receive unsolicited advice. Instead she asked a safer question.

"Have you decided if you're going to punish her?"

"She's grounded for two weeks, and she won't get any allowance for a month. I'd ground her for longer, but I know it's pretty lonely for the girls living out here during the summer. They really look forward to their trips to town."

"With the guests around now, surely it's a little easier for them," Beth said, thinking of Tad, who had actually danced twice with Tony tonight. It was a shame that Stacy's getting into trouble had to overshadow a wonderful evening for Tony.

"They still miss their friends. At any rate, if I catch Stacy drinking again I'll ground her for a month or more. And now, I think we're finished talking about my nieces for the night."

"We are?"

His expression purposeful, Lang set his coffee mug on the counter. He went over to the radio and tuned it to a station playing love songs. Beth smiled when she recognized the opening stanzas of "All I Have to Do Is Dream" by the Everly Brothers. It was definitely a night for fifties music.

"I never got to claim my last dance," he declared. He crossed the kitchen and took her into his arms. They began swaying together in time with the music, but within moments they gave up all pretense of dancing. Lang looked down at her, his eyes burning with a hunger that matched her own.

The tension which had been smoldering between them all night sparked to life. He tilted her face up, and his mouth claimed hers. It was even more devastating than the kiss he had given her in the sewing room, for they had a whole day of simmering hunger behind it. She opened her mouth and let him taste and explore her as he wished. In turn, she boldly reached up and ran her fingers through his hair. She had been longing to touch it for weeks now. It was just as thick and silky as she had imagined.

With a moan, he tore his mouth away from hers. His lips slanted across her face, kissing her cheekbones, her eyelids, the sensitive skin at the base of her neck. Beth wrapped her arms around his neck and held on for dear life. His face was rough with a day's growth of beard, but she didn't mind. She relished every moment of this kiss, every sensation in it, for Lang made her feel startlingly, beautifully alive.

He leaned back and stared down into her face. His expression was serious as he reached out one hand and traced the line of her jaw.

"Sweet Lord, your skin is just as soft as it looks. The first day I saw you in the parking lot of Danny's diner, I wanted to do this," he admitted hoarsely as he stroked his hand across her cheek. Little shivers traced down her back when he bent his head and gently kissed the line his fingers had taken.

He leaned back to look at her again, and this time his expression was more harsh. "Beth Richards, you're the most beautiful woman I've ever seen. I know you're trouble spelled with a capital T. I've done my damnedest, but I just can't stay away from you."

Before she could think of a fitting rejoinder, he framed her face with his rough hands and kissed her again. He moved closer, pressing her against the counter until their hips met. This time when she felt his hardness, she welcomed the sensation. She rejoiced in the knowledge that he wanted her, for right now her own traitorous body desperately wanted to join with his.

His mouth moved to claim hers again, and while their tongues met and mated he pressed against her in a delicious, primitive rhythm her body recognized and met. Vaguely, Beth was aware of the scent of coffee, the masculine spicy scent of Lang, the sound of the fire hissing and popping across the room. She didn't know whether she wanted to laugh or cry. She knew now with terrible exhilarating certainty that Bryce had been wrong about her. She wasn't frigid. She couldn't be frigid and feel as if her body were a torch waiting to explode into flames.

He cupped her buttocks and kneaded them, bringing her more tightly against him. Kissing the base of her neck, he lifted her up onto the counter and spread her knees wide with his hands. He stepped close so that their bodies touched once more. His gaze intent, he slowly undid the buttons of her blouse. He opened the garment just wide enough to place a reverent kiss on the top of the valley between her breasts.

He stood up again. His eyes never leaving her own, he slipped a hand inside her bra and touched her gently. She felt the tip of her breast harden against his palm. He shifted his hand and began to rub and roll her sensitive nipple between his fingers.

With each slow deliberate caress she felt an exquisite tug deep in her belly.

Suddenly, it was too much. It was too much to realize how much she wanted Lang. It was too much to realize she was capable of real passion, after thinking for years there was some sort of awful lack in her. It was too much, hovering on the edge of some kind of intense sensuous precipice to which Lang had brought her so quickly.

She reached out and shoved against his chest. She felt his hands tighten briefly on her shoulders, and then he let her go. He stepped back and ran a hand through his hair. She derived mild consolation from the fact he was breathing just as hard as she was. She slipped down from the counter and buttoned up her blouse with shaking hands. She wanted to walk away, but she wasn't absolutely certain her legs would work properly just yet.

She forced herself to look him straight in the eye. "I don't want this," she said fiercely. "I don't want you."

Lang shook his head wearily. "Lady, your body sure says otherwise."

"I don't care what my body wants. I don't want a relationship with anyone right now. I don't want to care about anyone but me right now."

"Well, I wasn't exactly looking for a relationship, either, but I'd say there's something going on between us. We'd be fools to pretend otherwise. And I was never one to resist a challenge."

"There isn't any challenge here," she declared, trying to keep panic from her voice. "There isn't anything going on here but basic animal attraction, and I, for one, refuse to be ruled by my instincts. We don't even like each other." She found herself echoing the disclaimer she had made to Elsie just this afternoon at the rodeo.

"I'm not so sure about that. I think I may like Beth Richards very much," he stunned her by admitting. "I just can't trust her, because I don't know who the hell she really is."

As she stared up at the rugged planes of his face, she felt the tide of emotion rise in her. "I'm just plain me," she said, swallowing back a sob. "I'm just plain me."

She hurried from the kitchen before she disgraced herself by bursting into tears. She knew he watched her leave, and she was relieved that he made no move to follow her. She fled Lang and his ranch house for the security of her own snug little cabin. She closed the door tightly and leaned against it. She could shut out Lang in a physical sense, but she knew she would have a difficult time shutting him out of her heart and thoughts tonight.

TEN

The next morning as she cooked breakfast, Beth dreaded the moment when she would have to face Lang again. What must he think of her? She had acted like a temperamental idiot last night. One moment she had encouraged his kiss, and the next moment she had run away from him.

What he had said about coming to like Beth Richards had touched a cord deep inside her. For so long she had wanted to be liked for her own personality and character rather than the name she carried, or the social connections her father's billions and her mother's fine New England bloodlines had given her. Throughout her life she had never been certain if her friends had honestly liked her, or just her family's incredible penthouse in New York City and the wonderful places she could take them on vacations.

Certainly Bryce Townsend, the first man she had cared for deeply, had only wanted her for her money and the status being married to her would give him. She had found that out to her despair and rage six months ago.

After that terrible day she had risked her father's fury, broken off her engagement, and left the only life she knew, to find out for herself who she was.

THE COWBOY AND THE HEIRESS 109

During the past few weeks at the Rafter N she had started to figure out that answer. She had left Katherine Elizabeth Harrison behind, and combined the middle name she had always preferred with her mother's maiden name. She thought she rather liked Beth Richards—and being Beth Richards. It meant the world to her that Lang might like her, too.

She had just started to mix up a large bowl of flapjack batter when Lang walked in and poured himself a cup of coffee. He often did that in the mornings, staying in the kitchen while he drank it, talking with her about his plans for the day before the rest of the people on the Rafter N were up and about. She hadn't realized until now how much these talks meant to her. She hoped with all her heart that last night's episode hadn't spoiled these quiet times they shared together.

He leaned back against the counter and watched her as she cracked eggs into the bowl.

After a long, awkward moment, he cleared his throat. "I got a little carried away last night. I wish I could say it won't happen again, but I can't promise you that."

"I got carried away, too, but I *can* promise you that it won't happen again," she said firmly.

He made a noncommittal sort of a grunt and sipped his coffee.

"Thank you for convincing me to come into town yesterday. I had a wonderful time," she offered.

"I'm glad," he said. Then he smiled at her, the warmth back in his lovely toffee-brown eyes, and she knew it would be all right between them.

He tilted his head back and drained the last of his coffee. Beth found herself staring at the corded muscles in his neck and forced herself to look away.

"We'll be taking our guests on an overnight in three days," he announced as he placed the empty mug in the sink. "Tucker and Elsie will give you some advice on what cooking gear to pack."

"Mr. and Mrs. Eldridge Mott will be thrilled." Beth had to grin. "At last they may be able to spot the shy and elusive Rocky Mountain ptarmigan, a new addition to their lifetime birding lists."

Lang smiled back at her. "And I thought fishermen could be a fanatic bunch. These bird-watching types have them beat to hell. If I can't find them some pine grouse and the ptarmigan, I'm afraid they're going to ask for their money back. If Mrs. Mott starts to kick up a fuss, she'll talk me into giving them a full refund in no time."

"I can't imagine that sweet old lady ever kicking up a fuss, and Mr. Mott is just an old pussycat with spectacles."

"Don't you be fooled by their scholarly grandparentish looks. That old lady has a mind like a steel trap, and the way she negotiated a twenty-five percent discount for them because they're both seniors still gives me the willies," he said with a shudder.

"Why, Lang Nelson, I think I've finally found something you're afraid of. The man who likes to ride eight hundred pounds of bucking bronco is running scared around a little old bird-watching couple from Cincinnati."

"Yep. I guess that just about sums it up. There's only one thing that scares me more."

"And what would that be?"

"That I might arrive in the dining room so late sometime that Tucker will have finished off one of your delectable desserts before I've had a chance to have two helpings myself."

With that Lang strolled from the room, leaving her

THE COWBOY AND THE HEIRESS 111

feeling ridiculously pleased—both for his compliment and the easy teasing way he had delivered it.

"What a glorious morning for a pack trip," Mrs. Eldridge Mott said to Beth, her lined face alive with excitement as they rode along the trail. "I was so worried that it might be rainy, but just as Mr. Nelson predicted, here it is a bright sunny day. My goodness, look at that Lazuli Bunting. Isn't his plumage just lovely, dear?"

"It certainly is," Beth responded obediently. She'd be feeling more excited herself—about the Lazuli Bunting's plumage specifically and this trip in general—except for the fact that she had stayed up until one o'clock last night organizing the food and packing her own gear.

"Has anyone ever told you that you look astonishingly like Katherine Elizabeth Harrison? She's the daughter of Peter Harrison, the telecommunications magnate, you know." Mrs. Mott was watching her, her blue eyes curious.

"People have mentioned the resemblance from time to time," Beth said vaguely, her heart starting to pound. If only she had gotten more sleep last night. Her mind wasn't clear enough to be fencing with this shrewd old woman this morning. "I can't see it myself."

"Nonsense. You look just like her. I saw her once, at distance of course, at a ballet opening in New York City. She was one of the most glamorous creatures I've ever encountered. Are you sure you aren't related to the Harrison family in some way?"

"Not that I'm aware of," Beth said weakly. She thanked her lucky stars that Lang was riding at the back of the column where he couldn't overhear this conversation.

"Well, I find it hard to believe such an uncanny resemblance exists without there being some sort of genetic link between your families. Now that I think about it, I haven't read anything about that young woman for months now, and I'm hopelessly addicted to the society columns, you know. Last I heard, I think she was supposed to be married, and what a handsome young fellow he was. I wonder why I haven't read about their marriage yet. It was supposed to take place this June."

"Look—what kind of bird is that?" Beth asked desperately.

Fortunately for Beth, the small brown bird which had just flitted across the trail was a species that Mrs. Mott didn't immediately recognize. Beth drew a huge sigh of relief as Mrs. Mott excitedly pointed out the bird to Mr. Mott. The two of them pulled their horses to a halt. Blocking the trail and oblivious to the fact that they were holding up the whole column of riders, they dove for their birding books. After consulting at great length, they informed their amused and exasperated fellow guests they were fortunate to have just seen a hermit thrush.

Lang rode up from the back of the line and diplomatically suggested that the Motts wait for the rest to ride on. The older couple would come along to tonight's campsite with Hank. That way they could stop and bird-watch as often as they wanted without holding up the rest. While Lang talked with the couple, Beth quietly eased her mount away from Mrs. Mott. For the rest of their stay, she was going to do her best to avoid being alone with the shrewd old woman from Cincinnati who knew far too much about a certain Katherine Elizabeth Harrison.

* * *

That night as they sat around the campfire, Beth was annoyed to find herself watching Lang. She told herself to look away from him, and minutes later she found herself staring at him again. *Katherine Elizabeth, the case you have on this man is getting worse by the day. The first time you had so much yearning in you for a male was when you had that terrible crush on Eddie Friehoffer in seventh grade—and Eddie hardly knew you were alive. The last time was the first day you met Bryce.*

Rather than dwell on that painful thought, she decided to enjoy looking at Lang instead. The firelight glinted off his sandy hair and threw the planes of his rugged face into stark relief as he talked and laughed with his guests. His cheeks were shadowed by a day's growth of beard, and small lines at the corners of his eyes deepened when he smiled. Rough and real, Lang definitely aroused stronger feelings in her than Bryce ever had.

The first day she met her father's new CEO, she'd thought he was the most handsome man she'd ever seen. With his striking black hair, gorgeous blue eyes, and fine patrician features, perfectly groomed Bryce Townsend had swept her off her feet with his determined courtship. Bryce had flattered her, and he had taken advantage of her deep-seated loneliness and insecurity. He had offered her the companionship and affection she had been starved for. She winced as she remembered how fast she had fallen for him. She had certainly made the task of wooing the boss's daughter easy. Despite the fact that she convinced herself that she loved him, she hadn't been in any hurry to get married, and that wariness had frustrated and angered Bryce. It wasn't until six months ago that she had realized just how much.

Lang Nelson was the complete opposite of a polished practiced sycophant like Bryce. Lang worked brutal hours, doing everything he could to save his ranch. On a night like this, he had to do something he particularly disliked—charm his guests. Bryce was remarkably good at dodging any sort of activity he disliked, and found time to spend hours at his various country clubs, playing golf and tennis. Even though Lang often irritated her with his high-handed way of ordering her about, she respected him in a way she had never respected Bryce.

Lang Nelson had hardly tried to court her. By his own admission, he had gone out of his way to avoid her. She had done her best to avoid him, too, but she couldn't seem to stop thinking about him. Shivers crept down her back and longing swept through her every time she thought of the kiss he had given her in the kitchen, the kiss she had vowed they wouldn't repeat.

Just then, Lang looked across the fire and caught her staring at him. Her cheeks flamed. They grew hotter when he raised one eyebrow in a very knowing amused masculine look. In that moment, she knew he had guessed what she was thinking. *Damn you, Lang Nelson. Damn you for being a cocky, far-too-handsome-for-my-peace-of-mind cowboy.*

She looked away from him haughtily, to hide her embarrassment and chagrin. If she couldn't get her unruly feelings toward her boss under control soon, she would have to leave the Rafter N. A wave of sadness washed over her at the thought. She had become so fond of Tucker, Elsie, Tony, Stacy, and even Lang, in such a short time.

That night it took Beth a long time to fall asleep

THE COWBOY AND THE HEIRESS 115

in the small tent Tucker had helped her erect on the side of camp. She hated small dark spaces, but she didn't want to complain. Tucker had warned her that people often had problems sleeping at high altitude. That had to be the reason why she turned and twisted restlessly in her sleeping bag, despite the fact that she was exhausted. A certain rancher with shaggy blond hair and a set of shoulders wider than the Mississippi had absolutely nothing to do with it.

When she did finally doze off, she began dreaming almost at once. Although she tried to stop it, she began dreaming *that* dream, the dark horrible nightmare which had plagued her for over a year now. It always started the same relentless way.

She was walking down a street on the Upper East Side in Manhattan. It was after midnight, not terribly late by New York standards. The street was quiet but well-lit, and there were other people out and about. There was no reason for her to be afraid. There was no reason for her to react with anything other than mild curiosity when she heard a vehicle pull up behind her.

Only when she heard footsteps running up fast behind her did she begin to worry. Only when she felt hard hands grasp her arms did she become frightened. She fought her assailant instinctively at first, and then she thought of her purse and the two hundred dollars inside it. She tried to turn and offer him the purse. She tried to make him understand he could have all her money, and her jewelry, too. When he started to pull her toward the van, she understood at last, and she was terrified.

She managed to scream once. Then she was inside the van, and they clamped something over her nose and mouth which smelled sickeningly sweet. She held her breath until her lungs burned, but at last she had to breathe in, and when she did she felt the world fade away from her. "No," she cried, fighting to stay conscious. If only she could keep her mind focused and alert. If only she could fight off the hands holding and shaking her . . .

"Shh, Beth, it's me. You're just dreaming. Hush now. Everything's all right. It's just a dream."

She fought off the black paralyzing terror to realize it was Lang beside her inside her tiny tent. He held her shoulders, and he spoke to her in a deep slow voice which began to calm her racing heart. Still, she found she was shivering, and she couldn't stop. She was frozen to the marrow of her bones. It was hard to believe she was safe in a tent instead of trapped inside that horrible, cold dark van again.

"I-I'm sorry. D-did I wake you?" she got out between chattering teeth.

"No. It's not all that late yet. I was just prowling around, making sure we'd stowed the food where varmints and bears couldn't get into it."

"I t-tied the food up in a tree j-just l-like Tucker told me to." Despite the lingering terror of her dream, she felt a flare of irritation to realize he doubted that she had done her job.

"Shh, now, I know you did. It's just second nature for me to check." He reached over and touched her hand to reassure her. "Christ, woman, your hands are freezing. You're freezing. It's no wonder—you've twisted yourself halfway out of your sleeping bag."

Gently he pulled the warm sleeping bag back up around her shoulders and zipped her in. She was afraid he was going to leave her. She didn't want to be alone, not yet, for she feared that her nightmare might return. Yet she was too proud to ask him to stay.

"That must have been one nasty nightmare you were having," he said quietly, seemingly reading her mind. "You could tell me about it. I'm no shrink, but I know that when Tony and Stacy tell me about

THE COWBOY AND THE HEIRESS 117

their nightmares right after they wake up they usually sleep well for the rest of the night."

As she stared up at his dim shadowy outline, she found that she did want to tell him. By the sheer force of his personality, big capable Lang might make her fear and her awful dream go away for tonight. It was too much to hope that he might help her to conquer the nightmare and her fear forever.

And so she told him how she had been kidnapped a year ago in New York. She told him what it had felt like when she had been forced into the van and drugged. She told him about the hot airless room where they had kept her for four days, blindfolded and terrified, while they negotiated with her father for her ransom.

Then, as suddenly as it had begun, her ordeal was over. Her father had paid the ransom, and the kidnappers had shoved her out of their van in Central Park in the middle of the night. She had proved to be one of the few victims lucky enough to survive her kidnapping.

That was all she told Lang, but her thoughts raged on. She still lived with the memories of what had happened to her. She had gone into counseling and taken a self-defense class from one of the best instructors in the country. She was determined that she would never feel that helpless again.

Her father had to live with his memories of her kidnapping, too, of a time during which ruthless, omnipotent Peter Harrison had felt helpless, frustrated, and frightened. His reaction when he got his daughter back safe and sound was to promptly hire a team of bodyguards which had been with her constantly after that day. She had tried to accept the bodyguards, for she knew they gave her father some peace of mind. At the start, they had given her peace of mind, too. After a few months, though, she had felt smothered by their constant presence.

Her father had also pushed her to set a date for her marriage to Bryce. Somehow he seemed to think she would be much more secure safely married to the man he had chosen for her. Bryce had stepped up his subtle pressure, as well. She had almost gone along with them. She was on the brink of saying "yes" to the June wedding they both wanted. Then she had overheard Bryce talking on the phone with a woman who was clearly his mistress, and her world had shattered again within the course of those two shocking grim minutes.

She had fled to her room, and within a crazed half-hour had come up with the plan to run away from her father and his watchdogs, her faithless fiancé, and the opulent privileged life in which she had felt increasingly uncomfortable. At the end of her frantic run she had landed at the Rafter N, working for the man who waited so patiently beside her. A man who was coming to mean far too much to her.

She sighed and reached out a hand to him. He took it between both of his. His hands were warm, and she could feel the calluses on his palms.

"I'm sorry you had to go through something like that," he said after a long time. "Did the police ever catch them?"

Beth let out a bitter laugh. "No. Despite the reward my father offered for their capture, no one ever caught a single man in that gang. They were professionals."

"I'd hunt each one down and make them pay for what they did to you, if I had the right," he said in a cold, implacable voice she had never heard him use before. He meant it, she realized with a shiver.

"Thank you," she said a little shakily.

THE COWBOY AND THE HEIRESS 119

"I don't suppose you're going to tell me who your father is?"

"No. Now you know he was wealthy enough to pay a hefty ransom for my return, but I think you already guessed I came from a rich family."

"You don't exactly talk or act like a woman born on the wrong side of the tracks," Lang pointed out dryly.

"And you're hardly the hick cowboy you'd like your guests to believe you are," she countered, hoping to distract him from the issue of her father.

"Touché." She heard the smile in his voice. "Now, if you're feeling a little better, I should slip on out of here. We all have a long day tomorrow."

She tightened her grip on his hand. She knew what he said made sense, but still she didn't want him to leave. Suddenly she was very aware that they were alone together in the small dark tent. A part of her mind warned her that she could be opening the lid to Pandora's box, but she didn't care. All she knew in that moment was that she didn't want Lang to leave without kissing her. After the cold terror of her dream, she wanted him to help her feel alive again.

He cleared his throat and shifted restlessly. The darkness made her bold. She raised her other hand and touched his face. He went completely still as she smoothed his cheekbones with her fingertips. Greatly daring, she let her fingers travel lower and trace his lips. A quiver went through her when she felt him kiss the tip of her finger. Then he pulled away from her touch.

"This isn't a good idea," he said, his voice gruff. "This isn't the right time."

"Shh," she said, using the same soothing voice he had used earlier. "I think this is exactly the right time." She freed her other hand from his grip and tugged his head down to hers.

He resisted her for a long moment, and then he gave in with a groan deep in his throat. Moments later, his big body settled over hers and his hands framed her face. She relished the feel of his weight pressing down on her. He kissed her, and the lingering chill from her nightmare vanished in a blaze of heat.

There was no doubt about it. Lang Nelson was one hell of a kisser. She had thought Bryce was skillful, but now she realized there was simply no comparison. There was a thoroughness in the way Lang went about kissing, despite the need she sensed in him, which made her breathless and dizzy. He sampled and tasted her mouth, exploring her and encouraging her to do the same. It was wonderful to be so completely the focus of a man's attention. *Bryce Townsend, eat your cold calculating heart out. I hope you play golf better than you make love.*

That was the last conscious thought she had for a very long time. She simply felt, and the sensations Lang gave her were remarkable. Instead of feeling claustrophobic, she liked the long weight of him on top of her. She found herself opening her legs as far as the sleeping bag would allow, until he was cradled between her hips. As he deepened the kiss, she shamelessly pressed herself closer to him. The core of her pulsed with delicious burning waves of need.

She let her hands range down his broad back. Boldly she reached under his jacket and slipped her hands under his shirt. He drew in his breath sharply when she touched his skin. He was warm, smooth, and firm beneath her fingers. Deprived of sight in the dark, she felt her awareness of her sense of touch become more intense. Slowly she explored the sides of his rib cage and the hard muscles across his back.

Once again, the darkness encouraged her to do something she never would have dared to do in the daylight. She slipped her hands down to the edge of his jeans. When she started to venture further, he stiffened.

"Whoa, there." He caught her hand and brought it to his lips and kissed her fingertips. He linked his fingers with hers and firmly pinned her hands beside her head.

He rested his forehead against her own, his breath coming in gasps. "Not that I don't want you to touch me. Right now I'm just about dying to have you touch me all over. Tonight's all wrong for us. You've got to be sure this is what you want."

His words chilled her ardor like a bucket of ice cold stream water. Of course he was right. She didn't know if this was really what she wanted. Damn Lang Nelson for being such a gentleman. Right now, she'd much rather he hadn't pointed that fact out to her. Tomorrow, however, she knew that she'd probably feel a great deal differently.

He sat up, and she let go of his hands.

"Sweet dreams, sweet Beth," he said, and then he kissed her on the forehead. The gesture was so tender and unexpected that she had to smile, despite the fact that her body was still boiling with frustrated desire. Then he unzipped the door of her tent and slipped out into the mountain night.

Beth let go a long breath and punched the pillow she had made out of her down jacket. Lang Nelson was definitely one of the most unpredictable, infuriating, and outrageously decent men she had ever met.

She was still remembering the feel of that last kiss and Lang's parting words when she fell sound asleep. And for that night, at least, she had no more nightmares.

TWELVE

The next morning Beth rose early, feeling surprisingly refreshed. It was so cold inside her tent that she could see her breath. Quickly, she put on her parka, hat, gloves, and boots and went outside to watch the first sunlight gild the tops of the high peaks bright gold. She had coffee ready, a blazing campfire burning, and a hot breakfast of scrambled eggs and bacon ready for Tucker, Lang, and Hank by the time the three men sleepily stumbled from their tent.

Tucker took one look at the fire and the coffee and smiled reverently. "Beth, I swear, I've thanked the Good Lord at least a dozen times that Lang decided to stop by Danny Parson's diner the day he hired you. If only I was thirty years younger, I'd ask you to run off to Mexico with me."

"If you were thirty years younger, I'd probably go." Beth smiled back at him.

Lang made no comment on this exchange. Instead, he headed straight for the coffeepot and poured himself a cup. She watched him as he stood by the fire. With some amusement she studied his weary face and decided he looked as if he had spent a restless night.

Her vanity had been hurt that he had turned

THE COWBOY AND THE HEIRESS 123

down her unspoken invitation last night. It was an invitation she had made to few other men. Deep down inside, however, she knew he had been right. She had been looking for comfort last night. She didn't want to make love with Lang Nelson. They could have no future together. She meant to move on after the fall hunting season ended. She wasn't ready to build a relationship with any man.

After he had eaten breakfast Lang finally spoke up to assign everyone their responsibilities for the day. "Tucker and Hank, I want you to look after the Buchanans, the Iversons, and the Smiths. They are probably going to want to spend most of the day fishing. I'll take the Motts up on Bighorn Ridge to look for ptarmigan. Beth, after you make pack lunches for everyone, you're free until it's time to start on dinner."

With that romantic exchange, he left his plate by the plastic tub beside her which served as their camp sink and went to check the horses. Shaking her head inwardly, Beth set to work on making breakfast for the guests.

She was busy for the next few hours, cooking and cleaning up. By the time ten o'clock rolled around, her camp kitchen was tidy, the guests had gone to their various pursuits for the day with the pack lunches she had made for them, and she had several wonderful hours of free time ahead of her.

Although she liked fishing, she was much more interested in hiking up someplace high to look at alpine wildflowers and the high peaks all about them. When she asked Tucker for a good trail recommendation, he'd told her Bighorn Ridge was the prettiest place she could reach from this valley.

She decided to take that trail, but she promised herself that she would stay clear of Lang and Mrs.

Eldridge Mott. Within a half-hour, she knew her choice had been a good one. The wildflowers were glorious. She particularly liked the delicate blue-and-white columbine and the vibrant magenta Indian paintbrush she saw beside the trail.

By noon she had hiked well above the timberline. She was tired and out of breath from the high altitude, but the view was worth the effort. Bighorn Ridge was actually a large alpine plateau. Beyond miles of open tundra she could see jagged peaks dotted with snowfields in every direction. She could also see Lang and the Motts walking along the southern edge of the plateau, which dropped away in a series of steep ledges and gullies. Relieved to discover that there was plenty of space for them all up here, Beth sat down behind a boulder out of the chill wind and ate her lunch. After she finished, she stood up and started taking pictures.

She was just putting her camera back into her pack when the alpine wind brought with it the sound of someone shouting. She looked up and saw that Lang and the Motts were only a quarter of a mile away. Lang was waving to her urgently. Mrs. Mott was peering over the edge of the ridge. With a cold shaft of foreboding, Beth realized she couldn't see Mr. Mott anywhere.

She slung her pack on her back and hurried toward Lang. By the time she reached the place where Mrs. Mott stood wringing her hands, Lang had vanished over the edge.

Tears streamed down the old woman's face. "It's my poor Eldridge. He saw a ptarmigan on a ledge down there, and he slipped on the gravel and fell. Mr. Nelson warned us to watch our footing, but Eldridge didn't listen to him."

Her heart in her throat, Beth walked to the edge

of the ridge. Mr. Mott lay on his back on a broad grassy ledge twenty feet below. He was wide awake and talking with Lang, but his right foot lay at an unnatural angle, and a dark stain was spreading quickly across his pants leg. From a first aid course she had taken a few years ago, she guessed Mr. Mott probably had a compound fracture. Lang had already opened up the first aid kit he always carried in his pack.

"What can I do to help?" Beth called down to him.

"For the moment, I want you to keep an eye on Mrs. Mott and make sure she doesn't fall down here, too," Lang shouted back grimly. "I called Tucker on the radio, and he's already on his way up here."

Beth took a deep breath and stepped away from the cliff. For the next half-hour, she did exactly as Lang had asked. She did her best to reassure Mrs. Mott, and she made sure that the agitated woman didn't venture too close to the edge herself.

At the end of that long thirty minutes, Lang reappeared. He walked straight to where Mrs. Mott sat and knelt before her.

"Your husband is going to be just fine. He doesn't seem to have any internal or spinal injuries. I don't want to move him, just to be on the safe side. Although he does have a compound fracture, I managed to stop most of the bleeding. I've got him all covered up with jackets and sweaters, so he shouldn't get chilled or go into shock. When Tucker gets up here with some splints, we'll immobilize that leg and get your husband ready to travel. Now I'm going to dial up a ride out of here for him."

Beth was startled when she saw Lang pull a small cell phone from his pocket. Although the device hardly fit his cowboy image, she realized how smart he had been to bring one into the back country. Within moments he was talking with the county sheriff, trying to arrange a rescue. Although Beth didn't want to eavesdrop, she couldn't help overhearing their conversation. Within a minute or two it became clear the sheriff was reluctant to call for the helicopter Lang wanted.

"Damn it, Ray," Lang argued, "Mott is seventy-two years old. He's stable now, but packing him out twenty miles on horseback with a compound fracture is going to be too hard on him. I'd say you've got to call for a chopper. Taking into account his age, and the amount of blood he's already lost, and the fact that he might have a back or head injury, we need a backboard and a chopper up here pronto."

There was a long silence while Lang listened to the sheriff, his brows drawn together in a fierce scowl.

"Yes, it's calm and sunny up here. If you wait too long to call Grand Junction, though, you know the afternoon storms will roll in, and then we'll all be in a real fix."

There was another long silence, and then Lang's features relaxed a little. "Thanks, Ray. Call us when you get through to the boys in Grand Junction."

He hung up and walked to the edge of the cliff. "How are you doing down there, Eldridge?"

The old man called back gamely to say he was fine. Two minutes later, the cell phone beeped. It was the sheriff calling back with confirmation that a rescue chopper would be leaving shortly from Grand Junction. Beth squeezed Mrs. Mott's hand encouragingly.

"You see, your husband will be in a hospital in no time," Beth told the old woman with a bright smile.

THE COWBOY AND THE HEIRESS 127

During the next two hours, Lang coolly and calmly directed the rescue chopper to their location on Bighorn Ridge and worked with its crew and Tucker to bring Mr. Mott up the cliff in a wire basket. Beth continued to keep an eye on Mrs. Mott, and lent a hand wherever else she could.

Shortly before she went to join her husband in the helicopter, Mrs. Mott turned to Beth and said quietly, "My dear, thank you for looking after me so well. I never forget a face, and I find it hard to believe Miss Katherine Elizabeth Harrison has a double in this world. Whoever you are, I hope you realize what a remarkable man Mr. Nelson is. I've seen the way he looks at you, and the way you look at him, and I hope you can find a way to reach across the social gulf separating you. As they used to say in the Old West, Lang Nelson is a man to ride the river with. There aren't many like him anymore."

With that, the dignified old woman walked to the helicopter. Beth looked after her, touched and troubled by her words.

The rest of the pack trip went by in a blur for Beth. She was exhausted from the strain and excitement of the afternoon. The guests were a subdued group around the fire that night, for the Motts had been popular with everyone. Beth tumbled into her sleeping bag at nine o'clock and slept soundly all night. The next morning she was glad to pack up her tent and cooking gear after breakfast and head back to the Rafter N.

That afternoon, Lang drove over to the hospital in Grand Junction to take the Motts their suitcases and clothing. It was late when he returned. He came to the kitchen to eat while Beth was tidying up from dinner and making preparations for breakfast the next morning. She felt a pang when she saw how tired he looked.

"How is Mr. Mott doing?" she asked as she gave Lang the plate of food she had kept warming for him in the oven.

"He sure is a game old gent." Lang shook his head as he sat down at the kitchen table and started in on his dinner. "When I came in, he was sitting up in bed and telling the staff all about his adventure. The rescue with the basket and the ropes fascinated him, and I gather both he and Mrs. Mott really enjoyed the helicopter ride. They said it was one of the most exciting things that had ever happened to them."

"It probably was," Beth said, smiling at the thought.

"The damnedest thing is, they both seem to feel that spotting a ptarmigan down on that ledge was worth a broken leg—although Mrs. Mott is a little put out because she didn't get a better look at the bird before Eldridge slipped and almost fell on the thing. The Motts make quite a pair. I can imagine them both happily hunting down birds to add to their life birding lists when they're a hundred. Then again, if they are always this accident-prone, they might not reach a hundred."

"I think they're sweet," Beth declared.

Lang responded with a very male, "Hmph," and concentrated on his plate. Beth let him eat in peace. From the crease between his brows, she guessed his thoughts were not particularly happy ones. She wondered if the possible legal ramifications of the accident were troubling him. The Motts hardly seemed the sort to sue, but one never knew anymore. When he finished his meal, he rinsed his plate and put it in the dishwasher.

THE COWBOY AND THE HEIRESS 129

"Do you want dessert?" she asked him. "There's some chocolate cake left."

"I don't think so, thanks. I'll just have coffee. Thanks for keeping some dinner for me," he added, and walked from the kitchen, his mind clearly elsewhere. Beth looked after him worriedly. If the man didn't want dessert, there was something seriously troubling him.

After she finished up in the kitchen, Beth went to her cabin. Despite the long day, she felt too restless to sleep. Tempted by the full moon outside, she decided to take a walk along the river.

It was lovely along the riverbank. Moonlight danced on the swirling currents and eddies in the water. The leaves of the cottonwood trees rustled quietly in the night breeze. She stood quietly for a time on the grass along the bank, simply enjoying the way the brilliant moon overhead turned the world all about her into shades of silver and shadow.

And then one of the shadows moved, and she realized she wasn't alone by the river any longer. Lang walked toward her along the grassy bank, his face pale and set in the cool wash of moonlight. As he drew closer, her treacherous heart began to race.

THIRTEEN

Lang came to stand beside her. For a time, they watched the moonlit river in surprisingly comfortable silence. When she looked over and saw he was still frowning, she decided it was time to take the bull by the horns. Lang Nelson did far too much of his worrying alone.

"I really don't think the Motts will try to sue, you know," she said quietly.

Lang looked at her and raised his eyebrows. "Reading my mind, now? What a multitalented cook you're proving to be, Beth Richards."

She ignored the sarcasm in his comment. She knew he had good reason to be in a foul mood tonight. Rather than be hurt or intimidated, she forged stubbornly ahead.

"I don't have to be a mindreader to tell that you're worried. Tonight was the first time since I've been here that you've turned down one of my desserts. Now, so far as I can see, you do most of your worrying about the ranch, or Tony and Stacy. Since the twins managed to avoid getting into trouble while we were gone, my powers of deductive reasoning tell me the future of the Rafter N is on your mind tonight."

Lang ran a hand through his hair and sighed.

"You figured that one out just right. Perhaps you should have been a detective."

"Not on your life. Detectives spend most of their time prying into other people's lives. I'm too busy figuring out how to live my own life to care about someone else's dirty laundry. But back to the topic at hand."

"I didn't know we had a topic." He mocked her by copying her cultured accent with wicked precision. Because the smile was finally back in his voice, she decided not to take offense.

"The topic for tonight's riverside discussion is the fact that you're worried that Mr. and Mrs. Eldridge Mott might sue you for criminal negligence. I don't think that you need to worry about that possibility. They like you, and they had a wonderful time in Colorado, rescue and all. You weren't negligent. Last but not least, the Motts got to see their ptarmigan."

"Thank heaven for that, or I would be expecting to receive a court summons any day," Lang admitted with a flash of his usual humor, but his face sobered quickly.

"I agree," he went on. "I don't believe that the Motts are going to sic a pack of lawyers on me, but their accident makes me realize how much my grand guest ranch scheme has put the Rafter N in jeopardy. I considered the possibility that we might incur some legal liability if we had a serious accident, but I told myself that I'd be careful, and I'd make damn sure my crew was even more careful, and we wouldn't have any injured guests. Now, during our second pack trip of the season, a seventy-two-year-old man falls off a cliff, and I'm the one who was supposed to be looking after him."

The frustration and anger in Lang's voice made Beth want to reach out to him. Instead, she kept her hands in her pockets and offered him a much safer kind of comfort—logic.

"Accidents do happen from time to time. If you and your staff are careful, and so far as I can tell, you have only careful caring people working for you, no one is going to be able to successfully charge you with negligence."

"It would be nice to think that, but we both know these days that people can sue and win cases for the most ridiculous reasons. My turning the Rafter N into a guest ranch put this whole place at terrible risk. I'm more like my father than I want to admit to anyone, myself most of all." His expression bitter, Lang began to pace up and down beside the river.

"All of my life I watched him dream up reckless scheme after scheme to get rich quick—and none of them ever came to anything. He was too lazy and weak to face reality. Running a ranch well is damn hard work. He could never accept that simple fact. His great plans and schemes just placed the Rafter N further and further into debt."

"I didn't know your father," Beth said firmly, "but I do know you, and you certainly aren't lazy." She was encouraged by the fact that he had halted his pacing to listen to her. "No one on this whole ranch works harder than you do. I know you aren't reckless, either. I'd be willing to wager my last three paychecks that you spent a long time when you studied the guest ranch business and thought through whether or not it could possibly work here."

"I did my homework, all right, but I still didn't think through the liability question carefully enough. I dismissed the need to purchase liability insurance because it was so expensive, and now I wish like hell that I'd bought it. I took a gamble—a

THE COWBOY AND THE HEIRESS

gamble which could cost the twins and me our home."

"I suppose you could have just let the bank foreclose, and then there wouldn't have been any risk or ranch left at all," she pointed out coolly.

Lang gave her a grim smile. "You have a point there, and in the long run that's probably the only point that matters. Deep down inside I know you're right. I just don't like facing the uncomfortable fact that I'm going to have to be ten times more careful about safety and ride everyone else hard about it, and hope like hell that we don't have any more guests go stepping off cliffs for the rest of this season."

"I know you won't, and I'll be careful not to give anyone food poisoning. By the fall, the Rafter N's reputation as one of the finest guest ranches in the West will be firmly established."

"Well, it might take a little longer than one season to accomplish that, but I like that notion mighty fine," Lang allowed.

He turned away from the river. Beth felt her cheeks heat as he studied her. Refusing to be intimidated, she studied him boldly in return. Why had she ever thought Bryce handsome? His smooth refined face was so bland compared to Lang's rugged features. She was coming to much prefer Lang's looks, with his strong jaw, hard cheekbones, and beautiful mouth.

"I like you mighty fine, too, Ms. Richards," Lang declared, a new note creeping into his voice. "You did a good job of keeping your head during all that excitement up on Bighorn Ridge. I appreciated your help up there."

A shiver went down Beth's back, a shiver which had nothing to do with the coolness of the night.

Katherine Elizabeth, it's time to head right back to your cabin, if you know what's good for you.

"And because I like you," Lang continued steadily, "and because I know you have some very wise doubts about getting involved with your cowboy boss, I'm going to give you fair warning. If you stay out here much longer, I'm not going to be able to keep my hands off you."

She made no move to leave and he stepped toward her, and then it was too late. Suddenly she was in his arms, and she realized with frightening certainty that she had been longing for this moment since he left her tent two nights ago. His head bent toward hers, his warm lips claimed her own, and the moonlit world beside the river vanished. All that mattered in this moment was this vital caring man who was holding her and kissing her as if he never wanted to let her go.

Someone moaned. Beth was amazed to realize it must be her. She wrapped her arms about his neck and kissed him back for all she was worth. He tasted like coffee, and his hair and jacket carried the fresh sweet scent of willows. Beside them, the water sighed and swirled along its course. Dizzy with moonlight and longing, she pressed closer, wanting to feel his hard length against her.

While their tongues mated and danced, he slipped his hands under her jacket and shirt. She shivered up and down as he caressed the sensitive skin of her rib cage.

"This is crazy. We're all wrong together," she protested when his lips left her mouth and she finally could draw in enough breath to speak.

"Right now, we feel just right to me," Lang stopped kissing the line of her jaw long enough to declare "That pricey perfume you wear is sexy as hell, and you feel like heaven in my arms."

"I don't use pricey perfumes." Beth couldn't help laughing. "That's plain old soap I'm wearing."

"Whatever it is, it smells good on you." He growled deep in his throat and nipped the skin below her earlobe gently.

Right then, she decided to throw away all the perfume she owned. He nibbled and tasted the base of her throat, sending a whole hot new wave of desire through her. He slipped his hands from beneath her shirt. Her breath caught when he reached up and unzipped her jacket. She could not tell him to stop—her vocal chords seemed to be paralyzed. As he deliberately unbuttoned her shirt, her heart pounded in her chest. When Bryce had made a similar move, she had dreaded what would happen next.

She was surprised to realize that she wanted Lang to touch her—she even wanted him to see her. With the same deliberate care which marked everything he did, he loosened the front clasp on her bra and pushed the garment aside.

Lang's face was intent, his eyes dark and serious in the moonlight as he looked at her.

"Lord, woman, you are just plain pretty," he breathed, and he reached out and touched the very tips of her breasts. The reverence in his manner humbled her even as his touch made her pucker and harden. He took his time, methodically exploring and caressing, while her insides grew warm and wet.

He sank to his knees before her in the grass, and her breath caught again. He waited, an ardent silent supplicant asking for her permission. She didn't trust her voice to speak. Instead, she placed her hands on his shoulders and urged him closer.

His mouth was magic. With clever lips and tongue,

he laved and worshipped her. She tightened her grip on his shoulders and sighed her pleasure to the moonlit sky. His silky hair and the cool night air brushed against her bare skin in a sinfully sensual combination of sensations.

Her legs had gone weak, and protesting was the last thing on her mind when he gently lowered her to the long grass. She just wanted to get closer to him—wanted to feel his bare skin against hers. He covered her body with his own and kissed her, long and hard. When he shifted away from her, she clung to him until she realized he was reaching for the snap on her jeans. Mentally, she urged him on. Then he hesitated.

"Hell," he said, and sat upright, disbelief and disgust evident in his tone. "As much as I want you, I just can't do this. I can't make love to a woman I don't really know."

She stared at him, dazed. In the heat of her passion, she had been willing to give him everything.

As the reality of what he had just said slowly registered in her mind, a cold hard shell settled about her heart. Despite what he had said about wanting her, she wondered if there was some sort of fundamental flaw in her. Maybe Bryce was right. Maybe she was frigid. She knew so little of lovemaking. Perhaps she had done something wrong, or perhaps she hadn't done enough. All she knew was that she had desperately wanted to make love with Lang tonight. She had tried to tell him that in every way she could with her body, and still he had refused her. She was too proud to say the words aloud and risk another humiliating rejection.

She was glad Lang probably couldn't see that she was blushing with shame and embarrassment. Hastily she redid her bra and buttoned her shirt.

"I'm sorry," he said, his eyes dark and troubled as he watched her.

"I'm sorry, too," she said, keeping her tone even and cool, "but not too sorry. I said it before. This," she gestured to them both, "whatever we have between us isn't a good idea. I just got a little carried away in the moonlight."

"I'm not so sure that we're such a bad fit for the long run," he surprised her by saying, "but in the short term I know it's wrong for us to make love when I don't even know your real name. If you ever do decide to trust me with the truth, I'll have you out in the moonlight again so fast your head will spin."

She would have smiled, but she still hurt too much for that. Instead, she simply nodded and walked away from him, her head held high.

As soon as she reached the safe refuge of her cabin, she mechanically got ready for bed. She stared at her reflection in the bathroom mirror for a long time. *Katherine Elizabeth, when are you ever going to learn your lesson? People have told you that you're beautiful, but whatever it takes to make a red-blooded man want you, you simply don't have it. Maybe you're better off without one.*

Cursing a certain stubborn rancher, her frustrated restless body, and her own stupidity, Beth took a long time to fall asleep that night.

Lang slammed shut the hood of the old Ford van and wiped his greasy hands on a rag. Whatever was wrong with that engine, it was beyond his ability to fix. It was just one more thing gone wrong in a thoroughly jinxed day. First thing this morning, Tucker had brought him the news that a cow had been struck by lightning and killed in yesterday's thunderstorm. Then Hank had told him beavers had dammed three irrigation ditches in the north hayfield. To make matters worse, his old Massey-Ferguson tractor, usually the most reliable piece of machinery on the place, had refused to start this morning. Now the van was dead, too.

Days like this happened all the time in ranching. Usually he could take them in stride. Usually he could take a deep breath and remember that he was damn glad he got to spend most of his day working outside on his own land instead of punching a time card for someone else in a stifling city job. However, today he felt too edgy and angry to be philosophical about all the things that had gone wrong.

He was only too aware of the reason for his bad mood.

His beautiful cook was driving him crazy. He still couldn't believe that he'd had Beth in his arms beside the river, exactly where he'd imagined her a hundred times in his fantasies, and he'd been the one to put on the brakes. She was coming to mean so much to him—too much to make love to her when he didn't really know who she was. How could their bodies be intimate when she didn't trust him enough to tell him why she was hiding on his ranch?

If she'd meant any less to him, he would have taken what she seemed so willing to give and enjoyed it. He'd told himself just a week ago that he could handle a light affair with Beth, if it helped him to get over his growing obsession with her. She was just a rich girl slumming it on a Colorado ranch for fun and adventure. She'd move on when she grew bored and go running back to the glittering luxurious world she came from—the same world where beautiful heartless Sonya belonged.

He'd known even a week ago, though, when he had

THE COWBOY AND THE HEIRESS

considered a superficial sort of affair with Beth, that he'd been fooling himself. He'd never been one to enjoy meaningless sex. Despite his best efforts to fight the feelings growing inside him, he cared for Beth now.

This morning she had looked at him with a reproachful expression in her mist-blue eyes which had twisted his heart. He hadn't meant to hurt her feelings. Hell, he'd done them both a favor by keeping things from getting out of hand last night. Couldn't she see it?

"You gonna try fixin' that van, or are you just gonna stare at it for the rest of the day?" Tucker asked as he came to stand beside Lang.

"I already tried to fix it, but it's too far gone for me." Lang swung away from the van, irritated that Tucker had caught him in the midst of his brooding. "I'm pretty sure it needs a new carburetor, and it's going to take some time to hunt one down. The transmission's on its last legs, too."

"We should just shoot the dang thing and put it out of its misery."

"I know, but we need it to ferry our guests to the airport." Lang sighed as he did the arithmetic in his head. He set some money aside each year to repair ranch machinery and vehicles, but a carburetor and a new transmission were going to take a big chunk out of it.

Tucker peered past him. "Ain't that Danny Parson's rig?"

Lang spotted the battered black pickup coming up the road. "Looks like it."

"Wonder what he wants. He's not exactly the sort to stop by for a little chat."

Lang wondered the same thing as he strolled to meet Danny. They were good friends, but Danny wasn't apt to take time away from his precious diner just to make social calls.

After he stepped down from his truck, Danny glanced around him approvingly. "Place sure is looking shipshape these days." One of his best friends since grade school days, Danny knew how frustrating it had been for Lang to watch his father run the Rafter N into the ground.

"Thanks. You want to come in for a cup of coffee?"

"Is Beth apt to be in the kitchen right now?"

"Most likely." Lang's heart fell. The serious look on Danny's face warned him that he wasn't going to like whatever news Danny had brought him about his cook.

"I think I'll take a pass on coffee for the moment. I may go fetch myself a cup a little later. I did bring Beth a couple of recipes she's been asking me for."

"I don't suppose you drove out all this way just to exchange recipes with my cook."

"She's easy enough on the eye, and sweet enough, too. I would have done exactly that if I thought I had a chance with her. After watching her watch you over the Fourth of July, though, I figure she's pretty well gone on you. It's a damn shame. I thought she had better taste."

"Either you're crazy, or you need to have your eyes checked. Beth doesn't even like me."

Danny shook his head and let go a belly laugh. "For a gent who attracts women the way you do, you sure are dumb about them."

"Did you come all the way out here just to insult me, or was there a more pressing reason for this visit?"

"There's a reason, all right." Danny's expression sobered instantly. "I thought you'd want to know that there was a fellow who arrived in town this morning asking if anyone knew of a beautiful, classy young woman traveling on her own. The picture he left with Ida over at the Co-op sure looked like your Beth all done up in real fancy clothes.

"Ida kept her mouth shut, because you put the word out that Beth wanted to be left alone. Most folks will probably do the same, out of respect for you, or because they liked what they saw of Beth over the Fourth of July. I watched this fellow bang on doors all over town, though, and he sure is a persistent type. Sooner or later he may find someone who'll tell him about your cook."

"Has he left town yet?" Lang asked, thinking fast.

"He hadn't as of lunchtime. I gave Juan the afternoon off and asked him to keep an eye on this guy while I hightailed it out here to talk with you. I'd be willing to bet he hadn't found anything by noon. He looked too frustrated and bored to have found a lead on her."

"Thanks, amigo. I owe you for this one."

"You don't owe me a thing. I like Beth, and I'm happy to help her out. This guy looked like a private detective to me, and probably an expensive one at that. You have any notion of who might be looking for her?"

"I'm pretty sure she's not running from a husband." Even as he said the words, Lang realized that he wasn't certain they were true. He'd noticed that very first day that she hadn't been wearing a wedding ring when she came into the diner. Beth just didn't seem the sort to go kissing one man if she was married to another. Yet, for all he knew, she might be married. Hell, she might even have children. How he wished he could give Danny a better answer. *She's worked for you for over a month now, you came damn close to making love to her last night, and you still know next to nothing about her.*

"A woman can get into all sorts of dangerous trouble these days," Danny said grimly. "You give me a holler if you need a hand out here."

"Thanks, Danny." Lang preferred to handle his own trouble, but if something really big and nasty came his way, he wouldn't hesitate to deal Danny in. Parson was just the sort of person you wanted beside you when the shit hit the fan.

"I think I'll just mosey along and have a quick visit with your cook."

"Just keep those big mitts of yours to yourself." The moment those words popped out his mouth, Lang was appalled.

Danny let go another laugh and shook his head. "I'm hardly going to make a pass at your lady while we're talking about pecan pie and sweet roll recipes. Amigo, I'm afraid you're a goner."

With that cheerful declaration, Danny turned away and headed for the house. Lang stared after him, torn between envy and anger. The last thing he had time to do this afternoon was sit at his kitchen table listening to the two of them go on about cooking. Yet the prospect of spending an hour with Beth sounded so good. He'd rarely had a chance to just sit and talk with her. No wonder she didn't trust him.

Maybe Danny's right. Maybe you already are a goner. And if that's the case, you're a damn fool. Sonya taught you that beautiful, rich eastern women aren't for you. You would think you'd have learned that lesson by now.

Lang turned away from the ranch house and stomped off to see what he could do to get his tractor fixed.

THIRTEEN

"I need to talk with you," Lang declared from the doorway to the kitchen.

Beth looked up from the Mornay sauce she was stirring and sighed. Of course, he had to pick this particular moment. If she didn't keep stirring the sauce it was going to curdle, and she was already behind on dinner, thanks to the nice long chat she'd had with Danny Parson that afternoon.

"Just once, you could ask if it's a convenient time for me," she told him tartly, "before you come barging in here expecting my full attention."

She almost grinned when she realized how assertive that sounded. For someone who had never been very good at standing up for herself or expressing her anger, she was definitely making progress. Lang, however, didn't look as though he appreciated her progress. In fact, he looked furious.

"I didn't realize I needed a formal appointment to talk with my cook," he gritted.

"Of course you don't. I just thought you could practice a little common courtesy. I can see now that was probably too much to expect."

His eyes narrowed at that. "If it's convenient for you," he said with sarcastic emphasis, "I'd like to talk with you in my office right now."

Beth looked at him curiously. He'd never asked her to come to his office before. What did he have on his mind? With a sinking feeling in the pit of her stomach, she guessed it might have something to do with what almost happened between them last night at the river.

"This Mornay sauce will be ruined if I come now, and your guests may have to eat their dinner an hour late. If that's all right by you, I'd be happy to come to your office."

That reply gave him pause, just as she had hoped it would.

"All right. I'll see you right after dinner."

"Yes, sir," Beth replied smartly. "By the way, I was right when I said a career in service would be wrong for you. You obviously should have been a drill sergeant in the Marines.

"Don't," he said in a quiet voice which gave her chills, "push me. Not today." With that he turned around and left.

Beth looked after him, sorry now that she had teased him. What had been so awful about today for Lang?

Throughout dinner, she wondered about that question and the reason why he wanted to see her. Butterflies were rampaging in her stomach by the time she finished cleaning up the kitchen and went to find Lang in his office. As she hesitated right outside his door trying to summon the courage to knock, she came to a discouraging conclusion. *Katherine Elizabeth, even though you are getting better at standing up for yourself during confrontations, you still dislike them intensely.*

When she knocked on his door, he called for her to come in. He was sitting at his desk, reading some papers. She was startled to see a pair of wire-rimmed

THE COWBOY AND THE HEIRESS 145

glasses perched on his nose. So her rough, tough western boss wore glasses. She liked the look, she decided after a few moments. Combined with the plaid flannel shirt and leather vest he wore, they made him seem like a scholarly cowboy. He took off his glasses, folded them, and placed them neatly in a case on his desk. To keep from grinning, she looked about his office curiously.

It was a very masculine room, with a river rock fireplace along the far wall crowned by a dramatic oil painting of Mt. Zirkel, and shelves and shelves of leather-bound books interspersed with pictures of Lang's family, trophies from his rodeo days, and western sculptures. It was also scrupulously neat. The order and control Lang exercised over the rest of his life existed here, as well.

The computer which dominated the right side of his big oak desk just didn't fit with her image of a rancher's office. Lang noticed her staring at the machine and quirked one eyebrow. "That comes in mighty handy for keeping up with beef prices and keeping records on my cows. The days of the isolated rancher struggling to raise cattle in the wilderness are long gone."

"I see," Beth said a little wistfully. The rancher's tools might have changed, but she didn't think the rancher himself had. Whether he sat behind a desk or on a horse, Lang Nelson embodied the spirit of the West to her, and he always would.

The smile left his eyes as he folded his arms on his desk. "I wanted to talk with you because Danny brought me some interesting news. He said there's been a man showing your picture around town today and asking questions about you."

The butterflies in her stomach suddenly turned into cold hard stone. Her father and Bryce must have somehow traced her to northwestern Colorado. But how? She had been so careful. She had taken such pains to hide her trail.

In the end, she supposed it didn't matter how they had discovered where she had gone. They had come far too close to finding her, and she wasn't ready to go back. She wasn't sure she ever wanted to go back.

"We talked for over an hour this afternoon. Why didn't Danny tell me this then?" she asked, desperately trying to hold on to her composure.

"I suppose because he knows I'm looking out for you, and because you work for me, and it's more than a little peculiar to have some stranger showing your photo around town."

A hot flame of anger started to melt that cold ball of fear in her belly. Men. They were just the same high-handed, unreasonable creatures whether they lived in the East or the West.

"I still think that man and his photo were my business, and I'll tell Danny that the next time I see him."

"You can tell him anything you want." Lang rose to his feet and came to stand before his desk. He crossed his arms, and his gaze bored into her. "But first, I want you to tell me why there's a detective knocking on doors all over Perrytown trying to figure out where you are."

Beth gripped the wooden chair arms hard and forced herself to meet his gaze squarely. "As I said before, that's my personal business."

"I'm making it my business now."

"I swore to you once that I've broken no laws," she said, fighting to control her anger. How dare he try to interrogate her like this?

"How do I know some irate, gun-toting ex-hus-

THE COWBOY AND THE HEIRESS 147

band isn't going to show up on my doorstep demanding to see you?"

"There won't be any husband arriving on your doorstep. I've never been married."

His face seemed to relax a fraction at that news. "Then who the hell wants to find you so much he's sent a private cop to Perrytown, Colorado? I can't keep you on as my cook unless I know more about you."

So, it had come to that. She had been afraid it would, in the end. "I can't tell you the answer to that question." *You wouldn't believe me if I did tell you, and you wouldn't believe my reason for leaving. My own father wouldn't.*

"None of this matters, anyway," she declared wearily and rose to her feet. "I'll be hitting the road first thing in the morning. You're going to have to find yourself a new cook." With that she left the room and closed the door firmly behind her.

She gained little satisfaction from finally having the last word in a confrontation with Lang Nelson. She headed straight for her cabin. She had brought so few things with her, it wasn't going to take long to pack.

She had just pulled her suitcases out from under her bed when someone knocked loudly on her door. Beth sighed. She should have known he wouldn't give up easily, not when he needed her services so desperately. She was sorry to leave Lang in the lurch. She understood now how important it was to the entire Nelson clan for this guest venture of theirs to be a success. However, she knew Elsie would help cover until Lang could find a cook to work for the rest of the summer. In the meantime, Beth had to look out for herself.

She simply couldn't afford to stay, not with her father's hounds hot on her trail.

Steeling herself for a second round with Lang, Beth opened the door.

He stood in the doorway, his expression bleak. His gaze went straight to the two suitcases that were lying on her bed.

"May I come in?" The fact that he thought to ask surprised her. She promised herself that she wouldn't let the fact that he had remembered his manners disarm her.

"If you promise not to start ordering me around within the next two minutes."

"For two minutes, eh? That could be a tall order." The sheepish look in his eyes did it. Lang Nelson just didn't look sheepish very often. She found herself moving aside and letting him come in. Suddenly, her cabin seemed a great deal smaller. Because he moved so well, she sometimes forgot what a big man he was.

He sat down in the old armchair in the corner of the room. His brown eyes were serious as he watched her.

"You called my bluff," he said simply. "I don't want you to leave. We need you here too much. You can keep your secrets. Just promise me one more time that you won't bring any trouble down on my family, and I'll stop prying at you."

I know you mean that promise right now, Lang Nelson, but I bet you can't hold it for long.

"It's not that simple," she said with a sigh and went back to her packing. "If a detective has gotten this close, it's time I moved on."

"I thought you might say that," Lang admitted. "I called Danny right after you left my office. He had one of the guys who works for him keep an eye on that detective all afternoon. Juan's pretty sure he didn't find anything. The detective looked bored and disgusted when he drove out of town around four o'clock in his rental car, heading toward Big Springs."

Beth let out a sigh of relief. Big Springs was the next major town to the south, in the opposite direction from the Rafter N. Surely he would have come straight to the ranch if he'd discovered where she was living.

Lang echoed her thoughts. "If anyone in town had told him about you, I figure he would have headed straight out here to be sure he'd found the right woman."

Beth sat down on the bed, her legs weak. "I can't believe a single person in Perrytown didn't tell him about me. Hundreds of people must have seen me over the Fourth of July."

"Yep," Lang said, "that's about right. But all those folks also know you're a part of the Rafter N now. Danny, Tucker, and Elsie helped put out the word that you'd rather not be found by anyone, and Perrytown looks after its own."

"I didn't know there were places like Perrytown left in the world anymore," she said with a shake of her head. "I'm grateful to all of your friends for keeping quiet about me, but that detective might come back." Regretfully, she got to her feet and resumed her packing.

"I don't know about that. Now that they've crossed this town off their list, it seems to me that the Rafter N is as safe a place for you as any."

She stared at the jeans she held in her hands while she weighed his words. She wanted so much to believe him. "I just don't understand how they traced me this far. I didn't use credit cards, and I never used my real name at any of the fleabag hotels I stayed in."

"You've got the kind of face people tend to remember," Lang pointed out dryly.

Beth looked toward the open door to her bathroom and grimaced at herself in the mirror. "So everyone keeps telling me. My mother was much prettier than I am."

"Then she must have had a face that could have launched a thousand ships," Lang said softly, his eyes never leaving her.

Beth felt her cheeks begin to burn. She'd been given hundreds of compliments in her time. Why did one from this man make her blush and become tongue-tied like a schoolgirl? "I'm not sure she could have given Helen of Troy a run for her money, but she was a lovely woman, inside and out."

"And so are you, and I don't want you to leave here unless you absolutely have to. You're much more apt to leave a trail that detective can find if you keep moving around. Now that you've found a safe place, you ought to stay."

He looked down at his lap then, his voice thoughtful. "Besides, I've been thinking that there's a second possibility here. Maybe you did cover your tracks well. Maybe whoever sent that detective after you knows you and guessed the western slope of Colorado was where you were headed. They might not have tracked you to Perrytown specifically. They're just guessing you might be somewhere in this region, and that detective is wandering from town to town just to make sure you aren't hidden hereabouts. It's a pretty darn expensive way to go about finding someone, but if money is no object—"

Beth forced herself to consider Lang's argument objectively. Of course, money was no object to her

THE COWBOY AND THE HEIRESS 151

father and Bryce. Despite the fact that communication had become strained between them this past year, her father knew her very well, indeed. Had he guessed how much she had longed to return to the western slope of Colorado?

She also wondered if Lang could be right. Now that the detective had checked out Perrytown and moved on, would she be safest staying in a place they had already searched?

"I can't make up my mind about this right now," she said, both to herself and the man waiting so patiently for her decision. "I'm going to do some hard thinking tonight, and I'll let you know my decision in the morning."

Lang unfolded his long length from the chair. When he started to speak, she braced herself for another round of arguing. Instead he said, "All right."

He crossed the room and laid one hand on her shoulder. With the other, he tilted her head up, his hand gentle beneath her chin. "If you do decide to move on and you need help, you just give us a call. You've got friends now on the Rafter N and in Perrytown, and we'll come a-running. Tucker, Danny, and I, we'll be the cavalry if you need us."

Tears stung her eyelids. "A trio of white knights at my service. What a lucky damsel in distress I am."

"I'm not sure anyone's ever called me a white knight before," Lang said, ironic humor back in his eyes. "And even though I'm damn sure that's a new job description for Danny and Tucker, too, I can't think of two men I'd rather have with me when the chips are down. They'd both go to hell and back for you. All three of us would."

She couldn't speak past the large lump in the back of her throat. He bent his head and pressed a short sweet kiss on her mouth. She had just started to get into the spirit of it when he lifted his head and stepped away.

"I hope you decide to stay." With that, he walked out the door to her cabin and left her alone to wrestle with her demons.

It was a long night, but by morning Beth had made her decision. She wanted to stay at the Rafter N. She loved it, and she was too fond of the Nelson clan to run at the first sign of trouble. Even if her father found her and she had to confront him here, she was coming to think she could do it—as long as she stood on Rafter N soil with Lang beside her.

The ranch house was dark and silent when she made her way to the kitchen to start breakfast. She had just finished making coffee when Lang appeared in the doorway and made a beeline for the coffeepot. Her heart did a flip-flop at the sight of him, his eyes still bleary from sleep, his thick hair looking as if he'd combed it with his fingers—if he'd combed it at all. She waited until he'd poured himself a cup and downed two swallows before she made her declaration.

"I'm staying—for the moment, anyway. If that man comes back looking for me, all bets are off."

Lang leaned back against the counter and studied her over the rim of his coffee cup. "That's fair enough. I'm glad. In fact, I should get down on my knees and thank the Good Lord. I don't want to have to drink the sludge Tucker brews in this coffeepot when he's on breakfast duty." Lang's tone was light and teasing, and the smile he sent her warmed her right down to her toes.

His expression grew sober. He placed his cup carefully on the counter beside him and stared down at it for a long moment. "Last night, after I left your cabin, I thought a lot about the two of us."

He looked up at her, then, and his eyes were sad. "I'm sorry I pushed you too hard there in my office. I care about you. Somehow I got the dang fool notion in my head that there could be something special between us. But I'll do my best not to ask you about your past from now on, and I won't be looking for anything more than friendship. I know better than just about anyone that we're worlds apart, and you've got your reasons for not trusting me. I expect we'll muddle along well enough for the rest of the summer, and you can go on your way when hunting season's over. Does that sound all right to you?"

Beth stared back at him, feeling stunned and sick. What he was proposing should have sounded perfect. She wanted to be left alone. She wanted him to stop prying at her. So why did she feel like crying? *You've been trying to push him away for weeks now, and he finally got the message. You should be happy that Lang Nelson is going to leave you in peace.* But she wasn't happy. She wasn't happy at all.

"That sounds just fine," she managed to get out past the large lump in her throat.

"Friends we'll be, then," he said, and he didn't look much happier than she felt. He changed the subject and talked about when he'd take her to town to stock up on groceries again. He left the kitchen shortly after that, and she was relieved to see him go. As she set about fixing French toast and bacon for twenty, she wondered why she felt as if she had just lost her best friend.

During the next four weeks, Beth saw relatively little of Lang. Haying had started, and Lang pushed himself harder than ever. He spent long hours out in the hayfields, running machinery, fixing it when it broke down, and making certain the entire operation ran smoothly. When he wasn't haying, he was making sure his guests were enjoying themselves.

The rare times when Beth was alone with him, Lang was always scrupulously polite and distant. He never lingered anymore in the kitchen when he came to fetch his coffee first thing in the morning, and she never saw him on the few evenings when she decided to take late night walks along the river. She began to wonder if she had imagined the longing she had once seen in his eyes, or the desperate need she had sensed in him when he had kissed her.

Trying to deny the strange ache in her heart, she threw herself into her job. She tried new recipes, enjoyed the guests, and spent more time with the twins. Tony and Stacy were constantly in and out of her kitchen. In the afternoon, the three often went riding. During these rides Beth learned that Stacy's crush on Billy Ferguson was growing stronger as the summer progressed. She wondered if she should tell Lang, because she knew he didn't approve of the boy. At the same time, she felt it would be disloyal to Stacy to relay information to Lang which the girl had shared in confidence. Beth decided uneasily to hold her tongue for the moment and hope that Stacy's infatuation with Billy flamed out quickly the way most high school crushes did.

It was on one of these rides that Beth discovered why her employer had never married. She was sitting with the twins beside a pretty waterfall on the upper reaches of the ranch when Stacy brought up that very topic.

"It's going to be weird if Uncle Lang ever gets married," Stacy said, hugging her knees and staring at the stream. "His wife would be like our step-aunt or something."

"I think Uncle Lang should get married and have a family of his own. He can't look after us forever," Tony countered staunchly.

Stacy wrinkled her nose. "But babies cry so much, and their diapers smell."

"Maybe he'd pay us to babysit," Tony suggested.

Stacy brightened at that idea. The girls were always trying to find ways to make money.

"Why hasn't your uncle gotten married?" Beth casually asked the question which had been on her mind for weeks now. "It seems like most of his friends are married."

"It's because of Sonya," Stacy said dramatically. "She broke his heart, and he's never gotten over her."

"Who was Sonya?" Beth asked.

"She was a beautiful, incredibly rich young woman from back east. She came out to stay with her parents at a dude ranch where Uncle Lang was working. He fell head over heels in love with her, and they spent tons of time together that summer. Uncle Lang wanted to marry her. He even drove all the way to Denver to buy an engagement ring. The night she was supposed to go back home, though, Sonya told him she had a fiancé waiting for her. Uncle Lang was just her last fling before she got married. He was crushed."

Tony rolled her eyes at her twin. "Of course, you know how he felt. This did happen before we were born."

"It happened the year we were born," Stacy said with great dignity. "And I do know how he felt because I got Elsie to tell me all about it one day. She said Sonya was the one great love of his life. That's why he's never gotten married. How could he ever get over that horrible woman using him like that?"

How could he, indeed? Beth thought sadly. Here was the missing piece of the puzzle. Now she understood why Lang had been so cool toward her when she first came to the Rafter N. No wonder he didn't trust her. From the start he must have guessed she came from Sonya's world.

Beth's eyes burned with tears. She looked away from the twins so that they wouldn't notice. He must have loved Sonya very much—and she must have wounded him deeply for him to have remained single all these years.

"You should be happiest getting that gorgeous body of yours wrapped and manicured at expensive clubs and spas," he'd said. "You should spend your days pampering yourself and buying designer dresses to wear to society functions where you could outshine some of the most beautiful women in the world."

Those words came back to haunt Beth now. That must have been how Sonya had spent her days. It hurt so much to think he must have been comparing her to that callous, cruel, young woman all this time. Then she remembered what he had said that morning after she almost left the Rafter N.

"Somehow I got the dang fool notion in my head that there could be something special between us." Surely he wouldn't have thought that if he truly believed that she was like Sonya. She clung to that idea during the ride back to the ranch house. She needed to hold on to something to keep from becoming completely depressed. What the twins had told her today made it even more clear than ever that she and Lang had little chance of building something special and lasting.

THE COWBOY AND THE HEIRESS 157

* * *

One night in mid-August, just after Tony, Stacy, and Beth had finished cleaning up from dinner, Lang came striding into the kitchen, his expression jubilant. Still dusty and sweaty from the hayfields, he picked up each of his giggling nieces in turn and swung them about in an exuberant twirl.

"We're done. We just got the last bale stacked. We are through with haying for this season. Ladies, we are heading into town to celebrate. We're going to have dinner and dance up a storm at the Wagon Wheel."

The twins whooped and cheered, for going into town on a weeknight was a real treat for them.

Suddenly, Lang seemed to remember that he wasn't alone in the kitchen with his nieces. He was still smiling, but his eyes were more guarded as he turned to face her. "Beth, I hope you'll join us, too. Tucker, Hank, and Jim are all coming in. You've worked just as hard as anyone this hay season."

He honestly wants you to go, she realized as she studied him. That fact warmed a part of her heart which had felt frozen since that morning weeks ago when he had promised to leave her alone. In fact, this was the first direct overture he had made toward her since then, and she felt bad about having to turn him down. However, she didn't think it was wise to go into town unless she absolutely had to. As much as it sounded like fun to go celebrate with the rest, she didn't want to tempt fate.

"Thanks for the invitation, but I'm feeling pretty tired tonight. I think I'll stay in. You all go and have a fine time."

Lang's smiling expression faded, to be replaced

by the polite mask she was coming to hate. "I'm sorry to hear that."

"Oh, please say you'll come, Beth," Stacy protested. "Seth Fields and his band will probably be playing. We'll all have a great time."

"And we'll help you practice your cowboy dancing," Tony offered with a shy smile. Beth started to waver, for she hated to hurt the twins' feelings, but Lang came to her rescue.

"Girls, that's enough. If Beth's feeling tired, it's not fair for you two to badger her into coming." The girls took one look at their uncle's stern expression, and they fell silent.

"Maybe I'll come with you some other time," Beth offered weakly.

"Okay," the girls chorused, and then they dashed off to change their clothes.

"Thanks for backing me up," Beth said to Lang, who had gotten himself a Coke from the fridge and showed no inclination to leave the kitchen just yet.

"Don't mention it," he said with a hint of a smile. "I've been on the receiving end of that kind of coercion from those two far too many times. At the risk of pestering you like the girls just did, are you sure you don't want to come in with us? You've been working damn hard, too, and you deserve some fun as much as anyone around here."

"I would like to, very much," she admitted honestly, "but I don't think it's a good idea."

He was quiet for a long moment. She let go a small sigh of relief when he finally seemed to accept her decision. She didn't want her first real talk with Lang in weeks to turn into a knock-down-drag-out fight.

"Are you going to be okay if we take everyone in?" he asked. "The Doogans, the Oliphants, and the Roes have been wanting to take in some local night life."

"I'm sure I'll be fine."

He looked away from her, and the silence between them began to grow awkward. "I'd better go get washed up, then."

Right before he stepped through the door, she said softly, "Congratulations on finishing your haying right on schedule."

"Thanks." This time he sent her a smile with real warmth and some self-deprecating humor in it. "It's probably the first time that's happened in the history of this ranch. Maybe you brought us good luck."

"I'd like to think so," she said to herself after he had gone. She wanted to think she had given him something more than providing good food for his guests this summer. Lang had already given her so much—a refuge first and foremost, a chance to work at a job that had given her confidence, and a new sense of self-worth.

Within an hour everyone had loaded up and headed to town. Beth wandered restlessly about the ranch house. Going to her own cabin sounded boring and unappealing. She slipped into Lang's study and looked for something to read. She was surprised to see that their tastes in popular fiction were similar. She ended up selecting a mystery she had never read by one of her favorite authors.

She went back out to the living room, switched on the stereo, and within minutes became totally engrossed in her book. She rose just once to fetch herself a cup of coffee.

Hours later, she was startled when she heard the front door open. She glanced at her watch and realized it was after midnight.

She couldn't see the front hall from where she was sitting, but she could hear voices clearly. Within moments she realized with a sinking heart that the trip to town hadn't gone smoothly for Lang and the twins.

"You're not my father," Stacy shouted at Lang. "You don't have the right to tell me who I can see and who I can't."

"I know I'm not your father, but I am responsible for you and helping you make good choices." Beth could hear the effort Lang was making to hold on to his temper. "Billy Ferguson is nothing but trouble."

"He is not. I love him, and if you won't let me see him I'll hate you forever!"

"You can hate me if you have to!" Lang yelled back at Stacy, and Beth found herself holding her arms tightly. "But I'm not letting you go out with a boy who drinks like Billy does. You of all people should know why I don't want you spending time with someone like that."

"You don't understand. Billy's not like my father. You don't understand anything." Stacy went storming up the stairs, sobbing hysterically. Beth winced when she heard the door to Stacy's bedroom slam shut.

"I'll go check on her in a little bit, Uncle Lang," Tony said quietly and went upstairs.

Beth sat frozen in her chair for a long minute, wondering what on earth she should do. She hadn't meant to eavesdrop on a family argument, but everything had happened so quickly, that she hadn't had time to slip out the other door to the living room. She rose to her feet, planning to use just that escape route and head for her cabin when Lang strode into the living room.

"Who left all these lights and the stereo on?" he

bellowed up the stairs, obviously thinking the twins had been careless.

"I did," she replied.

That brought him up short. When he saw her standing beside the big easy chair in the corner, he ran a hand through his hair and had the grace to look embarrassed.

"Hell, I guess you just heard my row with Stacy."

"It was pretty hard not to," she pointed out evenly.

"I caught her drinking a beer with that worthless Billy Ferguson again."

"So I gathered."

"The two of them were sitting in the front seat of a pickup behind the Wagon Wheel. At least they could have had the sense not to start drinking right under my nose."

"Did you ask Stacy not to leave the Wagon Wheel?"

Her question threw him off stride for less than a heartbeat. "Well, even if I did I sure didn't mean for her to go out in the parking lot and do her best to kill off a six-pack with Ferguson."

"Of course you didn't," Beth said soothingly.

"What am I going to do with her?"

She decided to take the risk of actually answering that question. "Well, for starters you might try talking to her rather than yelling. I think she really cares about this boy."

"Oh. And how did you figure that out?" he asked dubiously.

"Stacy told me."

"And did she tell you she's been sneaking around, meeting him behind my back whenever she could?"

Beth took a deep breath. "I definitely got the impression that she's been seeing him every time she goes to town."

Lang's brows drew together in a fierce frown. "After what happened at the dance, you must have known I didn't want her being around him. Why didn't you tell me?"

"Because she told me that in confidence, I wanted her to trust me, and I wasn't sure it was my place to tell you."

"My niece has been hanging out with one of the wildest boys in Perrytown, and you didn't think it was your place to tell me? Thanks a lot. Next you're going to tell me that you encouraged her to see this boy."

"I did no such thing," Beth denied hotly. "All I did was take the time to listen to her. I know you're busy this summer, but you've got to find a way to spend more time with your nieces. You can't order teenage girls around the way you order your hands and your staff. You're going to turn two sweet lovely girls into unhappy rebels."

As soon as she said them, she wished she could take those words back. His face never changed, but she knew she had hurt him.

"Thank you for that fine vote of confidence," he said in a quiet bitter voice. "Next time I'll remember that I hired you to be our cook, not our family counselor." With that, he left the living room and went straight upstairs.

She stood completely still for a long moment, clasping her arms tight to her chest. She wouldn't cry, not here and not now. *Besides, it's not you he's angry at. He'll be sorry for what he said in the morning.*

Beth made quick work of turning off the lights and the stereo. She wanted nothing more than to leave the house and retreat to the quiet and privacy of her own cabin. So much for trying to help. The Nelsons weren't her own family, and she should have steered clear of their domestic battles. Still, she couldn't help wondering what Stacy had meant when she said Billy wasn't like her father.

Had Brian had a drinking problem, like Langdon Sr.? His alcoholic father had clearly left his mark on Lang, but had there been two people with drinking problems in this family? That might explain the fury she had heard in Lang's voice tonight. It really wasn't any of her business. Nothing that happened tonight in the Rafter N ranch house was.

As Beth walked to her cabin through the still starlit night, though, her heart ached for Lang, Stacy, and sweet Tony, who was caught between them.

FOURTEEN

Beth was just starting on breakfast in the kitchen the next morning when Lang walked into the room. For once, he didn't make straight for the coffeepot.

"I think Stacy's run away," he said, his eyes dark with worry. "The old Ford pickup is gone, along with her coat and backpack."

Beth blinked, trying to digest what Lang was saying. She knew both girls could drive—Lang had taught them so that they could help with ranch work.

"Are you sure she just didn't go to town to be with one of her friends?"

"I just called Billy's mom. He's gone, too."

"Surely they can't get far."

"With a truck full of gas, they can get far enough to land themselves in a world of trouble," he replied grimly. "I'm going into town to check around and make sure she's not staying with a friend. Then I'll go to see the sheriff."

When he started to leave, Beth stopped him. "You should eat something first."

"Thanks, but I don't feel much like eating."

"Then take these muffins and a thermos of coffee for later," Beth ordered. She quickly wrapped up four blueberry muffins and filled a thermos for him.

"About last night," he said gruffly while she worked, "I'm sorry I snapped at you. I know you were just trying to help."

"I'll accept your apology if you'll accept mine. I know you try to spend as much time with the girls as you can."

"Obviously, I need to find a way to spend more."

Her heart twisted for him. "I'm sure Stacy's going to be fine. I predict that she'll probably stay away just long enough to scare the heck out of you. Then she'll walk right back in here, safe and sound."

"I'd like to think you're right, but she was furious with me last night, and we Nelsons are plenty stubborn. The third time I ran away from home, I made it all the way to Salt Lake City."

"How old were you?" she asked, impressed despite herself.

"Fourteen," he said with a wry twist to his lips. "I finally hitched a ride back home because I ran out of money, I knew my mom would be worried sick, and I missed my horse."

Beth laughed because she thought he wanted her to, but a pang went through her when she realized he hadn't said anything about his father being worried about his runaway son. After arranging to call in every hour to see if anyone on the ranch had heard from Stacy, Lang left for town.

As much as Beth longed to be with Lang, she realized there was very little she could do in Perrytown to help him. In the meantime, on the Rafter N there were meals to prepare and guests to feed. As the day wore on, Beth grew increasingly grateful for mundane tasks which kept her mind and hands busy. She eventually decided the best way to help Lang was to keep an eye on poor Tony.

After helping Tucker search for Stacy in all of her

favorite spots around the ranch, Tony wandered restlessly around the house. At last Beth put her to work in the kitchen, baking bread and cookies.

Lang returned to the ranch well after dark. Elsie, Tucker, Tony, and Beth all met around the kitchen table while Lang wolfed down the supper Beth had saved for him. Between bites, he explained what the local law officials were doing to look for Stacy and Billy.

"They can't officially broadcast a missing persons report on them until they've been missing for twenty-four hours, but Charlie and Earl went to high school with me, and they've passed the word to all the troopers within three hundred miles of here to keep a lookout for Stacy and Billy and the truck."

"You're sure she didn't drop any hints about where she might go?" Lang asked Tony.

Tony looked so close to tears that Beth reached out a hand to comfort her. People had been asking Tony that question about her twin all day long.

"I don't know where she went, Uncle Lang. I promise I'd tell you if I did know."

The catch in Tony's voice had Lang kneeling beside her chair in a heartbeat.

"I know you would, sweetheart."

Tony sobbed aloud and threw her arms around Lang's neck. "I'm sorry I didn't tell you that she'd been hanging out with Billy. I never thought they'd go do something so crazy."

"Shh, now, I know you didn't," Lang told her gently. "Everything's going to be all right."

Beth looked down at the table, remembering when he had said much the same words to her. How she hoped they would prove true this time, for Stacy.

Suddenly, Tony sat up and brightened. "She's always talked about going back to Denver because we

THE COWBOY AND THE HEIRESS 167

had such a great time last fall when you took us there."

"Denver, eh? That's a good clue," Lang said lightly. "I'll tell Sheriff Tomlinson that the next time I talk to him."

Beth glanced across the table. Lang was hiding his dismay well. A big city like Denver had to be one of the last places he wanted Stacy and Billy to head for. Lang went to his office soon after that to make more phone calls. The rest of them stayed around the table talking until Elsie suggested that they play gin rummy. That kept them busy until midnight, when Lang came into the kitchen and insisted that it was Tony's bedtime. Weary from their long day of work, Tucker and Elsie slipped away to their cabins after Lang promised that he would wake them the moment there was any news of Stacy.

"You should try to get some rest, too," Lang told Beth when he returned to the kitchen after getting Tony settled for the night.

"I couldn't sleep," she said simply. "Would you mind if I stayed here for a while?"

"I'd appreciate the company. I know I won't be doing much sleeping tonight. Let's go to the living room. We might as well be comfortable while we wait for the phone to ring."

When they went into the other room, Beth purposely chose the big easy chair in the corner where she had read the night before. She hoped Lang might catch some sleep on the big leather couch before the evening was over.

"What did Stacy mean when she said Billy wasn't like her father?" She hadn't meant to ask the question, but somehow it popped out, anyway.

Lang rubbed his face with his hands. When he lowered them again, he looked inexpressibly weary.

"I suppose this is one more ugly family secret we can't hide from you any longer. I'm surprised that someone hasn't told you already. My brother Brian was an alcoholic, just like my father. They say it's a disease that often runs in families. I don't know if he learned to drink from Dad, or he started drinking hard to attract Dad's attention, or whether there's something inside us Nelson males that makes us susceptible to alcohol.

"Drinking's also a part of the cowboy myth, although folks in these parts don't like to talk about it much. Plenty of men around Perrytown have serious drinking problems. And Brian was very much a cowboy. He was charming and fun and handsome, a real chip off the old block, most folks said."

Beth winced at the anger in Lang's voice. She had been right to think much of his fury last night was really directed at Brian and his father.

"At any rate, Brian drank to get drunk from the time he was eighteen. In his mid-twenties he fell in love with Sue, the twins' mom. She wouldn't have anything to do with Brian until he stopped drinking. For her sake as well as his own, he dried himself out. He stayed sober for a couple of years, and we all thought he had it licked. He and Sue got married, and a year later the twins were born. When the twins turned five, he fell off the wagon. No matter what Sue or the rest of us said to him, Brian couldn't stay sober.

"He was drunk as a skunk the night he lost control of his pickup. He spun out right into the path of an oncoming semi, and he and Sue were killed instantly."

"Do the twins know all this?"

"They do, which is why I'm surprised Stacy has

been giving Billy Ferguson the time of day. Usually both of the girls frown on drinking."

"Teenage girls aren't exactly the most rational creatures in the world."

"Lord knows that's true." Lang flashed her a rueful smile. "The girls used to be so easy. I'm beginning to wish I could send them away to the moon until they're some safe sane age like twenty, and then bring them back home again."

"There are a million parents of teenage girls out there who probably feel the exact same way you do."

"But I'm not their real parent, you see," he said softly, "and sometimes that makes it ten times worse. I can't help wondering how Sue and Brian would have handled last night. Surely they would have done a better job."

"You have to enforce the rules and limits you feel comfortable with. Stacy and Tony will understand and respect you for that in the end. I just think you need to find a way to spend more time with the girls, so you all can keep talking to each other."

She winced inwardly when she thought of how little talking she'd ever been able to do with her own father. "They love you very much," she plunged on stubbornly, "and they'll share what's on their minds if you give them half a chance."

"I know," he acknowledged. "You've got a good point there. Summer is always the busiest season in the ranching business. I'll be able to spend more time with them now that haying's done."

The guilt and worry she saw in his face made her long to reach out to him. She wanted to find some way to distract him from the horrible gnawing worry which must be eating him alive right now. The first notion that popped into her mind was hardly appropriate. As much as she liked the idea of necking with Lang on that comfortable big couch, he'd most likely turn her down cold. She still hadn't forgotten the way he had rejected her by the river that night.

All in all, suggesting a card game seemed like a much safer idea. "All right," she said cheerfully. "Elsie happened to mention the fact that you fancy yourself quite a cribbage player. Of course, I have a hard time believing anyone raised west of the Mississippi could possibly play the game properly."

"Is that so? We Nelsons never refuse a cribbage challenge." He rose to his feet and went to fetch a cribbage board and some cards. She moved to the couch so that they could place the board before them on the coffee table.

"Does the little lady from the East dare to play muggins?" he asked in his best drawl, referring to the most cutthroat way to play the game.

"Of course." She met his disdainful grin with one of her own.

They cut the deck to see who would have the first crib. Beth won, which meant she dealt first. Soon, they were deeply involved in a serious card game. Lang played quickly and decisively. Beth soon realized they were evenly matched in terms of their skill, which meant luck was going to be the deciding factor. Luck was with her during the first two games, much to his frustration. In the second round, no matter how well he played, Lang couldn't make up for a series of poor hands and cribs, which allowed Beth to "skunk" him, the ultimate indignity in cribbage.

"I think you're dealing off the bottom of the deck," he said with disgust when she trounced him a second time.

"I never cheat," she informed him loftily. "I don't have to." As she watched him shuffle the cards, a

THE COWBOY AND THE HEIRESS 171

thought occurred to her. "Do you know how to deal off the bottom?" she asked with great interest.

"Nope. I never played enough poker to make it worth my while to learn. Tucker can do it, though. That old devil's like a magician with cards."

"You love him very much, don't you?"

"He's my real father, as far as I'm concerned. My own father was never really there when it counted."

The closed look on his face discouraged her from asking any more questions about his father. She wondered if so much of Lang's self-control and so much of his need to order the world around him came from living with someone who was frequently out of control.

Halfway through their third game, she glanced up from the cards. Lang was staring at her lips. Slowly, he lifted his gaze to meet hers, and the stark longing in his eyes made her shiver. Deliberately, he placed his cards on the table.

"It's your turn to peg," she protested, for she didn't trust him, or herself. All of a sudden, she realized how quiet and intimate the living room seemed. Everyone else in the old ranch house was fast asleep.

"I know it is, but right now my mind's not on the cards."

He reached out a hand and gently brushed her lips with his thumb. Beth closed her eyes. How could her entire body come burningly alive at one simple touch from this man?

"Lord, woman, how I've wanted you," he breathed the words like a prayer. "The last month has been the longest of my life."

"I . . . I thought you weren't interested in me in that way anymore. Not since that night beside the river. You've hardly spoken to me in four weeks."

"I'd have to be dead not to want you," he said with a pained laugh. "And I haven't talked with you much because I can't stay in the same room with you for more than a minute or two before my body goes haywire on me. There's only so much of that a man can take."

He shifted closer to her and reached out a hand. She closed her eyes as he caressed her cheek. She could match his fire, but his tenderness undid her completely.

He leaned forward and covered her lips with his own. Although his kiss was gentle, she sensed at once how much he was fighting himself to keep it that way. He did want her. A very female side of her gloried in that realization. For the past month she had wondered how and why he had found her wanting.

Of their own volition, her arms went around his neck. She shifted closer until their legs touched. She was aware of his thigh, hard and warm against her own as he deepened the kiss. Within moments, he had kindled the fire in her blood once again. No man had ever made her want like this. With a wistful pang, she wondered if another man ever would.

Greedy to make the most of this stolen moment, she opened her eyes and tugged his shirt loose from his jeans and slipped her hands under it. She relished the feel of his upper chest, hard and supple beneath her fingers. Kissing her fiercely now, he eased her back against the pillows. In the quiet room, she could hear the rustle of their clothing, the creak of the leather sofa, the quick intake of their breaths, and the pounding of her own heart.

She knew this was hardly the place or the time for them to make love, with one of his nieces asleep upstairs and the other one lost out in the night.

Surely, though, it would do no harm to anyone if she savored being in his arms just a few minutes longer. She had felt so lonely this past month, and now Lang made her feel complete again.

Kissing the sensitive skin at the base of her neck, he made quick work of the buttons on her blouse. He dipped his head and kissed the swell of her breasts while his fingers cleverly teased and touched her through the thin fabric of her bra. Her breath caught when he kissed and sucked at her breast, the silky material turning sensuously cool and damp against her skin.

In turn, she allowed herself to slip her fingers through his hair, relishing the soft silky feel of it and the warmth of his strong body lying next to hers. He smelled even better than she remembered, the wonderful, musky male odor of him mixed with the scent of the fresh outdoors.

Beth stilled, hardly daring to breathe as his hand slipped lower, exploring the contours of her belly with maddening thoroughness. His touch made wonderful shivers trace all over her, but it also made her pulse with an almost painful need even lower in her body. When she was certain she couldn't bear the anticipation any longer, he eased his hand beneath the band of her jeans. Before he even touched her, she felt a rush of warmth between her legs. He caressed her center and sent a shaft of pure intense pleasure rioting through her body. She waited, hoping he would touch her again.

Then the phone rang. They hesitated for a long moment, fighting off the passionate daze engulfing them. Muttering an oath under his breath, Lang sprang for the phone. As she hastily buttoned up her blouse, Beth prayed it was Stacy, and that she was all right.

"Stacy, honey, are you all right?" she heard him ask.

There was a long silence while he listened to Stacy talk.

"That's all right, honey. We'll work this out after you're home again." He paused again to listen, and then he said firmly, "You stay right where you are. I'll be there to pick you up in six hours. I love you, sweetheart."

He hung up the phone and released a deep breath. "They're a little shook up, but they're all right. The truck broke down in a rough area of Denver, and some gang kids stole their money. Stacy had the sense to drag Billy to the closest police station, and that's where they are now. They're just fine."

When she heard the catch in his voice, she was across the room in a flash. She wrapped her arms around him. He buried his face in her neck and hugged her, hard.

After a long moment, he sighed and leaned back so that he could see her face. "I know this is a lot to ask, but how would you like to drive to Denver?"

"I'd love to," she replied promptly.

"I figure if you're along you can spell me at the wheel if I need a break. More important, you'll keep me from shouting at Stacy and throttling Billy. We're probably just going to turn around and come right back, which means you'll have a good twelve hours in a truck ahead of you," he pointed out apologetically.

"I'll do anything to escape slaving over a hot stove for a day, boss."

"I'll have to remember that," he said with a glimmer of his usual dry humor. "Thanks for saying yes," he added, and pressed a short, firm kiss on her lips before he stepped back from her. "I've got a couple of phone calls to make. Could you let Tucker and

THE COWBOY AND THE HEIRESS

Elsie know where we're headed? We'll leave here in a half-hour or so."

She was relieved and amused to see Lang was back to giving orders. Heart singing because Stacy was all right and Lang wanted her company, she went to tell Elsie and Tucker the good news.

It was three o'clock in the morning when they left the ranch house. Despite the lateness of the hour, Beth felt wide awake as Lang swung the truck onto the highway and headed toward Denver. The black mountain skies overhead were full of stars. It seemed as if they were the only two people awake in the world as the truck rolled along the dark, empty highway.

For a time she let Lang drive in silence while she watched his profile in the dim light thrown off from the dashboard controls. "Tell me about your father," she said at last.

Lang shot her a sardonic look. "Is this the price of your company tonight?"

"I'd hardly call it that," she countered, refusing to back down. "I just want to understand you and your family better."

"There's not much to understand," he said shortly. "My father was a chronic alcoholic. He was so charming and sincere that he had us all believing time and time again he might be able to sober up, but he could never break the hold booze had on him."

"You said he was never there when it counted," she prompted him gently.

"You really are after your pound of flesh tonight."

"No," she said slowly, "that's not it at all. I'm trying to understand why you were so angry at Stacy for being with Billy. I think you may still be furious at your father and at Brian for wasting their lives. You'll be able to handle the twins better if you can come to terms with that."

She saw the almost physical effort he made to hold back another biting retort. He was quiet for a long moment, and then he said with a sigh, "If I had loved them less, I could have accepted their drinking. But they were the bright stars in our family. I'm the plodding one. Dad was one of those outgoing charismatic people who can light up a room. He probably inherited the gift of gab from the Irish side of our family. He could out-yarn Tucker, and make the most impossible dreams seem possible. I was ten when I found out the hard way that he couldn't make those dreams real, or keep his promises. By the time I was fourteen I realized he lived in a fantasy world that was destroying the real world where the rest of our family lived."

"What happened when you were ten?"

Lang stared straight ahead at the road, his expression bleak. "He promised to drive me to Denver. The two of us were going to go out to a fine steak dinner, stay at the Brown Palace Hotel, and see the finals of the National Western Stock Show, where just about every rodeo star I idolized at that time was going to be competing. I'd been counting down the days to our big trip for weeks. The night before we were supposed to leave, my father went to Grand Junction with some friends and tied one on. He never came home that night. By the time my mother and I found him sleeping it off in some fleabag hotel there, it was too late for her to drive me to Denver in time to see the rodeo."

He was quiet for a bit. "That wasn't the first time Dad disappointed me, but it was the first time I realized that I never was going to be able to count on him, not the way other kids could count on their parents. His drinking got steadily worse during my teenage years, and we started to fight all of the time.

"Dad was never a mean or abusive drunk, but the drinking seriously affected his reflexes and his judgment. Ranching can be dangerous work, and Mom and I both worried constantly that he was going to get seriously hurt. After he died I tried going away to college, but I had to drop out after my third year. Mom wanted me to keep on with my studies, but I knew it was too much for her to run the ranch, and try to keep Brian in line."

"So you had to give up your own dreams."

He shrugged his shoulders philosophically. "That part of it wasn't so bad. The Rafter N always came first with me. I had wanted a chance to take a good look at the rest of the world before I settled down to ranching. Rodeo riding let me do that pretty well. I had plenty of opportunity to ramble around the West on weekends."

"In the end, Dad's drinking was hardest on Mom. I've always thought the stress of living with him during those final days when his liver failed was part of the reason why she developed breast cancer. Dad's drinking was also hard on Brian. Being the oldest, I at least had some good memories of Dad before the drinking ruined him. Poor Brian just knew him as a drunken sot—red-rimmed eyes, bloated belly, and all. The shame of it was, Brian needed a strong father more than I did."

Lang sighed. "Even though I understand the reasons why Brian became an alcoholic, I don't know if I can ever forgive him for killing himself and Sue, and leaving Stacy and Tony without parents. Don't get me wrong—I don't mind raising my nieces. The girls have already given me so much more than I've ever given them. I just wish they had a real mother and father to bring them up right."

"They have a wonderful man serving as their surrogate father," Beth defended him stoutly. "You're going to bring them up just fine."

His lips twisted in a mirthless smile. "If I'm doing such a great job, why are we driving to Denver right now to retrieve two teenage runaways?"

"Because Stacy is stubborn and has a temper, and you're stubborn and have a temper. From now on the two of you are going to do a better job of listening to each other."

"I sure as hell hope so."

He looked so worried and uncertain that she decided it was time to distract him again. "Tell me a happy memory about your father."

"All right." He sent her a real smile this time. "But only if you tell me one about yours. It's time I found out more about my mysterious cook. Fair's fair."

"That's a deal," she said, scrambling to think of a memory she could share with him without revealing too much about herself.

Lang launched into his story, "Well, when I was five years old, Dad won the calf roping event at the National Western. Now that's a real, big official rodeo, but when he heard he'd won he waved me down out of the stands and rode around the ring once with me sitting in front of him on the saddle. You don't usually take a victory lap in rodeo, but he did that night just so that I could share his big win with him. I'll never forget that moment, a whole stadium full of folks clapping and looking at the two of us. That was my Dad at his best.

"And now," he said with a glint in his eye, "I do believe it's your turn. Start talking, lady."

FIFTEEN

Beth clasped her hands tightly in her lap. She was ready with a story that would reveal something to Lang about her and her father, but not too much.

"When I was in sixth grade, I had a project due for school. We were each supposed to come up with an idea for our own business and make plans for implementing and marketing it. That topic was right up Dad's alley. We must have spent hours together, making tables and plotting graphs. He never took the project over. He was just there to offer ideas and help me when I got in over my head. In the end, we wowed my social studies teacher, and she had me make a presentation about my business in front of the whole school.

"That was back in the days when my father was involved in my life in a good way." Beth looked down at her hands. "Somewhere along the line, that involvement turned into a determination to control me—in part because he lost what little faith he had in my own abilities and judgment.

"To be absolutely fair, I'm not sure that I've ever shown him that I can be capable of taking care of myself. Most of my life I've drifted from job to job, never really settling into anything." *Mostly because the jobs you took were ones Dad wanted you to, not ones you wanted. Striving for corporate success never was and never will be something you enjoy.*

"I bet you never sank your teeth into something you cared about." Lang's words echoed her own thoughts with eerie precision. "You've taken hold and done a fine job in my kitchen this summer."

"And I've held this job for several weeks now." Beth shook her head and smiled. "That's not exactly a huge demonstration of my commitment or staying power." She was warmed by his defense, just the same.

"Does your father know where you are now?"

"That one crosses the line, boss."

Lang didn't look the least taken aback by her sharpness. "That means he doesn't. The man's probably worried sick about you, if the way I've been worrying about Stacy for the last eighteen hours is anything to go by."

"He'll live," Beth replied flatly. "Believe me, he'll live." The great Peter Harrison was too busy managing his billions to be too upset by the minor irritation of one missing daughter—especially since she had made it very clear that she was leaving her old life of her own accord. He had probably moved heaven and earth to find her—but mostly because he didn't think she could take care of herself.

Lang was quiet after that, either digesting what she had said or thinking about Stacy. As Beth stared out at the dark shadowy landscape slipping past, a nagging voice in the back of her mind kept intruding on her thoughts. *Lang's right. You should find some way to let Dad know you're safe. Somewhere between his office and the board room he'll worry about you in his own way.*

She made up her mind on the spot. She'd send a postcard from Denver to her cousin Lisa, the only relative she could consider trusting with her secret. Lisa had been urging her for years to strike out on her own and make a real life for herself. Beth smiled when she thought of her flamboyant cousin, who had thumbed her nose at generations of their conservative family to become a movie star. Denver was far enough away from Perrytown that even if her father persuaded Lisa to tell him where the card was postmarked, she didn't think it could do too much harm.

Beth caught herself yawning widely. Two minutes later, she yawned again.

"Won't hurt to catch a few winks," Lang suggested. "I'm wide awake right now."

"All right, I'll try to sleep, but only if you promise to wake me up if you want me to take over driving for a while."

"That's a deal."

It was plenty warm inside the cab, so she took her jacket off and folded it to make a pillow. She placed the jacket on the doorframe and leaned her head against it. The jacket kept slipping, much to her irritation.

"My shoulder's probably softer than that door," he said after she adjusted the jacket for a third time.

With all the hard physical work he did, she almost doubted that claim, but she didn't want to hurt his feelings by turning down his invitation. Surely things couldn't get too out of control between them while he was driving down a highway. Feeling like a high school girl with a serious crush on her date, she scooted across the bench seat and lay her head on his shoulder. The worn denim of his jacket was soft under her cheek. She thought she would be too aware of him to be able to sleep, but within minutes she dozed off.

When she woke up, they were in Denver.

"So much for helping you with the driving," she said with disgust as she stretched and looked around her curiously. She had only been to Denver once before, but she had never forgotten its spectacular setting at the base of the Rocky Mountains.

"I enjoyed watching you sleep. How you can look so pretty with your mouth hanging open is beyond me. You even snore, but you do it in a very ladylike dignified fashion," he said, the beautiful golden glints in his eyes quite evident as he teased her.

"I do not snore in a very ladylike dignified fashion," she countered indignantly.

"Would you rather I said you snored like a lumberjack?"

"I'd rather you told the truth and admitted that I don't snore at all."

"Cross my heart, hope to die, you do snore, Beth Richards," he pledged with mock seriousness. His expression sobered suddenly. "There's the station."

They were both quiet as he parked the truck. After he switched off the engine, he leaned forward and rested his forehead on the steering wheel. "Christ, I don't want to blow this."

She placed a hand on his shoulder. "You won't," she said confidently.

After raising his head from the wheel, he put his hand on top of hers and squeezed it. "I'm glad you're here." The smile in his eyes warmed her through and through.

"Well, let's go get them," he said with a sigh of resignation.

Lang had agreed to drive Billy back to Perrytown as well, for Alice Ferguson had been afraid that her old car might break down on such a long drive.

Lang didn't blow it. When he saw Stacy, he opened

THE COWBOY AND THE HEIRESS 183

his arms and she flew to him, tears streaming down her cheeks. As Lang gathered his niece close, Beth's eyes filled with tears of her own.

In that moment, she realized the painful truth. Despite her best efforts to harden her heart against him, she had fallen head over heals for this big, complex, caring man. Yet how could she be a part of his life when she still wasn't sure who she was? She had come so far to find out whether she could stand on her own two feet and build an independent life for herself. How could she even dream of loving Lang when she was sure he wouldn't risk losing his heart to another young woman as rich as Sonya?

Beth stared dully at her feet, wishing the earth would open up and swallow her. *What a stupid, idiotic thing to do. You've just begun to enjoy your freedom, and now your foolish heart is tearing itself apart over a man you can't have.*

Suddenly, Stacy was before her. "Uncle Lang said I should thank you for coming all the way to Denver to help pick me up. I am glad you came," she added in a diffident tone, very unlike her usual bouncy self.

When she saw more tears welling up in Stacy's eyes, Beth reached out and hugged her. "I'm just glad you're all right. You gave us all a scare, your uncle most of all."

"I know. It was a pretty dumb thing to do. But he can't tell me who to like and who not to like."

Beth let go of Stacy and held up her hands. "I'm not getting involved in this. I just want you to realize how much he loves you, and that he's doing his best to keep you safe."

Lang had to fill out some forms at the police station, and then they all went to the garage where the truck had been towed. While Lang arranged to have the truck fixed, Beth went off to buy a postcard to mail to her cousin. Next, Lang took them to a family restaurant where they shared an awkward uncomfortable lunch.

Stacy did much of the talking on the way home, which was fine with Beth. She needed time to come to terms with the idea she had fallen in love with Lang Nelson.

Poor Billy sat beside her, pale and withdrawn. Lang hadn't tried to throttle him, but he had sent several scorching glances the young man's way.

When they reached Billy's modest, one-story home in Perrytown, it was nine o'clock at night. Beth had to give the boy credit for standing his ground. Before he got out of the truck, the young man turned to face Lang and cleared his throat.

"Mr. Nelson, I'm sorry we took your truck. I know we must have made you really worry, but we didn't know what else to do. I really like Stacy, and I want to keep seeing her."

"Despite what you think, Billy, I don't have anything against you," Lang replied, his expression somber. "If you clean up your act, you're welcome to date my niece. I just don't want her spending time with a fifteen-year-old who drinks. You stop drinking, you can see Stacy. It's that simple."

"But everybody drinks."

"Not the boys who want to date my nieces. You'd better think on that."

Billy sent Stacy a beseeching look, but she was staring down at her hands. Beth climbed down out of the cab to let Billy out. He strode to the door, where his mother was waiting. Lang raised his hand to Alice Ferguson. The two of them had talked frequently during the past eighteen hours. Beth had received the strong impression that Lang actually

THE COWBOY AND THE HEIRESS

liked Alice, but he was exasperated that she didn't keep her wild son on a shorter leash.

Beth was tired to the marrow of her bones by the time they drove through the gate to the ranch. Tony, Elsie, and Tucker came out onto the porch when the truck pulled up. As soon as Stacy jumped down, Tony was there hugging her twin, and the others weren't far behind her. As Beth watched them all crowding around Stacy, a lump rose in the back of her throat. *Even though you care about them, and they care about you, you're not really a part of this family.*

Wondering if she ever would find a place where she belonged, Beth turned away to go to her cabin.

"Aren't you going to come in with us for a bit?" Lang's question stopped her in her tracks. She looked over and saw he was studying her across the hood of the truck.

"Elsie said she made one of her famous, prize-winning German chocolate cakes. Why don't you have a piece with us?"

"Thanks, but I'm still feeling full from that dinner we had back in Rifle. I think I'll just turn in."

"Are you sure you're all right?"

"I'm fine," she lied, swallowing down the irrational tears which were welling up from out of nowhere. "I'm just feeling a little tired."

"Then I'm officially giving you the morning off. Don't you dare report to work until eleven o'clock."

"That's hardly necessary. I just had a day off."

"I don't think riding twelve hours in a truck constitutes anyone's idea of a great way to spend a day off."

He had such a stubborn expression on his face, that she knew she didn't have the energy it would take to convince him that she could and should work. Being able to sleep in tomorrow did sound wonderful, but she wondered with a little pang if anyone in his family would make sure that Lang caught up on his sleep, as well. He did such a good job of looking after everyone else, but there was no one to look after him.

Which wasn't really any of her business, either, she reminded herself sternly. Still, she found herself saying, "I hope you take the morning off, too. Elsie can handle breakfast, and Tucker can handle the guests."

"I think I may do exactly that," he surprised her by saying. "Someone pointed out to me recently that I ought to find more time for Tony and Stacy. I thought I might spend the morning with them sorting out what just happened and generally getting caught up with my nieces."

He walked around the hood of the truck and placed his hands on her shoulders. Beth glanced toward the door to the ranch house, but everyone had already gone inside. Before she could voice a protest, Lang took her into his arms. He tucked one lock of her hair back behind her ear and kissed her tenderly.

It was so sweet to be held like this. It was so sweet to be kissed as if she were special and precious to him. Yet, her awareness of her true feelings toward Lang was too raw and new. She was afraid she might blurt out the truth to him if he held her much longer. At last he released her shoulders and stepped back.

"That's to say thank you for staying up with me last night," he said with one of his slow devastating smiles, "and for driving all the way to Denver and back with me."

"Hmm, maybe we should try driving to Alaska sometime," she managed. Before she threw herself back into his arms, she forced herself to turn away and head for her cabin.

"You say the word and I'll start packing my truck the day after hunting season ends," he called after her.

She raised a hand to acknowledge his joking comment, but kept walking toward her cabin. She was afraid that if she looked at him again, she'd beg him to run away with her to Alaska and beyond. Disgusted, she tried to give herself a stern talking-to. *You know he's not for you. He knows he's not for you. If you want to stay on at the Rafter N for the rest of the season, you're going to have to avoid being alone with him.* Yet, as painful as it was going to be to see Lang every day, she wasn't sure she could bear to cut short her time with him.

She smiled sadly when she realized that at least one good thing had come out of all this. Lang was going to spend his morning with the girls, instead of doing ranch work or seeing to his guests. He had listened to her. That, in a nutshell, was one of the greatest differences between Lang and her father.

On the surface they seemed frighteningly similar, for they were both strong forceful men used to commanding and taking charge. Both could be stubborn as mules, particularly when they were convinced that they were right. However, Lang could listen when the welfare of his family was at stake, something her father had forgotten how to do after his wife died.

How she missed her mother tonight. She wished she could talk with her about her feelings for Lang. Did being in love have to hurt so much? Trudging up the steps to her cabin, Beth had never felt more alone in her life.

SIXTEEN

Beth finished kneading her bread dough and set it aside in a bowl to rise. She had time these days to bake bread and make fancy pies and try out new recipes, for September was proving to be a much quieter time on the Rafter N than August had been. They had fewer guests, and the twins were off at school during the day.

Beth sorely missed Tony and Stacy during the weekdays. She hadn't realized just how much she had liked their popping in and out of her kitchen. Stacy had settled down considerably since she had run away. Soon after their return, Billy had decided that seeing Stacy meant more to him than drinking beer. The two of them now went out regularly with their friends on weekends. Beth's relationship with Elsie had deepened into real friendship. She enjoyed the older woman's company, and she was grateful for the fact that Elsie continued not to ask her too much about her past or background.

Her relationship with Lang had changed after that trip to Denver. Although he still worked hard getting the ranch ready for winter, he seemed to seek her out more. He started lingering in the kitchen again, when he came to fetch his coffee in the morning, talking with her and even helping her to prepare breakfast. Conscious that her time at the Rafter N was fast coming to an end, Beth was determined to savor the bittersweet time she had left with him.

One warm afternoon late in the month Lang walked into the kitchen when she was frosting a cake. He went to the sink and drank a glass of water. Beth watched him surreptitiously. His sandy hair was slightly damp from sweat, and he had a streak of dirt across one cheek which gave him a particularly rakish look. As he tilted his head back and drained the second glass with masculine gusto, she was struck all over again by what a vital and beautiful male animal he was. When she found herself staring at a bead of water clinging to his lower lip, she forced herself to look away and concentrate on the cake. He sauntered over to the cookie jar and helped himself to three homemade oatmeal cookies. As he ate them, he watched her work.

Just when she was starting to feel self-conscious he said, "You sure make that look easy. That time I tried to make a birthday cake for the twins, the frosting got all over me and the kitchen. Hardly any of it stuck to the damn cake."

"Well, you make herding cows and riding bucking broncos look easy, so I guess we're even," she said, trying to hide a smile.

Lang leaned back against the counter, relishing this chance to talk with Beth. Her neat, precise movements as she smoothed the icing onto the cake fascinated him no end. He loved looking at her hands. Her fingers were long, slim, and elegant. It was far too easy to imagine the way he wanted her to stroke and explore him with those hands. It was too easy to remember the tantalizingly brief times she had touched him and set his senses on fire.

"I still think riding a bronc is easier than making

a birthday cake from scratch," he said, forcing himself to concentrate on their conversation. "Before you know it, I'm going to have a chance to see you herd cows. We should be leaving next Tuesday for the high country."

Soon they all were going on a real cattle drive. The Rafter N leased land up in the National Forest each summer. Most of his cows spent the summer grazing on that land, and in the fall he drove them back down to the Rafter N's home pastures to spend the winter. This year Beth was going along to cook. Tucker, Hank, Elsie, Tony, and Stacy were all going, too, along with four guests who wanted to participate in a cattle drive.

"I'm looking forward to this trip," she admitted.

"We all usually enjoy it, if the weather holds. About the third day or so, though, I start appreciating the fact that I don't have to drive my cows over a thousand miles like the cowboys coming up the trails from Texas used to do."

"I'm glad we don't have to worry about rustlers or Indians, and I'm glad I can look forward to a hot shower at the end of the drive."

He smiled at her sally, and then decided to take the plunge. "I've been thinking," he announced, trying to keep his tone deliberately casual. "Before we head off on this adventure, how would you like to go out to dinner with me this weekend? You deserve to sit down to a meal you didn't cook for a change."

He held up a hand to forestall the refusal he could tell was coming. "Before you say 'no' let me tell you what I have in mind. We could drive over to Steamboat Springs and eat in some nice quiet restaurant. That's a big resort town, and few folks know me over there. If anyone recognized you from those photos that detective was showing around, they still wouldn't know where we came from. Surely there's no big risk in that."

"I'm sorry," she said, her lovely, gray-blue eyes wide and troubled. "I can tell you spent some time planning this, but I don't think it's a good idea."

He felt his smile fade. "All right then, we can take the twins along if you don't want to be alone with me."

"That's not it at all," she said and looked down at the cake. "I just think it's much smarter for me to stay at the Rafter N."

He was silent for a long moment while he fought down his disappointment. *Nelson, when are you going to learn your lesson? This woman wants nothing to do with you, except maybe a quick roll in the hay.* Yet she meant too much now for him to be able to settle for that.

"Beth Richards, or whoever you are," he said in a cool tone, "you are a woman of many talents, but you are a lousy liar. Either you're scared to go out with me, or you just plain don't want to. In either case, I read your message loud and clear."

He stalked from the kitchen and headed for the horse barn, one of his favorite retreats when he was troubled. Feeling the way he did about Beth, it was going to be a long time until the end of hunting season. As much as it tore him up to be around her every day, he still couldn't wish for her time at the Rafter N to end soon. He walked into the tack room to fetch his rig. He felt like riding, and he needed to check a section of fence Tucker was worried about along the upper hayfield.

As he strode out to the horse corral to catch up a mount, he wondered why he felt so blue just because Beth had refused to go out on a real date with him. He couldn't possibly have been fool enough to lose his heart to another eastern gal. He could be as stupid as the next man, but surely he hadn't been foolish enough to make the same mistake twice.

Lang hardly spoke to Beth over the weekend. Clearly she had hurt his pride—and possibly his feelings, as well. Saturday night, as soon as she finished cleaning up the kitchen after dinner, she escaped to her cabin. There she spent a restless frustrating evening trying not to think about what it would have been like to go out with Lang.

Instead, she tried to concentrate on where and what she should do when hunting season came to a close and she left the Rafter N. Somehow all the adventures she'd planned to have when she left her father's home no longer sounded so appealing. She still wanted to find work on a ranch, but she couldn't imagine any job suiting her better than the one she had now. Maybe she should try something completely different. She could start her own small catering company, or work as a cook in a restaurant. Moving to a new town, though, didn't sound exciting. It sounded hard and lonely.

How long was it going to take her to get over Lang? She certainly didn't intend to spend the rest of her life yearning for him, but she was afraid she was going to endure a great deal of pain before she managed to purge the need for a certain kindhearted domineering rancher from her system. All in all, it was a long time before she fell asleep that night.

Friday morning dawned cool and clear. As she hauled her gear down to the horse barn, Beth decided she was very grateful that the twins were coming along on the drive. She hoped they would help provide a safe cheerful buffer between her and Lang.

After breakfast they all gathered by the horse barn, where Lang and Tucker had already loaded the horses into trailers. Tony and Stacy were in tearing spirits. They loved the fall cattle drive, for it gave them a chance to camp out three nights in a row with their uncle and miss a day of school. The twins' enthusiasm was contagious. By the time they all piled into a caravan of pickups, Beth saw that everyone was smiling with anticipation.

They drove up to an old logging road that took them into the heart of the allotment which Lang leased from the Forest Service. There they unloaded the horses, and Hank and Elsie started to set up camp.

Beth wanted to stay and help, but the older woman wouldn't hear of it. "I've been on more of these things than I can count," she said with a twinkle in her eye. "You go on and help gather up those cows. There'll be plenty of chances for me to ride later."

Once they were organized and ready, Lang divided everyone up and assigned them areas to search for cows. He sent Beth off with Tony and Tucker to scour the northwest portion of the leased land. As they started off her heart beat a little faster, and her mouth was dry. She hoped she wouldn't disgrace herself by falling off her horse before the day was over.

It took them almost two hours of steady riding just to reach the farthest section of the land they were to search. They dismounted long enough to eat a quick lunch, and then they started combing the aspen groves and spruce forest for cows. After spending months in the high country, the cattle were like wild creatures and spooked easily.

Beth soon discovered that herding cattle through such rough country was a real challenge to her horsemanship, but it was also great fun. She quickly developed tremendous respect for her mount, Rusty. The sturdy sorrel gelding was surefooted and quick, and he seemed to sense when the cows they were chasing were about to dart back into the cover of the trees.

She was sore, tired, and exhilarated by the time they pushed their little herd of fifty head into the big meadow below camp. There a hundred other cows and their calves already grazed, tired and hungry from the day's drive.

She found Lang fixing a loose shoe on a pinto mare by the makeshift horse corral. "How did it go today?" she asked Lang as she dismounted.

"Well, the Coopers and the Nortons are still alive and in one piece," he said as he glanced up from driving nails into the mare's hoof, "and they all seemed to have had a great time today."

With a pang of guilt she suddenly realized that what had been a wonderful exciting day for her was probably a day full of worry for Lang. Her guilt eased a little when he let go of the horse's hoof, straightened up, and smiled at her. "It's days like these I'm mighty glad that I'm a rancher."

"I can see why. I had so much fun chasing cows today." She smiled back at him. "I'm very grateful to Elsie for taking over the camp kitchen so that I could play cowgirl."

He stared at her, and something in his expression changed. "Christ, you're so damn beautiful," he said as if the words were torn from him. He reached up a hand to touch her cheek. Then he must have thought better of it, for he let his hand fall.

She stared back at him helplessly, suddenly aware of the pull between them. The desire she had tried to keep ruthlessly buried for weeks now flamed to life once again. How could he do this to her with just a few words and a single burning look? She wanted him to touch her. She wanted him to kiss her in that devastating way he had. Before she embarrassed herself by begging him to do exactly that, he turned back to the pinto mare.

"I'm glad you enjoyed today," he said in a semblance of his normal voice. He leaned over and picked up the hoof he'd been working on. "You'll probably be sore tomorrow."

"I'm sore now," she managed to get out. "I'd better go wash up and help Elsie with dinner," she said hastily, and with that she fled.

The next morning, Lang blessed his lucky stars that the drive continued to go smoothly. By noon they had finished gathering up the four hundred head he had grazing on his allotment. After lunch they started the cows back down the logging road toward the Rafter N.

Around three o'clock, the skies started to darken. Tucker rode up beside him. "We're in for a boomer of a thunderstorm."

"I know," Lang said gloomily. "We'll probably see some hail, too." It had been too much to hope their good luck would last. He made up his mind quickly. "Tucker, you ride on to the new camp and take the twins, Beth, and the guests with you." He glanced around. That left him just Hank to help keep control of four hundred head, which could get tricky if the weather turned wild.

"Let me help, too," Beth suggested steadily. She had ridden up beside them while he and Tucker were talking. "You know you're going to be short-handed."

"Driving cattle in the pouring rain is a miserable business," he warned her.

"I'm not going to feel like a real cowgirl until I have a chance to try out my slicker," she said with a game smile. "Please. It would give me a chance finally to be of some real use on this drive."

While Beth gazed at him so hopefully, he found it impossible to say no. He knew how important it was for her to feel she was making a difference. "All right, you can stick with us," he said, hoping like hell that he wasn't going to regret that decision.

Within an hour, he was very glad he'd sent his paying guests ahead to their warm dry tents. The sky overhead had turned ominously dark. That meant they were going to be hit by hail, which could be vicious in the high country. The far-off growl of thunder from lightning striking the peaks high above them was almost constant now. After making sure that Beth had put on her slicker and her cowboy hat to protect her head, Lang went back to driving the restive cows as fast as he dared.

Unfortunately, they were in open country now, where the forest had burned forty years ago. If the cows stampeded, they were going to scatter to hell and gone, and it could take him and his crew days to gather them up again. If he could just move his herd another two miles down the trail, there was a large meadow below the burn surrounded by trees which would hold the cows nicely for the night.

The wind strengthened, and the cows began to

bawl nervously. Then the first wave of hail arrived with a roar. Marble-size pellets of ice sliced down from the sky, stinging and burning every living creature they hit. The cows hated it, particularly the exposed leaders. They tried to stop and turn around, but Lang yelled and cursed at them. Hank did the same from the far side of the bunch. Lang had to smile when he heard Beth shouting in a most unladylike voice while she drove the cows on from the rear.

The first wave of hail eased up, and just when they had caught their breath a second wave hit with the force and roar of a freight train. Lang gestured to Beth to go find shelter in a grove of trees, but she stubbornly remained in her position. He gave Appy, his appaloosa gelding, an encouraging pat. A fine cowhorse, Appy didn't like the hail any better than the cows did, but he kept plodding forward into the storm. The lead cows balked, lowing and bawling miserably. The entire bunch started to mill and rush about. Just when Lang was certain that the animals were going to bolt, the hail eased up, to be replaced by curtains of cold drenching rain.

Slowly, the cows began to settle and move forward again. They didn't like rain, but it didn't drive them into a frenzy the way hail did. Lang winced when he felt a cold trickle of rain slip down the neck of his slicker. The best rain gear in the world couldn't keep anyone warm and dry in a mountain storm like this one.

He glanced back at Beth several times as they continued to push the cows onward through the driving rain. She and Rusty did a fine job of forcing the stragglers onward. He grinned when he heard her shout one of Tucker's favorite profanities at a particularly stubborn cow that wanted to wait out the storm in the shelter of a tree with her calf.

He stopped grinning when the cow and her calf bolted from the herd. Beth sent Rusty charging after them. He called to Beth to let them go, that he could send someone later to round them up, but she couldn't hear him over the noise of the cows and the rain. He watched admiringly as she clung to Rusty's back like a burr as the agile cow horse darted in and out of the aspens and leapt over knee-high spruces. How had an eastern gal learned to ride like that?

Suddenly, Rusty stumbled on the wet ground and fell to his knees.

Lang felt trapped in a nightmare. As if it were all happening in slow motion, he saw Beth catapult over Rusty's head, her slicker a bright yellow blur, and then she landed heavily on the ground and lay still.

His heart frozen in his chest, he wrenched Appy around and sent him pounding toward the place where she lay. Fragments of thought raced through his mind. He'd been so foolish. Why had he let her stay? He'd been so desperate to share her company that he'd allowed her to remain in a situation which he knew could turn dangerous. If she was hurt, it was all his fault.

He slid quickly from his saddle. She was lying on her back, her lovely face pale and still. His stomach twisted when he saw that her eyes were still closed. As he knelt down beside her, he breathed a silent prayer: *Please, don't let her be hurt. Please, don't let her be hurt.*

Thank heaven she was breathing. He was just about to start checking for injuries when her eyes fluttered open.

"Wh-what happened?" she asked dazedly.

THE COWBOY AND THE HEIRESS 199

"You were chasing after a cow, and Rusty stumbled."

"I fell off, didn't I?" She looked so crestfallen and disappointed that Lang had to hide a smile.

"Well, I think there were some extenuating circumstances involved. I've been tossed off a horse a time or two exactly the way you were."

"You're just saying that to make me feel better," she said suspiciously.

"It's the gospel truth." He noticed her shiver. "It's also the gospel truth that you are getting soaked lying there. Does anything hurt?"

"Other than my pride, I don't think so."

"Can you can sit up?"

"I don't know why not." She struggled upright and then closed her eyes. "Whew. I am feeling a little dizzy." After a long moment, she opened her eyes and declared, "There, it's better now."

"How many fingers am I holding up?"

"Two." She made a face at him, "and you need to wash your hands before you eat any food I cook for you."

"I'd say you don't have a concussion, then," he said, relief washing over him. He picked up her hat and placed it on her head.

"You sit here while I check out old Rusty."

"I hope he didn't get hurt," Beth said anxiously.

"Cowhorses are a sturdy bunch," Lang said absently as he ran his hands gently down Rusty's forelegs. He led the gelding several paces forward and then led him back toward Beth. Rusty seemed sound enough.

He stood beside her, wishing like hell he could order up a warm dry limousine. "I know it may not seem like a great idea right now, but riding a horse is the only way we can get you back to camp."

She lifted her chin and met his gaze squarely. "I don't mind getting back up on Rusty. I know he d-didn't mean to t-toss me off," she said, her teeth starting to chatter.

Lang bit back a curse when he realized her jeans were soaked now, as well as her hair. It was probably forty degrees out, enough to make him feel cold, and he wasn't wet the way she was. They still had an hour and a half ride ahead of them through the freezing rain, which showed no sign of letting up.

Lang made his decision just as Hank came riding up.

"Is she all right?" Hank asked in a low voice. Lang was pretty sure that Hank was halfway in love with Beth, but too shy to say much more than hello to her.

"She didn't get hurt, but she did get soaked and shaken up from that fall, and I don't want her developing hypothermia. Push the cows on to that meadow just below the burn on the right side of the trail. It's maybe a half-mile from here. I'm going to take Beth over to Baxter's old cabin to warm up and dry out. I'll call Tucker on my handheld, and let him know what happened. He'll come up to relieve you in a few hours."

"Okay, boss," Hank agreed. Before he rode off, he said to Beth, "You did real good during that hail and all."

"Th-thanks, Hank. I'm sorry I fell off."

"Happens to us all. You should have seen the header the boss took at the spring round up last year," Hank told her with a shy smile, and rode off.

"Y-you don't have to take me to any cabin," she said, starting to shiver so hard her slicker rustled.

Lang ignored her and maneuvered Rusty around until the sorrel gelding was standing right next to her. He held the reins while she climbed stiffly into the saddle.

"I mean it," she said urgently. "You c-can't leave Hank alone with all those cows."

"Hank will be just fine, and so will the cows," Lang countered, heading for his own mount. "Right now, it's you I'm worried about." He winced when he saw the way she was shivering and holding her arms close to her body. "You are a case of hypothermia waiting to happen. You were probably cold, wet, and tired before you fell off Rusty."

He mounted Appy and rode back to catch up Rusty's reins.

"Y-you're not going to lead me like some little k-kid on a pony ride, are you?" she asked indignantly.

"Last time I checked I was still your boss, which means you are going to do exactly as I say until I get you safely back to camp."

"B-bully," he thought he heard her say to his back, and then she was quiet.

Lang started off, leading them back the way they had come. Carefully he watched the right side of the road for the trace of an old trail. None too keen on visitors or vandals, Baxter purposely kept the trails to his cabin overgrown.

Baxter Elijah Pierson was an eccentric old hermit who owned an old trapper's cabin on one of the last pieces of private land in this section of the National Forest. Baxter spent much of his time prospecting, convinced he was going to find a modern day bonanza. Baxter had been one of his father's drinking buddies. The old man wouldn't be happy to have visitors, but he wouldn't be able to turn them away, either.

Lang glanced back at Beth worriedly. She had

huddled down in her slicker, and she looked to be half-asleep. Sleepiness was definitely one of the signs of hypothermia, a condition which could lead to death if a person's body temperature was allowed to slip too low.

He needed to find Baxter's cabin, and he needed to find it fast.

SEVENTEEN

Five minutes later, Lang spotted the trail he'd been looking for. After he pointed Appy down it, he looked back at Beth. Her eyes were closed now.

"Hey, don't you go falling asleep on me, Ms. Richards," he told her sharply.

Her eyes fluttered open and she looked at him dazedly. "Who's Ms. Richards?"

"In theory that's you. I knew you weren't using your real name. I don't suppose you'd like to tell me your real one?"

"I don't believe we've been properly introduced," she said in a crushing tone.

One long look at her glazed eyes told him she wasn't teasing him. Lang bit his lip and tried to remember all he'd ever read about hypothermia. He thought becoming irrational was one of the signs of the condition. He urged Appy to walk a little faster.

At last they reached the secluded aspen grove surrounding Baxter's cabin. The cabin's shutters were all closed, and there was no sign of Lilly, the jenny mule Baxter rode down the mountain to the place where he kept his pickup. Lang dismounted by the door and helped Beth to do likewise. Bless his old-fashioned heart, Baxter didn't have a lock. He just used a sturdy two-by-four to bar the door against bears and other scavengers.

Lang swiftly unbarred the door and pulled Beth inside. "Sit here," he said and pushed her gently into an old rocking chair beside an ancient stove. "I'll be back in a moment."

He led the weary horses around the cabin to a small shed out back. In a few minutes he had stripped off their gear. He'd find water and hay for the animals later.

He hustled back inside and swiftly lit Baxter's old kerosene lantern. The cabin was surprisingly neat. He tried speaking to Beth as he built a blazing fire in the old stove, but she only mumbled in response.

The small cabin would heat quickly, but Lang knew he had to get Beth out of her wet jeans and warmed up now. Sighing, he knelt before her and tugged her boots off. He had a strong feeling that when Beth regained her senses she wasn't going to appreciate the textbook way to warm hypothermia victims.

"I'd like a pair in a size eight," she told him suddenly.

If he hadn't been so scared for her, he would have smiled. "I'll see if we have another pair in the back," he offered.

"Thank you," she said graciously, and lapsed back into silence. If she thought it was odd that the shoe clerk kneeling before her was tugging off her wet socks, she gave no sign.

"All right, let's stand you up and get these wet jeans off. This wasn't exactly how I imagined the first time I went to bed with you," he told her wistfully.

"That's all right," she patted his shoulder. "I've never much cared for the color yellow, either."

THE COWBOY AND THE HEIRESS   205

He spared a half-second to wonder if this was the closest he was ever going to be to seeing her intoxicated. If her behavior right now was anything to go by, she would probably be a happy, polite, and very correct drunk.

Right after he had reached this conclusion, she stood up and leaned over to whisper in his ear, "Every night I fantasize about going to bed with you."

He swallowed hard, wondering if he'd heard her right.

"And we're absolutely, unbelievably, off-the-charts fantastic together."

"That good, eh? Here I thought I was the only one imagining us in the sack." The odd, unfocused look in her silver-blue eyes and the paleness of her cheeks reminded him it was time to get back to business.

Trying not to touch any more of her than he had to, he started to strip off her sodden jeans. Unfortunately, the wet denim clung to her skin stubbornly, and he had to touch and see a great deal of her long slim legs to work her loose. By the time he had gotten the jeans off, his own body was fully aroused. Grimly he did his best to ignore the sensation. Surely he should be used to it by now. He'd endured more sexual frustration in one summer around Beth than he'd had in his entire lifetime.

After he peeled off her slicker, he discovered that her jacket and shirt were damp, too, where water had trickled down the back of her slicker. Setting his jaw, he quickly unbuttoned her flannel shirt. He couldn't help but notice how pretty and creamy white her skin was. The quick glimpse he caught of the rest of Beth in her very feminine pink nylon bra and panties was enough to fuel his fantasies for weeks to come.

The fact that her skin was so cold and clammy to the touch made him even more worried. He bundled her into a thick quilt from Baxter's bed. He pushed her back into the rocker. After he unfastened her braid he used the cleanest towel he could find to dry her hair as best he could. He had fantasized about this, too, freeing her hair and running his fingers through its thick, silky strands. Now, though, he had no time to relish or enjoy the experience.

Once he had patted her hair dry, there was nothing for it but to strip down to his own skivvies. After he had finished, he shoved the old iron bedstead closer to the stove. Then he dragged back the covers on the single mattress, hoping like hell that Baxter had changed his sheets recently. Lang picked up Beth and carefully laid her down in it. He slid in beside her and pulled the covers up around their necks. He was afraid that in her irrational state, she might object to him joining her in the bed. Instead she simply sighed and cuddled close. Gently he turned her onto her side so that he could wrap himself around her.

She was cold all over, from her feet to her hands, and everything in between. What if this didn't work? What if he couldn't raise her body temperature? Was she sleeping now, or was she unconscious? If he had to, how quickly could he get her down the mountain to medical treatment?

Although these questions tormented Lang's mind, his body couldn't ignore the fact that a woman he had wanted quite desperately for weeks now was in his arms, and she was next to naked. Heat rose in his cheeks when he hardened again. *What sort of a man gets a hard-on for a woman who could be in a coma for all he knows?* He eased his hips a little away from her and tried not think about how soft she felt against him, or how her hair still smelled faintly of roses.

Gradually, his body heat warmed the bed, and slowly Beth's body warmed, as well. Once, he slipped out from under the covers to build up the fire in the stove and to heat water he'd drawn from a rain barrel outside. In a while, he wanted to try waking her and getting hot sweet fluid and some food down her. He also hung up their damp clothing to dry. Then he dove back under the covers with Beth.

An endless hour later her skin temperature seemed normal to him again. He dressed quickly and went to tend the weary horses. It was dark outside now, and the rain was still coming down in torrents. He was glad he'd opted for Baxter's cabin instead of pushing on to camp.

When he returned inside, he went to the bed to check on Beth. He was reassured to see that her cheeks had some color in them now. How could she look so damn beautiful after what she'd been through today? The answer came to him as he gazed down at her. Beth possessed the bone-deep kind of beauty which would stay with her until she was eighty. Just looking at her like this made him hurt.

He forced himself to turn away. He called Tucker and gave him an update on their situation. Raiding Baxter's rough wooden shelves without compunction, Lang fixed soup and hot chocolate for Beth, and coffee and beef stew for himself. When her soup was ready, he carried a mug of it over to the bed. As much as he hated to wake her, he needed to be certain that she hadn't slipped into a coma.

He reached out and shook her shoulder gently. "Hey, sleepyhead, you need to wake up."

He gave a silent prayer of thanks when her eyes fluttered open almost immediately. Her dreamy blue gaze fastened on him at once.

"Hello, there," she said, and the warm sleepy smile she sent him had his body tightening all over again.

"How are you feeling?" he asked.

"A little tired, I guess." Her eyes widened as she glanced about the cabin uncertainly. "Where on earth are we?"

"This is an old trapper's cabin. You fell off Rusty while we were driving the cows through a hailstorm. You got soaked through and started turning hypothermic on me, so I brought you here to warm up and dry out."

"I remember bits of it now," she admitted. Suddenly she frowned and peeked at herself under the covers. "How, exactly, did you warm me up?" she asked, her formal correct accent returning with a rush.

"I used body heat, and before you start thinking the worst, I didn't touch a damn part of you that I didn't have to." *I wouldn't still be tight as a young bull about to cover his first cow if I had.*

"I'm sure you were a perfect gentleman," she said, her expression apologetic. "I'm sorry to be such a nuisance."

"Whatever else you are, Beth Richards, a nuisance is not the first word that springs to mind." A totally feminine distraction guaranteed to drive a man crazy was more like it. "Now, if I remember my first aid correctly, I'm supposed to ply you with hot fluids and plenty of food. See if you can drink this down."

She sat upright, carefully keeping the blankets

modestly tucked up under her armpits. "Have you eaten?"

"I was just about to."

"Could you come over here to eat?" she asked so hopefully that he didn't have the heart to tell her the last place he wanted to be right now was sitting on that bed next to her. She looked far too tempting, her glorious golden hair tumbling loose about her bare shoulders. Somehow he would have to find a way to keep his hands and his revved up body to himself.

And so they had a picnic supper on the narrow old bed before the stove, and every moment of it was sheer torture for Lang. He had no idea what they talked about while he watched the way she cupped her mug. He kept thinking about her elegant hands cupping various parts of him instead. She sipped the soup, and he wanted to sample those full lips of hers again. The light from the old lantern shone off her hair and burnished it bright gold. The lovely pale skin of her shoulders was driving him mad. It would be far too easy to lean over and press a long lingering kiss on her collarbone. Abruptly, he rose to his feet and went to fetch her shirt, which was dry now.

She eyed him quizzically as he shoved the shirt at her and turned around to face the stove.

"Thank you," she murmured, and put the shirt on.

The tension inside him eased only a little. The memory of what she looked like without that shirt on was far too vivid and fresh in his memory. As soon as they finished supper, he busied himself with washing up the pots and plates. When Beth offered to help him, he turned her down flat.

"I worked hard enough getting you thawed out.

I'd rather you stayed put right where you are in that warm bed."

"All right." The way she lifted one eyebrow let him know he'd been boorish.

There wasn't much he could do about it. Intense sexual frustration had a way of making a man rude. When he couldn't find another chore to keep him occupied inside the cabin, he went outside to check on the horses. He stayed out in the shed for a long time, hoping to cool off the fire in his blood and give her time to fall asleep again. He planned to bed down beside the stove when he went back inside. He knew he'd just about reached his limit in the self-control department. If he went anywhere near her again tonight he'd end up in that bed with her, claiming what he'd wanted from the first day he saw her at Danny Parson's diner.

Lang was gone outside for so long that Beth began to worry that something had happened to him. Because she was getting chilled again, she slipped down under the covers, but she knew she wouldn't be able to sleep. Surely it didn't take this long to make sure the horses were settled for the night. She was just about to get dressed to check on Lang when he stepped inside.

After he took off his wet slicker, he glanced at her and frowned. "You're still awake," he said, sounding irritated.

"I was starting to worry that Grizzled Pete had gotten you," she said lightly. Grizzled Pete was the hero of some of Tucker's most gruesome and ghastly ghost stories.

"Not hardly," Lang said with little humor.

THE COWBOY AND THE HEIRESS 211

She watched in growing dismay as he started to make a bed for himself before the stove.

"You are not sleeping on that cold hard floor tonight," she protested.

He looked up from where he knelt. She was stunned to see the tumult in his gaze. "If you're inviting me to share that bed with you, I'm warning you that it's not a wise idea. Not tonight." There was a strained set to his features she had never seen before.

"I'm not on my deathbed. You did a wonderful job of taking care of me. I feel much better now. You-you wouldn't bother me in the least." She bit her lip, wishing she could handle this situation with a little more poise.

"Well, you sure as hell would bother me," he said tightly. "Let me spell it out for you, lady. I'm doing my damnedest to act like the gentleman my mother raised me to be, but if I join you in that bed neither of us is going to get much sleep tonight."

She stared back at him, feeling her cheeks begin to burn. Now she understood why he had been so short with her. She'd grown increasingly aware of him all night until her body ached and tingled with longing, but she hadn't realized he'd been feeling the same way.

She drew in a deep breath. She would be leaving the Rafter N in less than a month. This might be the last time she would be alone with him. This might be her only chance to discover what it was like to share her body with the man she loved. She knew she would regret it for the rest of her life if she didn't make love with Lang tonight.

"I've always thought sleep was a rather overrated commodity, myself," she forced herself to say boldly.

"Don't joke about this," he said in such a fierce

tone that she had to restrain an urge to dive under the covers.

"All right. I want you to share this bed with me tonight." She met his gaze levelly. "I want you to make love to me. No—I want to make love with you," she corrected herself. "I want it more than I've wanted anything in my life." As soon as she said the words, she realized they were absolutely true.

"Damn it, you're not the kind of woman to go around having flings."

"No, I'm not," she agreed. "And I doubt you're the kind of man who enjoys casual sex, either. This wouldn't be casual, and it wouldn't lead to a fling. I know we don't have a future together. But you matter to me, and I think—I hope—that I matter to you, as well."

He bowed his head and was silent for a long moment. "You matter, all right," he said in a gruff voice. "So much that I don't know if we should do this if we don't have any sort of future."

Sensing that his barriers were weakening, she slipped out of bed and knelt beside him.

"Then let's be together tonight and pretend we have a lifetime ahead of us."

"Hell, I'm no good at pretending. It doesn't really even matter anymore that I don't know who you are. I want you so much . . . just looking at you twists me up inside." He lifted his gaze to hers at last, and the longing she saw in his beautiful brown-gold eyes made her throat go tight.

Instinctively she understood he wouldn't make the first move, not when he wasn't sure it was right. *What if he rejects you? Idiot. There's so much more at stake here than your pride.*

Heart pounding, she placed her hands on his broad shoulders and kissed him. For one long horrible moment, his lips remained still and unresponsive against her own. Then he groaned and wrapped his arms around her and kissed her back with feverish intensity. Giddy with relief and happiness, she felt her desire rising fast to meet his.

Lang wanted her. That prospect was glorious, wonderful, and frightening, all at once. What if she disappointed him, just as she had disappointed Bryce? It was hard to concentrate on that fear.

Soon it was hard to concentrate at all. Lang was doing such delicious things to arouse her senses. His lips ranged across her face and the sides of her neck. He paused and kissed the sensitive skin beneath her ear. She gasped when he nipped at her earlobe. His hands smoothed her sides, rousing her sensual awareness and making her long for him to touch the rest of her.

In turn, she boldly undid the first two buttons on his shirt and slipped her hands under the soft flannel fabric. His skin and body were warm and hard, supple and utterly fascinating. She stroked what she could reach and wished she could explore farther. He must have sensed her frustration, for he made quick work of the rest of his buttons and tugged his shirt off.

She leaned back to appreciate the view. His upper body was lean and fit, his well-defined muscles formed by years of hard physical work rather than pumped up artificially in a gym. She smiled when she saw his rancher's tan—brown neck and forearms, paler skin on the rest of his torso. His neck was strong, his shoulders almost intimidatingly wide while he knelt so close to her. His chest was lightly furred with dark hair that tapered to a V above his jeans. Lang was magnificent, and for tonight he was all hers.

"Lady, do you like what you see?" His tone was teasing, but she thought she saw a flicker of uncertainty deep in his eyes.

"Cowboy, those eastern gals don't know what they're missing."

Giving in to impulse, she leaned forward and kissed the skin just above his heart. With a moan, he cupped her buttocks and molded her closer against him. When she felt his hardness thrusting between her hips, a primitive thrill of feminine satisfaction shot through her. He reclaimed her mouth, and they kissed, tasted, and explored until they were both breathing hard.

Just when she realized that kneeling and kissing weren't the most comfortable combination in the world, he urged her to her feet and swung her up into his arms. Kissing her all the while, he crossed the distance to the narrow bed in three strides. He placed her gently on the bed and turned to wrench his boots off.

When he had finished, he lay down beside her and threw one leg across her thighs, the worn denim of his jeans pleasingly rough against her bare skin. His expression intent, he raised himself up on one elbow and slowly began to undo the buttons of her shirt. After he released each one, he thoroughly kissed the skin he had exposed, sending wonderful, sensuous shivers all over her.

After he had undone every button and spread her shirt wide, he reached down, flicked open the clasp on her bra, and pulled the garment away from her. Beth drew in a breath and stilled the impulse to cover herself. She gazed at his face instead. The smoldering look she saw in his eyes reassured her.

"Cowboy, do you like what you see?"

"Lady, I don't care anymore where you're from.

I just know you're the most beautiful thing I've ever seen," he said hoarsely, and then he bent his head and kissed the tips of her breasts and teased her gently with his teeth. She found herself arching against him. She was taut and aching by the time he finished with the first, and wild with need by the time he finished lavishing such delicious attention on the second.

She smoothed a hand along his taut belly and boldly slipped it inside the front of his jeans. She stroked him once, and he drew in a sharp breath. He drew her hand away and kissed her fingertips. "Much more of that, woman, and this show's going to be over in a real hurry," he admitted. "And I want to make this as good as I can for you."

"But I want to hurry." She shifted restlessly against his hard leg, which continued to keep her pinned against the mattress. Her body felt as if it were on fire. A wonderful, coiled sort of tension was building deep inside her, and she needed to find relief from it soon.

"Shh, now," he said, his deep voice gentle in her ear. "I've been waiting for this night too long to rush any of it."

The hot waves of arousal swept through her as he reached out and began to caress and play with the tips of her breasts. She swallowed hard when his hand ventured lower, tracing slow sensuous patterns across her belly.

She closed her eyes when he shifted his leg and began to massage the sensitive skin along the insides of her thighs. She raised her hips to help him slip off her panties. She moaned aloud when he traced the outside of her folds with his fingertips. How could a man with such large hands be so dexterous? How could Lang know how exactly how she liked to be touched when she didn't even know herself? She felt a rush of warmth when he slowly entered her with his fingers.

"Lord, woman, you're tight." She was dimly aware of the roughness in his voice.

"I don't—I haven't done this all that many times," she heard herself confess. There had been one boy in college, a young chef in cooking school, and then Bryce. She had been too shy, and the men she encountered too intimidated by her father, for her to have had much experience with sex.

"Lucky me," she thought she heard him say, but he was gently rubbing her female center with his thumb, and the tight coil inside her suddenly crested and released. She bucked against his hand as the waves of exhilarating pleasure seemed to go on and on. She clung tightly to his shoulders, knowing he was her anchor in a sea of sensation.

When she could actually think again, she found he was holding her close. *So that's what all the fuss is about.* Beth smiled languidly and stretched her arms above her head. She was twenty-six years old, and because of Lang Nelson she finally knew what pleasure her own body could give her.

A kind caring cowboy had just given her this magnificent gift, and he had yet to take his own pleasure. She felt a rush of remorse when she glanced up at him and saw the strain etched on his features. One look at his hungry eyes, and the tension began to build inside her all over again.

He pressed a kiss on her forehead. "You got your breath back now?"

She nodded, not quite trusting herself to be coherent yet.

"Please tell me you're protected." He said the words like a prayer.

She nodded again.

"Good," he said, a glimmer of humor in his brown eyes. "I don't usually bring condoms on cattle drives." Then the humor vanished, to be replaced by a scorching look that made her insides melt.

Relentlessly, he spread her knees wide with his hands. He stripped off his jeans and briefs and lowered himself over her. An exquisite pulse shot through her when she felt him probing at her entrance. Just moments ago, she had felt so relaxed and nerveless. She couldn't believe that she would be able to climax again. Yet, as he slowly pushed all the way into her, she realized that he could very well take her over the edge again. With Lang inside her, she felt wonderfully stretched and full.

She gasped as he slowly withdrew and then sheathed himself in her again. She had never felt such intense pleasure. She raised her hips to meet his next thrust. To her delight, the sensations grew stronger.

"I don't—I'm sorry, I can't wait any longer," he ground out suddenly. He held her hips tightly and plunged into her again and again. She rose to meet him, her body tightening and reaching for that place he had taken her before, and then he thrust into her a final time. As his big body shuddered in climax, he called out her name in a guttural shout. She hardly noticed he had shoved her shoulders up against the old bedstead, because her own release slammed into her with stunning force.

She opened her eyes at the height of it, and saw he was watching her, his eyes black with passion and tenderness. Afterward, they collapsed into each others' arms and lay panting while a warm lassitude stole over them. Beth knew she would never forget this night, lying beside Lang in the old narrow bed while the lantern washed the cabin with soft golden light and rain pattered on the wooden roof overhead.

After a time, Lang raised himself up on one elbow and stared down at her. "Are you all right? I didn't mean to get so rough." His worried, apologetic tone touched her.

"I'm more than all right. That was fantastic."

"I hope it was absolutely, unbelievably, right off-the-charts," he said, an odd smile she couldn't quite read lighting his eyes.

"A ten on the Richter scale wouldn't come close," she said with feeling. She laughed when she saw a very self-satisfied expression cross his face.

"I did mean to take that a little slower," he admitted, playing with a lock of her hair.

"I'm glad you didn't. I've been fantasizing about us tearing the clothes off each other for months."

"I've been thinking about this since the first day I saw you in the parking lot at Danny's diner," he confessed.

"You have? I thought you didn't have much use for me there at the start."

"I didn't like who I thought you were."

Beth swallowed hard. It was time to face the ghost in his past who scared her the most. "The girls told me about Sonya."

He sighed and rolled onto his back. "I figured someone probably would, sooner or later."

"Do you still think about her?"

"Every once in a very long while, I suppose. Usually I just thank my lucky stars that she didn't say yes when I proposed to her. We would have made each other miserable. I did wonder when I first saw you if you might be like her. I think I realized within the first twenty-four hours that you two were quite different. Sonya was a taker. You're a giver through and through."

The compliment warmed her, but Beth didn't let it distract her. "Is she the reason you never married?"

Lang stared at her for a long moment, and then he let loose with a gust of laughter. "Is that what the twins told you?"

She decided not to mention the fact the twins had gotten their information from his loyal housekeeper. "Basically, yes."

"As much as my teenage nieces probably relish the melodramatic notion that I've been carrying a torch for Sonya all these years, I can honestly say that that torch burned itself out a long time ago. I've never married because I never found someone in Perrytown I wanted to spend my life with. End of story."

The real humor and exasperation she heard in his tone convinced her. Lang was over Sonya. She wondered, though, if he could ever truly trust a woman who came from a rich privileged background.

"Now," he said, changing the subject in a stern voice, "you've had a long, hard day, and after what you've been through I think you should get some sleep."

She gazed up at his weary face and swallowed her disappointment. So much for hoping they might make love again. Lang had to be exhausted after a long day of looking after his guests, driving cows, and rescuing his cook. At least she could look forward to sleeping next to him all night long in a very narrow bed.

As she snuggled closer to his warm body, the back of her hand brushed against something hard and hot. She moved her hand away in surprise. Lang had been lying next to her fully aroused, and he hadn't said a word. She raised herself up on one elbow and looked down at him indignantly. "You were going to let that go to waste?"

"After what I put you through today, I figured you needed sleep more than another round with a horny cowpoke like me."

"Well, you figured wrong, mister."

He sent her a slow sensual smile which took her breath away. "If you're so set on taking advantage of me, I've often wondered how good a rider you really are."

She was silent for a long moment while she digested his meaning. To Lang's delight, a wave of delicate pink rose in her cheeks, but she replied gamely, "I'd be happy to show you, cowboy."

The sultry promise in her smoky blue eyes made Lang's pulse race. He lifted her up and positioned her so that she was straddling his hips. He didn't slip her shirt off, for he wanted her to have some protection from the cabin's cool drafts. The glimpses he caught of the rosy peaks of her breasts through the gap in her shirt were tantalizing enough. Hell, he'd still probably get turned on by Beth if she wore a paper bag.

She bent her head and spread kisses across his chest and the base of his neck. He loved the silky feel of her hair against his skin. He was drowning in her sweet rose scent. He tried to enter her, but she wriggled away, forcing him to wait while she drove him crazy with her clever mouth. Taking her time, she thoroughly kissed his neck, shoulders, and chest.

At last he could wait no longer. With a groan, he held her hips and thrust upward. She was just as tight and velvety hot as he remembered. At first she set the pace and kept it slow. She raised and lowered herself deliberately, allowing them both to enjoy the delicious friction.

Knowing there was only so much a man could take, he reached up and caressed the sensitive tips of her breasts. He rotated his hips, changing the angle of his penetration, and she gasped in pleasure. They both went wild, their bodies tangled and straining together. She rode him hard, and he loved every minute of it. He had wanted for so long to see her like this, free of constraint and convention. She was just as generous in her loving as he had known she would be.

They peaked at the same moment. While her body shuddered and tightened around him, she called out his name. In the depths of his own passion he still heard her, and he thought that he had never heard such a sweet sound.

Afterward, it seemed like the most natural thing in the world to pull her close. He curled himself around her, and they both fell into a sound sleep.

When the first gray light of day came seeping through the cabin shutters, Lang was wide awake. By lantern light, he had been watching Beth for the last hour. She looked younger in her sleep, her face pillowed on her arm, her cheeks flushed and rosy, her long, blond hair all tousled.

As he stroked a lock of that hair with his fingertips, he realized the sobering truth at last. He didn't just care about Beth. He loved her with all his heart. It wasn't only her remarkable beauty that drew him. He loved her giving spirit and the sweetness in her. He loved her enthusiasm, and the way she managed to take joy in every day. He had worked so hard for so long that he had almost forgotten how to enjoy his life until Beth had made him see and appreciate the world of the Rafter N from her perspective.

She'd even helped him realize all over again how wonderful the twins were. More importantly, she'd made him see that his nieces needed his time more than anything. She seemed to care a great deal about them, and the girls clearly loved her.

Beth might not be from his world, but she fit remarkably well here. Lang drew in a deep breath. He might be crazy, but he was going to do his damnedest to keep her. He knew that if he let her walk away a month from now, his own happiness would vanish with her. Given half a chance, he thought he could make her happy. Something must have been terribly wrong in her old life to make her run away from it.

He frowned as he considered that mysterious former life of hers. Before he could fight the battle to win her heart, he had to know what he was up against. When they returned to the Rafter N he was finally going to find out who Beth was, and what she was running from.

EIGHTEEN

Beth was tired but happy as they rode up to the horse barn. The Rafter N's fall cattle drive was officially over. Lang's cows and their calves were settled in the outlying pastures, eating their heads off now that the three days of constant walking were through for them.

She shifted her weight in the saddle, wincing a little. She was sore from more than riding. Last night Lang had slipped into her tent and made love to her with a single-minded intensity that had set her senses afire. She smiled at the memory. She now knew with glorious certainty that she wasn't frigid. Her body began to heat at the very thought of Lang's magical hands touching her.

She refused to worry about the future. She was going to hold on to the next four weeks and enjoy every single day and night that she had left with Lang. Perhaps she could even earn his trust and prove to him that she wasn't like Sonya. Perhaps the new life she had been searching for was right here on the Rafter N.

Dreamily she wondered if he would come to her cabin tonight. Based on the last two night's experiences, she might not get much sleep if he did, but who cared about sleep? Her daydreaming came to an abrupt halt, and her stomach tightened into a cold hard knot when she saw the tall, distinguished-looking man with iron gray hair striding toward the horse barn beside Elsie.

"Hello, Dad," Beth greeted her father, wondering how he managed to look quite so at home wearing a suit on a ranch in northwestern Colorado.

She glanced over at Lang. He was studying her father with interest. With a sigh, she realized she could hardly hide the truth from Lang any longer.

"Dad, this is my boss, Lang Nelson. Lang, this is my father, Peter Harrison."

She watched Lang. It didn't take long for the name to register, for her father was one of the five richest men in the world and enjoyed the notoriety to match. He'd built a vast financial empire based on telecommunications and computer technology. For a moment Lang looked startled, and then his expression became impassive.

"It's a pleasure to meet you, Mr. Harrison," Lang said politely. "Welcome to the Rafter N."

"It's not a pleasure to meet you, and I'll be here just long enough to talk some sense into this daughter of mine." Having dismissed Lang with his customary brusqueness, her father addressed Beth. "It's nice to know that while I've been worrying myself sick about you, you've been off playing cowgirl." The look in his gray-blue eyes, so like her own in color, was cold and hard.

Before she could defend herself Lang spoke up for her. "Beth has been doing very little playing this summer. For the past three months she's been working damn hard, cooking three meals a day for my hands and guests."

"Don't," Beth said quietly, putting a hand on Lang's arm. "It's time I finally stood up to him."

She turned to confront her father. "I'm twenty-six years old. I've every right to do what I want with my life. I sent you a postcard right after I left to let you know I was fine, and I sent one to Lisa. If I had called, you would have traced those calls and tried to bully me into coming back home."

"You sent all of two postcards in four months." Her father shook his head in disbelief "You could have been kidnapped again, for all I knew. I'll never understand you. I send you to the best cooking schools in the world, and you end up working at a dude ranch. This little adventure of yours is over as of this minute. I've got a helicopter waiting in town, and the jet is ready in Grand Junction. With any luck, I can still make my meetings tomorrow in New York."

"You can make those meetings easily, because I'm not going back with you. I agreed to work here through the end of hunting season, and I'm not going to leave Lang in the lurch."

"So that's the way the wind's blowing."

She hated the knowing look which came into her father's eyes at that moment. She had always hated the way he was so sure he understood people and their motivations.

"I'm sure Bryce will understand that you had to sow a few wild oats before the wedding," her father said with a mirthless smile.

"Just who is Bryce?" Lang asked tightly.

"Why, Bryce Townsend is Elizabeth's fiancé," her father replied promptly. "Didn't she tell you?"

"I didn't tell him because I have no fiancé," Beth got out between gritted teeth. "I told you and I told Bryce it was over. It's not my fault you two arrogant males can't understand that fact."

For the very first time in her life, she was actually

standing up to her father. She could hardly enjoy the sensation, though, for at the mention of her ex-fiancé Lang's expression had grown remote and cold.

"Perhaps it's time we stopped airing family matters in front of strangers," her father suggested icily.

"These people aren't strangers. They're my friends, and they've shown me more respect and caring this summer than you have in my entire life. However, I do agree that it might be more polite and considerate if we talked in private."

Lang stepped forward and took Rusty's reins. "Elsie and I can handle dinner tonight," was all he said to her, and the emptiness in his gaze chilled her blood.

Beth stared at his back as he led her mount away. She had to quell the urge to run after him. Stubbornly she fought down the tears burning in her eyes. Tears wouldn't do her the least bit of good with either of these men.

"Let's go down by the river," she told her father. The grass down there might be damp, but it was his problem if his thousand dollar Ferragamo shoes got ruined.

When she reached the river, she turned to face her father. Dimly she realized she was standing in the very place she and Lang had almost made love. Perhaps she could draw some sort of strength from that.

"I'm not going back with you," she declared.

"You've fallen in love with that two-bit rancher, haven't you?"

"There's nothing two-bit about him. He's an intelligent hardworking man. In fact, he reminds me a little of you, back in the days when you still had a heart."

THE COWBOY AND THE HEIRESS 227

Her father completely ignored her jibe, the way he always did when she made comments he believed were beneath his notice. "That hardworking rancher just happens to be up to his neck in debt. I had him checked out as soon as my detectives finally found someone who remembered seeing you in Perrytown."

"Somehow that doesn't surprise me." One of her father's favorite axioms had always been "Information is power."

"I own a majority position in the company that owns the bank that holds his note. If you don't come back home where you can be properly protected, I'll make sure they foreclose on this ranch."

"You can't do that." Even as she said the words, she knew he'd find some legal way to do exactly that. The financial and legal resources her father had at his command were enormous. If she didn't leave now, Lang would lose the ranch—and the Rafter N meant everything to him. A vise seemed to be tightening around her heart. She would have to leave here to protect Lang, his ranch, and his family. As soon as she returned to the East with her father, though, nothing would induce her to stay under his roof again.

"Believe me, I can influence that bank, and I will if you push me to it. I also understand that one of Nelson's dudes had an accident here this summer. I can make sure there's so much bad press about Nelson's guest venture that he won't see another paying guest set foot on this ranch."

"All right," she said coldly. "You've made your point. I won't have you destroying a decent man because of me. I'll go pack. But understand this: It will be a very long time before I forgive you for this, and I won't marry Bryce."

Her anger seemed to surprise him. "You know I only want what's best for you."

"I know you believe that, which is why I'll probably have to forgive you some day. Right now, I can only see a domineering father who is hell bent on destroying his daughter's only chance at happiness because it doesn't fit with his perfectly thought-out plan for her future. Lang Nelson is the only man who ever respected me and taught me how to respect myself. You should be grateful to him instead of threatening everything he cares about."

For once, she finally saw her father rendered speechless. She stalked past him and headed for her cabin.

Lang was in the horse barn sorting through the last of the pack gear from the drive when Peter Harrison came to find him.

"She's agreed to leave with me tonight," the older man announced.

"All right," Lang said, his heart heavier than a boulder in his chest. What an idiot he had been to think he had a chance with Beth. At first the news she had a fiancé had thrown him for a loop. It had felt as if the disaster with Sonya was happening to him all over again. For the five most horrible minutes of his life, he'd believed he had fallen for another rich girl who had used him before she settled down.

After those first five minutes passed, Lang realized that he believed Beth when she faced her father and told him she had broken off her engagement. She never would have run from a man she loved and meant to marry. Would she walk away from him and the Rafter N now, because her father demanded it?

THE COWBOY AND THE HEIRESS 229

If only they could have had a few more weeks together. He knew he had been on the brink of getting her to trust him, and he thought he had seen real caring in her gaze. Now he might never know how she truly felt about him.

"I want your promise that you won't try to contact Beth once she's left here," Harrison insisted.

"I can't give you that promise," Lang replied, studying the worn bridle he held in his hands. Who would have thought that one of the richest men in the world would be standing in his tack room? And right now he hated that man's guts.

"I'll write you a check for a hundred thousand dollars this instant if you swear you won't try to keep her here. If you do contact her in any way, I'll make sure your bank rescinds your loan."

"If you weren't her father, I'd tear you apart for even suggesting you could buy me off," Lang said, fighting the impulse to plant a fist in Harrison's face.

"If money won't motivate you, then I suggest you consider this. Elizabeth was born to a life of privilege. If she marries you, I'll cut her off without a cent. What kind of life could you offer her here? Would she work herself into an early grave cooking for your guests and your hired hands? She is used to the finest things money can buy."

"And that made her happy?"

"Of course it did," Harrison brushed off his question. "Elizabeth has never been a particularly focused individual. Once she marries and settles down, I know she'll find contentment."

You could make her happy. You could make her contented right here on the Rafter N, an urgent voice said in the back of Lang's mind. Yet he had always been a pragmatist. His father had taught him the danger of believing in impossible dreams.

Lang walked to the doorway and looked over the hay meadows of the ranch he loved, the truth a bitter taste in his mouth. The bank owned more of his ranch than he did. His guest scheme had yet to prove whether or not it would make the difference to the Rafter N's future. He might have years of hard work and financial uncertainty ahead of him. What kind of life could he offer her, indeed?

Lang sighed and turned away from the door. "Look, I'll do what you ask, but not because I give a damn about who you are, or all the money you've made. I'll let Beth go because I'm not sure I can provide for her properly. But I sure as hell hope you'll stop and ask yourself why she ran away from that life—and the man you seem so set on having her marry, if he made her happy."

"Elizabeth has always been afraid of commitment."

"So much so that she ran halfway across the country and landed in Perrytown without a cent to her name? She committed herself to doing a hard job on this ranch, and she's done it well all summer. You don't give her enough credit."

"I believe I know my daughter a hell of a lot better than you do."

"I guess being one of the richest men in the world means you're always right. Now, go collect your daughter and get off my land."

Lang turned his back on one of the world's most famous billionaires and went back to sorting through the pack gear. After a long moment, Harrison went striding from the barn. Lang stared sightlessly at the saddlebags in his hands while he considered his options.

As much as he longed to saddle up a horse and gallop off to one of the most remote portions of the ranch, he had to stay. Watching Beth drive away was going to be one of the most painful experiences he'd ever endured, but he had to see her one more time. He couldn't let her go without saying goodbye.

He was just about to head back to the ranch house when the twins came to find him.

"Beth's ready to go now," Stacy said, her eyes already red from crying. Under his breath, Lang cursed Peter Harrison for making the twins face another abrupt loss.

"Is she really going to leave?" Tony asked him, her blue eyes puzzled and concerned.

"It sounds like it, honey."

"We thought you really liked her, and she really liked you," Tony persisted, watching his face carefully.

"Well, liking is a long way from loving," he said, deliberately trying to keep his voice casual.

"We're all going to miss her, but I think you're going to miss her most of all," Tony said quietly, and she stepped forward and gave him a hug.

"That we are," Lang said, feeling his throat go tight. He couldn't believe his nieces were so grown up that they were offering him comfort now. He slipped his arms around them and started for the house.

"Beth did say we could come visit her in New York," Stacy said, perking up at the thought. "If her dad's really that rich, I bet their apartment is incredible."

"Maybe you'll have a chance to do that some day," Lang agreed. *But you won't, old son. In a few minutes, your lady is going to drive out of your life forever, and big macho ranchers don't start leaking tears in front of their family and hired hands.*

They arrived at the porch steps just as Beth came outside and gave Elsie and Tucker a final hug each. Her father waited impatiently beside the silver limousine which looked so out of place parked in the Rafter N's gravel drive. Beth walked down the steps and gave each of the twins hugs as well.

And then the moment Lang had been dreading arrived. Beth stepped in front of him. Her eyes were suspiciously bright, her face a little pale, but her voice was steady.

"I'm so sorry I can't stay for hunting season, but I think it's best for everyone that I go now."

"We'll manage. You've two week's wages coming." As soon as he blurted those words, he felt like a complete idiot. A few hundred dollars was less than pocket change to a daughter of a billionaire.

"I want every penny of that paycheck," she said, obviously reading his mind. "I'm proud of that money. I'll send you my address when I reach New York so that you can mail my paycheck to me."

That was something, anyway. He'd have one letter from her he could hold on to forever.

"Thank you for giving me a chance to prove myself," she continued. "I've learned so much about me, and the Beth I want to be, working here this summer."

"I'm glad. You take care of yourself back there," he managed to say past the grief tightening his throat. He stared at her then, trying to impress on his memory every detail of her appearance so that he could still dream about her when he was a wizened up old man forty years from now.

She stepped forward and pressed a quick kiss on his cheek. "You always take care of everyone else, but make sure you take care of yourself too," she said, a catch in her voice. Before he could reach out and hold her close, she slipped away.

Like a man trapped in a nightmare, he watched helplessly as she walked away from them all, her head held high. The driver helped her into the limousine and closed the door behind her.

As Lang watched the fancy limousine glide down the dirt road toward town, he wondered how long it would be before he felt like smiling again.

Beth barely spoke to her father during the long flight back to New York. The opulence of her father's G-5 private business jet, which she had always taken for granted, now seemed oppressive to her. After she pointedly ignored his attempts at making conversation, he went to work on one of the computers built into the jet while she stared dry-eyed out of a window into the night.

She kept seeing Lang's face and the anguish in his eyes right before she left. Why hadn't he tried to stop her? If he had asked her to stay, she never would have been able to walk away from him. She'd been so sure he was coming to love her. But he hadn't said a word, and now she would never know if they could have had a chance together.

When they reached the elegant apartment building her father owned on Central Park South, Beth got out of the limousine and followed him into their private elevator. She didn't mean to stay in their penthouse apartment that night, but her father had said Bryce would be waiting for them, and she needed to confront her ex-fiancé one last time.

As soon as the elevator doors opened, she saw Bryce. He strode toward her, his arms outstretched, his handsome face full of phony concern. As she studied him, she wondered why she had never noticed that his chin was a trifle on the weak side and his charming blue eyes were really set a bit too close together.

"Elizabeth, I've been so worried about you."

"I've told you a hundred times I prefer to be called Beth. If you touch me, I swear I'll kick you in your private parts so hard you'll be rolling on the floor," she told him sweetly.

She would have laughed at both men's shocked expressions if the situation had been any less dire.

"Elizabeth," her father said sternly, "there's no need to be crude."

"Perhaps not, but I do find a need to be specific and to the point. Bryce, I won't marry you because you are a lying sycophantic jerk. I know you arranged my kidnapping because I heard you talking about it with your mistress on the phone. I know you only wanted to marry 'the old man's frigid bimbo daughter' for our money and our family connections."

"Please, Elizabeth, you're overwrought," Bryce said smoothly. "You must have completely misunderstood something I said jokingly to a friend."

"I don't know how you managed to con my father, but you'll never con me again. I know exactly what you are, and if I could prove what you did to me I'd have you locked behind bars." She drew enormous satisfaction from the fact that for the first time suave sophisticated Bryce looked rattled.

"Beth, what you're saying is preposterous," her father broke in, his color high. "Bryce loves you. He's perfect for you."

"No, he's perfect for you, because he loves money and power and you have plenty of both. I think he staged that kidnapping because he knew I was having second thoughts about marrying him, and he wanted to make me more emotionally dependent on him. If you really loved me half as much as you claim you do, you'd fire him and have some professional thugs beat his face in." She couldn't help remembering wistfully what Lang had said about wanting to hunt down the men who had dared to scare her so.

"I don't believe it for a moment."

"Of course you don't, Daddy," she said, her heart breaking for them both. "I'm just your daughter, and he's the man who shares almost all of your waking hours, working by your side, sharing your dreams of making your telecommunications empire even greater. That's why I ran away in the first place, because I knew you wouldn't believe me, and you would try to intimidate me into marrying a man who could do something so despicable to his fiancée."

She drew in a deep breath and forced down the tears she refused to shed in front of either of them. "Well, one thing I decided out west is that I'm never going to let anyone intimidate me again, especially you two. I'm going to stay at the St. Regis until I figure out my plans. Bryce, if you so much as try to call me I'll go to the press and tell them what you did. They won't be overly concerned about whether I have proof or not."

Deliberately, she turned her back on them and headed for the elevator.

"Beth, sweet girl, for heaven's sake, stay here and let's work this out," her father pleaded.

She glanced over her shoulder, her defenses weakening. He was finally starting to sound like the caring father she remembered from her childhood, but her resolve hardened. If she gave in now she would lose the whole game, and she would never be free of her father's well-meaning manipulations.

"I'm sorry, but I won't live in the same household with a man who has so little respect for me and my opinions. Good-bye, Daddy. And by the way, Bryce darling, I know for a fact now that I'm not frigid."

With that parting salvo, she stepped back into the elevator and punched the button for the lobby. As soon as the doors slid closed, she gave a wild cowboy yell and then she burst into tears.

NINETEEN

Wearily, Lang shut down his computer and stared out the window of his study into the cold winter dusk. The numbers from last summer looked good. Beef prices were up, and bookings for guests next year were already trickling in. Many were from repeat customers, like the Motts. Beth would have laughed with him about that, and shared his pleasure in the Rafter N's success. She didn't know how well the guest venture had gone in its first year, nor was he going to have a chance to tell her.

A thousand times he'd considered picking up the phone and calling her. A hundred times he'd considered hopping on a plane to see her. It wasn't Harrison's threat which stopped him. It was his own inner fears. Whatever it took to keep a beautiful, talented, sophisticated woman like Beth happy, he clearly didn't have it. He'd reached beyond his world when he fell in love with Sonya, and she hadn't taken him seriously from the start. Beth was a completely different sort of woman, but she came from Sonya's glittering privileged background. Peter Harrison made more money in a minute than a Colorado rancher would make working hard all year long.

He rose to his feet and began to pace back and

forth across his study. He came from a long line of foolish dreamers. He'd been a fool to reach for a star as bright as Beth, and now he was done with dreaming. But it was a bitter thing, learning to live without dreams, and without his sweet Beth.

He hated going to the kitchen now, for his memories of her there were particularly vivid. It was too easy to picture the way she used to stand at the counter, singing along to the radio while she worked. It was too painful to remember the way they talked and shared the first coffee of the day while the rest of the household slept. In his weakest moments he remembered the time he had kissed her on the kitchen counter, and a fiery longing swept over him, so intense that it was physically painful.

Tony's cheerful voice interrupted his brooding. "Hey, I thought you were going to help us with our science project tonight."

"I'll be there in a moment." He made an effort to smile at his niece.

She must have sensed his bleak mood, for she came into the study and perched on his desk.

"We got a letter from Beth today," she said, avoiding his eyes. Not for the first time he wondered if Tony was turning into a mind reader. "She says her new catering business is going really well, and she promised she'd send us some purple platform shoes. She said you'd probably hate them, but they're really in right now."

Stacy wandered in and came to sit beside her twin.

"Platform shoes I can handle," he informed them both. "I just don't want Beth sending you any more miniskirts. I was afraid Sheriff Tomlinson was going to arrest you two for indecent exposure when you started strutting around town in them."

"Uncle Lang, you're just so square sometimes." Stacy rolled her eyes at him.

"Yep," he said, trying on the word for size. "Square sums me up just about right. Now, how about you two hip teenagers and this square uncle of yours go spend some time on that project for the science fair? If turtles won us third place last year, I know your guinea pig experiment is going to bring home a blue ribbon to the Rafter N."

He followed them from the room and shut the light off behind him. At least he had the twins. During many of his worst moments, they managed to cheer him up. He was grateful, too, for the link they maintained to Beth. Through them, he knew she was well, and busy with her new business. She never mentioned her fiancé or plans to get married in her letters. He was damn glad she seemed to be successfully resisting her father's pressure to marry that Bryce fellow. Not even the twins would be able to help him if he discovered that Beth was going to get married.

Sighing, he went to see if he could help the twins devise a clever way to prove guinea pigs were color-blind.

Beth put the last plastic container of chopped cucumbers into the cooler and closed it with a flourish.

"That's it. We're ready to load up and head out to the Smythe-Cramers." She smiled at Sandy, her energetic partner, and they started loading coolers into the van. After four months of hustling for clients and working long hours, Beth was delighted that their catering business was finally starting to pick up steam. Tonight they were providing hors d'oeuvres and finger foods for a party of two hundred people.

Since she had made up her mind that she wanted to start her own business, Beth had thrown her heart and soul into this new venture. She wanted to prove to herself as well as to her father that she could build something worthwhile on her own. She had rented a tiny space in Soho for her kitchen, and she had used the money she had saved from working at the Rafter N to put a down payment on a used van. She had gotten in touch with Sandy Ferguson, one of her best friends from college. Sandy, a talented but currently unemployed graphic artist, helped her create a logo, print up cards and flyers, and paint the van, and they were in business.

From the start "Gourmet on the Go" had been a time-consuming proposition, but Beth didn't mind putting in long hours. She wanted to keep busy. It was the only way she kept from missing Lang all day long. She felt as if something vital had been torn from her when she left the Rafter N. She hadn't realized how central Lang had become to her happiness, to her very being, until she suddenly could no longer see him every day.

The nights were the worst. Before she drifted off to sleep she couldn't help picturing his strong handsome face, the way his serious brown eyes lit up when he smiled or the way he raked a hand through his hair when he was perplexed. She couldn't help remembering the sound of his deep voice, the timbre of his laugh, and the feel of his hands on her body when he loved her.

She told herself it would grow easier with time. She told herself it was probably for the best that she had left when she did. They probably never would

THE COWBOY AND THE HEIRESS 241

have been able to work out the differences between them.

Nevertheless, when her father called her she could barely bring herself to speak with him. She forced herself to answer his questions politely, but she refused to attend any of the functions he invited her to. She wasn't ready to spend time with him yet, and she was afraid he might try to set her up with some other young man he considered to be a good prospective husband candidate. Someday, she supposed, she'd have to start dating again, but right now she couldn't bear the thought of seeing anyone.

She had just come back inside the kitchen to pick up another load when her father walked in the front door of the shop.

"Hello, Beth," he greeted quietly, and looked around him. He had come by once before, just when they were getting started. "You've done a lot with this place."

"Sandy did most of the decorating. She's got a gift for it."

"You've got a gift, too. Ruth Cassidy raved to me last week about the party you catered for her."

"I can't imagine you came all the way down to Soho just to compliment my cooking."

"Actually, I was planning to do exactly that, and then something even more important came up. My detectives presented me with proof today that Bryce was indeed the mastermind behind your kidnapping. I fired him an hour ago, and I'm pressing charges. He'll probably spend a good long time behind bars."

Her father paused and searched her face quizzically. "There's time for me to have someone beat his face in before he's arrested—if you'd still like me to. I already gave it a good start. I'm quite certain

I just broke his nose." He gazed down at his hand with a kind of surprised satisfaction.

"You hit Bryce?" Although she knew her father had a temper, she just couldn't imagine suave controlled Peter Harrison hitting her ex-fiancé.

"After what he put you through, I wanted to tear him apart with my bare hands," he confessed. "It's not the way I usually do business, but my head of security said he'd be delighted to beat Bryce to within an inch of his life for you."

Her lips twitched. "I think just knowing he's in jail will be satisfaction enough for me. His tennis game is going to get really rusty in there."

"With his pretty face, his tennis game is the least of his worries in the slammer," her father said with a grim sort of relish.

"At any rate," he said in a more serious tone, "I'm sorry I didn't believe you. I realize I probably haven't been listening to you for a long time now. I understand that it could take you years to forgive me. I had no right to try to browbeat you into marrying anyone. Your mother would have had my hide for that." The wry, self-deprecating tone of that admission melted some of the ice around her heart.

"I just want you to know that I won't follow through on any of those threats I made against Lang Nelson if you decide to go back to Colorado." He paused and cleared his throat. "He seemed like a good man. I liked him, and I think he loves you very much."

"If he really loved me, he would have asked me to stay," Beth countered sadly. "If he really cared, he would have written or called me here in New York. I haven't heard a word from him since he sent me my last paycheck."

"Hell," her father said, looking uncharacteristically uncomfortable. "I guess I'd better tell you all of it. While you were packing, I went to Nelson and tried to buy him off. He wanted to punch me, but he said his regard for you held him back. When I realized money wouldn't motivate him, I told him he could never provide you with the kind of lifestyle you were used to. That was when he finally agreed not to contact you again."

"Oh, Daddy, how could you?" She felt sick when she thought of how angry and insulted Lang must have been.

"I thought he was a just an opportunistic, fortune-hunting cowboy. I couldn't believe he didn't know who you were. I wanted to protect you. I just wanted you to be happy."

"By pushing me into a marriage with an ambitious unprincipled rat?"

"At the time I believed that rat could take good care of you," her father said mildly. "And obviously, I was very, very wrong. You might be happy to know this whole fiasco with Bryce has shaken my confidence in my ability to read people and their motivations," he admitted with a surprising glimmer of humor. "But enough about me," he said briskly.

Beth groaned mentally and braced herself when she saw that intent look on his face which meant her father was about to pursue and execute some important agenda of his own.

"Are you going to contact Nelson?" he asked.

"I don't know," she said as she thought about Lang and how much had been left unresolved between them.

"If I said you should, I wouldn't blame you if you did the exact opposite. But you looked happy when you rode up with him that night, more happy than I've seen you look in years. Maybe you should give him a call. If you want to fly out to Colorado, I'll tell Geoffrey to put the G-5 at your disposal."

Beth just stared at her father, wondering if she were dreaming.

"At this rate, we may need a private jet to deliver this food on time," Sandy said from where she had been waiting patiently in the doorway. "Two hundred people are going to wonder where their food is a few hours from now. We're going to be late— really late if the traffic's bad."

"Could you save some time if I helped you load up?" her father asked with uncustomary humility.

"You bet. Thanks, Dad." Beth grinned and handed him a cooler. "And thanks for coming down here to talk to me tonight." She wondered what the Smythe-Cramers would say if they knew one of the richest men in the world had loaded their food into a catering van.

She also wondered what the answer was to the question her father had asked her. Was she going to try to see Lang Nelson again? She knew she would have to call or write, if only to apologize for what her father had said to him.

If she took the greatest gamble of all and went to see him, how would Lang react? She was still pondering that question as she locked up her shop and headed for her van.

TWENTY

Lang pulled into the parking lot of Danny Parson's diner. It was May now, and the most hectic part of calving season was finally over. He was still plenty busy, getting the guest cabins into shape, dragging the hayfields, and fixing his haying machinery. Just like last year, his most vexing problem was trying to line up a good cook for the summer. Elsie's niece, Julia, had promised to take the job. Then her younger sister, Mary, who was pregnant with twins, was put on bed rest, and Julia wanted to help her sister for the summer.

Starting to get seriously worried, he had put the word out a week ago that he was looking for someone. Danny Parson had left a message with Elsie yesterday, saying he might have a line on a cook. So here Lang was back at the place where he'd hired himself a hell of cook last June, and bought himself a year of heartache to boot.

His lips curved when he remembered the way Beth had told that trucker off in her ladylike way, right there in the parking lot. Beth had caused him a world of hurt, but looking back on last summer he was still damn glad he had hired her. She had given him and his family so much. He still missed Beth so fiercely sometimes that he ached for her.

But he wasn't sorry he'd gotten to know and love her. He wasn't sorry at all.

Telling himself he had no time right now to sit around moping about Beth, he left his truck and headed for the diner. As soon as Lang stepped inside, Danny spotted him and came out of the kitchen. He showed Lang to a booth and sat down across from him.

"You don't come by here much anymore."

"Been too busy," Lang lied. He was never too busy to enjoy good coffee and good food. The truth was, it was too painful for him to come to Danny's diner. Just driving by this place made him think of Beth. Right now, he was haunted by the memory of their first talk in this very booth, when he'd done his level best to discourage her from working for him.

Looking excited and pleased, Sally came by and poured him a cup of coffee. Wondering idly what she was so fired up about, Lang savored his coffee.

"You found someone yet to cook for your outfit this summer?" Danny asked him.

"Nope. That's why I stopped by. Your message said you might know about someone."

"Well, I hired myself a new cook a few weeks back. Now the business is turning a nice profit, I figured I deserved to take some time off occasionally. Of course, with my luck, someone's probably going to come along and hire her away from me. She cooks like a dream, but prefers working on ranches more than she likes the restaurant side of the business."

An odd prickle of awareness suddenly swept over Lang. Just then he spotted a flash of gold through the window to the kitchen. Danny just sat there grinning at him.

"Hell, she's not here, is she?" Lang rose to his feet, and then sat down again abruptly, feeling as if he'd been kicked in the stomach. "You son of a gun. Why didn't you tell me she was working here?"

"Calm down. You don't want Beth to see you all worked up like this. Have some pride, amigo," Danny said, obviously enjoying himself hugely.

Before Lang could tell him exactly what he thought of that suggestion, Danny turned and shouted toward the kitchen, "Hey, Beth, there's someone here to see you."

Beth came hustling out of the kitchen a minute later. She slid to a dead stop when she spotted him. Her cheeks were flushed from working over Danny's hot grill, her beautiful hair pinned up in a neat bun, and she wore a simple white apron. Lang thought he'd never seen her look more pretty.

As they stared, speechless, at each other, Danny chuckled and slid from the booth. "I reckon I can take over for a bit," he said to Beth and sauntered back to his kitchen.

"Hello, Lang," she said at last and clasped her hands tightly together.

"What the hell are you doing here?"

She gave him a tentative smile and gestured to her apron. "I think that's pretty obvious."

"I mean, what the hell are you doing in Perrytown?"

Her smile faded. She crossed her arms and looked him up and down. "I decided I liked living in the West better than the East, and I'd appreciate it if you'd stop swearing at me."

Suddenly he became aware of all of the customers in the diner who were watching them both with great interest, people he'd known since he was a kid. He'd be damned if he was going to have the most important conversation of his life in front of an audience. Lang stood up, grabbed her wrist, and pulled her none too gently outside.

"I want you to take your hands off me," she said in her most glacial, lady-of-the-manor tone the moment they reached his truck.

He'd really managed to tick her off now. "I'm sorry," he said, letting go of her wrist and raking a hand through his hair. "I'm just so surprised to see you. Why didn't you come out to the ranch to see us? The girls will be happy to know you're back."

"I was working my way up to it." Looking him straight in the eye, she said, "The question is, are you happy that I'm back in Perrytown?"

Her question took him by surprise. The whole situation had turned him upside down. Minutes ago he had been mooning over her in the parking lot like a lovesick bull, and all the while she'd been scrambling eggs in Danny's kitchen. Of course he was happy she was back. He was also petrified, because he wasn't quite sure what her being here meant.

He must have hesitated too long, for her hopeful expression grew frosty.

"Well, you don't need to worry about my pestering you out at the ranch," she declared in a cool voice. "I'll just visit with the girls when they come to town. I might not stay in Perrytown all that long, anyway. There're plenty of places around Colorado and Wyoming that I want to explore. That's why I got a job with Danny while I figured out where I wanted to live."

It was the vulnerable set of her lips which gave her away, and the fact that she wasn't looking him straight in the eye anymore. Beth had always been a lousy liar.

For the first time, he allowed himself to hope. "Of course I'm happy you're back," he said slowly.

"Happy isn't a big enough word to describe how I'm feeling right now. But I'm also just plain terrified, because I don't know why you're here."

When she moistened her lips with her tongue, Lang felt a pang of desire shoot through him. After just a few minutes with Beth, his old awareness of her as a woman was back, stronger than ever. *Now, Nelson, this is no time to start reacting like a randy teenager.*

"I came back to see if my leaving had been a mistake," she confessed. "My father forced me to go with him that day. He said he owned the company that owned your bank, and that they could find some excuse for pulling your loan if I didn't go back home with him. I couldn't bear to let that happen. I'd promised you at the start of the summer that no harm would come to you or your family because of me, and I know how much the Rafter N means to you."

"That interfering son of a bitch," Lang breathed. He should have punched Peter Harrison when he'd had the chance.

"I told him that I thought much the same thing when we reached New York. I refused to stay with him, and we've barely been on speaking terms since."

"I'm sorry if getting involved with me put a strain on your relationship with your father."

"You have absolutely nothing to be sorry about," Beth said briskly. "It's all his own fault. He wouldn't believe me when I told him that my ex-fiancé Bryce instigated my kidnapping. When we were still engaged, I heard Bryce talking about it on the phone to a woman who obviously was his mistress. I knew Dad would never believe me, so I walked out."

"So that's why you ran away," he said, digesting

her words. "You know, my offer to hunt that skunk down for you still stands."

"I appreciate that," she told him with a breathtaking smile. He longed to cross the distance between them and take her into his arms, but his gut told him the time wasn't right yet.

"My father was finally convinced by evidence his own investigators brought to him," she continued, "and now he's going to put the formidable resources of the Harrison empire to work making sure Bryce is convicted of kidnapping. Dad was so furious he even broke Bryce's nose when he fired him."

Lang had to smile at that. "There's hope for your old man yet."

"Just when I thought he was irredeemable, he came through for me. He even suggested in his own convoluted way that I ought to come see you again."

"Now that surprises the hell out of me. I got the impression he thought I was just about the lowest form of life for even daring to look at his daughter."

"Actually, he told me that he liked you."

"I'd hate to be someone the man disliked," Lang said fervently. The longing and loneliness he saw in her mist-blue eyes decided him. It was time to take the biggest gamble of his life.

"I'm grateful he suggested that you come back." He stepped forward and took her hand. He stared down at it because he didn't dare look her in the eyes just yet. What he had to say was too important, and he wasn't good with words. "I've thought about going to New York to fetch you home a thousand times."

"Why didn't you come?" she asked, her voice husky with strain.

"Pride kept me from it at first," he admitted. "It's not easy for a man to realize that the woman he

THE COWBOY AND THE HEIRESS 251

loves could probably buy his ranch with her weekly allowance. There's so much I couldn't give you, things that you had been used to, a whole way of life you'd be giving up if you lived on the Rafter N with me. Then, as time wore on and I started seeing things between us a little more clearly, I realized most of that probably didn't matter."

He looked up at her, then, and willed her to understand him. "What did matter is that I wasn't sure that you could be happy with me. I never finished college. Hell, I'm thirty-six years old and I've never been east of St. Louis. There's so much you've seen and done. I'm just a Colorado cowboy, and ranching's all I really know."

"There's so much I've seen and done, all right, and none of it made me happy." She squeezed his hand. "The happiest I've ever been was last summer on the Rafter N. It's the first place that ever really felt like home to me—the first place I ever felt really needed. And you're the first man who has ever made me feel that what I had to give mattered."

He saw the tears in her eyes, and he couldn't wait any longer to hold her. He slipped an arm around her waist and pulled her close. When one tear slipped down her cheek, he wiped it away gently with his fingertip. "What you have to give matters. What you are matters," he said gruffly. "You're the sweetest, most loving woman I've ever met."

He decided it was time to take the second biggest gamble of his life. He'd gone and told her he loved her. He might as well plunge right off the cliff. Nelsons never did anything by halves.

"Katherine Elizabeth Harrison, will you do me the honor of being my wife?"

"I would be the one honored, but I can only say yes on two conditions."

His heart fell when he saw how serious she looked. Right about then, he'd have agreed to just about anything, even if she asked him to give up the Rafter N and move to New York with her.

"I want you to try harder to ask me to do things instead of telling me. That's how we keep getting sideways with each other. I've lived with a man who told me what to do most of my life. I won't live that way anymore."

"All right. I'll give it my best shot. You may have to hit me over the head a few times with a frying pan when I slip up. Cowboys can be a bit slow when it comes to changing their ways. What's condition number two?"

"You have to promise never to call me Elizabeth or Katherine again," she said, and the laughter and joy he heard in her voice made him grin.

"Now that could be a tough one," he said, shaking his head. "A man's got to have something he can tease his wife about."

"I'm sure you'll find plenty of other topics, but those names are strictly off limits." She wagged one elegant finger under his nose.

"I'll be happy to call you Darlin' for the rest of your days, if you'll just say you'll marry me."

"God, I love the way you say 'Darlin,' " she said, her eyes dancing. "That or Beth will do just fine."

"Good, because I'm tired of all this talking." He dipped his head and finally claimed her mouth with his own. She wrapped her arms around his neck and kissed him back for all she was worth. Lang became so consumed in the kiss and in the joy of having Beth in his arms again that he quickly forgot he was standing in the parking lot of Danny's diner.

"I think we have an audience," Beth murmured when they finally came up for air.

THE COWBOY AND THE HEIRESS

Still holding her in his arms, Lang swung around and swore under his breath. Sure enough, most of Danny's customers and staff were standing by the windows of the diner. Danny opened the door and stuck his head out.

"After a kiss like that, I sure hope the two of you are getting hitched, or I may have to call Ray Tomlinson and ask him to arrest you for indecent behavior."

"We're getting married, all right, just as soon as we can arrange it."

Lang grinned when he heard the chorus of cowboy yells and cheers from inside the diner. He looked down at Beth, and his smile faded. "I hope you don't mind me making that announcement. No one can keep a secret for long in Perrytown."

"I wouldn't have it any other way. I think I may love your town almost as much as I love you, and your nieces."

"Speaking of Tony and Stacy, we'd better hustle out to the ranch before someone decides to call them with our news. The girls are going to go crazy about this. I think they've been hoping for months now that I'd break down and go fetch you back from New York."

He paused and cleared his throat. "You won't mind helping me raise them, will you?"

"I don't mind at all, but the responsibility of it scares me. Even though I was a teenage girl once, I'm not sure I know how to raise one well, much less two."

"From what I saw last summer, I thought your instincts were dead on."

"At least we can worry together about curfews and boyfriends. I think Tony and Stacy will make lovely bridesmaids. I'll probably sew sky blue dresses for them. I'd love to make my own dress, as well."

He laughed and swung her around in a circle. "The daughter of one of the richest men in the world wants to make her own wedding dress. Beth Harrison, you never cease to amaze me."

And then a more sobering thought struck him and he set her back down on her feet. "Does this mean I've got to put up with months of wedding frou-frou and planning?"

"You'd better believe it," she said with relish. "I'm only going to get married once. I promise I'll sew as fast as I can between cooking meals this summer."

"I don't want you to feel like you have to do the cooking. Beef prices are up, and our bookings look good. I can hire someone else to be the Rafter N cook this summer."

"You aren't letting a complete stranger anywhere near my kitchen, Lang Nelson."

"Yes, ma'am. You sure got bossy while you were off in the big city."

"You're damn straight I did," she said with a very credible Western accent. "And now that that's all settled, I want you to give me another kiss, cowboy, even if Danny calls the sheriff on us."

"Always happy to oblige a lady," Lang said in his best Western drawl, and he did exactly that.

BOOK YOUR PLACE ON OUR WEBSITE AND MAKE THE READING CONNECTION!

We've created a customized website just for our very special readers, where you can get the inside scoop on everything that's going on with Zebra, Pinnacle and Kensington books.

When you come online, you'll have the exciting opportunity to:

- View covers of upcoming books
- Read sample chapters
- Learn about our future publishing schedule (listed by publication month *and author*)
- Find out when your favorite authors will be visiting a city near you
- Search for and order backlist books from our online catalog
- Check out author bios and background information
- Send e-mail to your favorite authors
- Meet the Kensington staff online
- Join us in weekly chats with authors, readers and other guests
- Get writing guidelines
- AND MUCH MORE!

Visit our website at
http://www.zebrabooks.com

COMING IN MAY FROM
ZEBRA BOUQUET ROMANCES

#45 WILD ROSE #1: WIFE IN NAME ONLY
by Marcia Evanick

__(0-8217-6603-1, $3.99) Sue Ellen Fabian is a beautician with a secret dream she knows will never come true in her small town. Still, if she can't have a family of her own, she'll channel her love of children towards her cherished godsons. There's nothing she won't do for the motherless boys—even marry a man whose heart she knows she can never claim . . .

#46 KISS THE COOK by Jacquie D'Allessandro

__(0-8217-6604-X, $3.99) Melanie Gibson has her hands full caring for her beloved grandmother and working to secure a bank loan for her new catering service. The last thing she has time for is Christopher Bishop, the sexy financier with the devilish goods looks of a practicing playboy. But Chris is determined to show her that love is the sweetest dish of all.

#47 ADAM'S KISS by Patricia Ellis

__(0-8217-6605-8, $3.99) When Adam Larsen tries to convince Amelia Appleberry to sell her property, all of his tactics are in vain. And every time he is near her, Adam finds himself completely enchanted. But he is unwilling to admit to himself that he wants the lady more than the land—unless Amelia can show him that love is all he really needs . . .

#48 SEDUCING ALICIA by Tracy Cozzens

__(0-8217-6606-6, $3.99) Top scientist Alicia Underwood is devoted to her research. Hiding her beauty—and her broken heart—behind a microscope feels much safer than taking a chance on a man. So why is she suddenly so attacted to the company's hunky handyman, whose glittering eyes and devastating grin are sweeping her off her feet?

Call toll free **1-888-345-BOOK** to order by phone, or use this coupon to order by mail.

Name _____
Address _____
City _____ State _____ Zip_____
Please send me the books I have checked above.
I am enclosing $_____
Plus postage and handling* $_____
Sales tax (in NY and TN) $_____
Total amount enclosed $_____
*Add $2.50 for the first book and $.50 for each additional book.
Send check or money order (no cash or CODs) to:
Kensington Publishing Corp., Dept. CO, 850 Third Avenue, New York, NY 10022
Prices and numbers subject to change without notice. Valid only in the U.S.
All books will be available 5/1/00. All orders subject to availability.
Visit our web site at **www.kensingtonbooks.com**.